THE RIDE

IN THE AIR AND
THROUGH THE COURTS

by Patti Day

CreateSpace

This novel is based on some true events, however, the situations, characters and locales have been fictionalized, enhanced and modified. The opinions expressed in this book are solely the opinions of the author and do not represent the opinions or thoughts of the publisher.

THE RIDE
IN THE AIR AND THROUGH THE COURTS

CreateSpace
http://createspace.com

ISBN-10 1453693572

ISBN-13/EAN-139781453693575

PRINTED IN THE UNITED STATES OF AMERICA

Acknowledgment

To my friends who supported me
and helped complete this book.

TO:
Joan Dameron whose help and insight
I truly appreciated.

Lauryn Casasanta for her web design

Shari Corbett for making the cover speak

Zanne Kennedy for formatting and more

In Honor of

my mother, my angels and my husband who gave me
the chance and strength to succeed.

In Memory of

Hunter who will be in my heart and mind forever!

EXCERPT

An American court of law is in many ways un-American. In our everyday lives we Americans celebrate the subversion of the social order; everywhere a visitor to our country looks he will find a poor American boy trying to make good, usually with the encouragement of his society. An American courtroom is designed first and foremost to preserve the social order, to keep the poor boy down. The judge sits on a raised dais from which he can condescend to the lawyers, the lawyers stand up so that they may condescend to the seated witness, and the witness, though he may have no one to whom he can plausibly condescend other than perhaps the curiosity seekers on the hard benches at the back of the room, at least has the comfort of his upholstered chair. If anyone dares to step the slightest bit out of line, a large man emerges from the back to shout, "Order in the court!" If the judge decides he needs to relieve himself, the large man appears again to shout, "All rise!" And everyone in the room stands and waits stupidly until the judge has ambled off to pee. There is not a "please" or a "thank you" or a "by your leave" in any of this. Our democracy's system of justice is a feudal society in miniature.

"THE NEW NEW THING", By Michael Lewis
W. W. Norton & Company, Publisher

*"BUT LIFE GOES ON LIKE THE PAGES IN A BOOK,
AND WE GO ON. ONE CHAPTER ENDS AND ANOTHER BEGINS."*
TINA MORGAN

CHAPTER ONE
OCTOBER 14, 1990

It was the end of the perfect vacation, Tina thought, relishing the crisp feel of the desert air and taking in the picturesque view of the sparkling, blue sea. Tina was glad that they had decided to go on this trip. She didn't know Hunter's neighbors Russell and Christina very well, but they had invited Hunter and Tina to fly with them to Baja Del Sol for an Aerostar airplane convention. Since Russell and Christina were busy with the convention, Tina and Hunter had days of leisure, all to themselves, and it was just what the doctor ordered. Getting away from the daily routine they had left behind in Las Cruces brought out Hunter's romantic side more than ever before. Hunter and Tina had met at a singles' party two years earlier, and they had been together ever since.

It was times like this when Tina wondered why she just didn't marry the guy. After all, he made her feel like a princess, and he was secure, stable, and good looking. No, he was more than good looking, and that in itself was the problem. At 6' 2", Hunter towered over Tina's 5' 2" petite frame. His blue eyes twinkled and his gaze never failed to take her breath away. He loved her—she knew that. But his humbleness, charm, high cheekbones, and perpetual tan attracted other women, too. He was confident in his own skin, and he certainly could have afforded the designer clothes that many of his country club neighbors wore, but clothes didn't matter to him. His plain style only accentuated his other qualities. In fact, he was almost perfect, Tina smiled inwardly.

Tina nodded and smiled at the shopkeepers as she quickly traversed the shops up and down the hilly streets of old Baja Del Sol. The colorful baubles, Mexican trinkets, and interesting art called to her, *Buy me, Buy me!* She glanced at her watch. She had been gone for an hour and a half. A little boy about six years old followed her out of the last shop with hand-carved wooden turtles, and Tina gave him a quarter as she walked quickly and empty handed back toward the condo. She wanted to spend the last minutes in paradise with Hunter.

"You didn't find anything?" Hunter asked, as Tina breezed through the door.

"Nothing I couldn't live without," she answered. "We'd better pack so we can get the taxi and pick up Russell and Christina at their hotel."

The taxi driver helped load the luggage in the trunk and they drove to the Ericksons' hotel. "Hi," Christina said casually as she smiled broadly, her bags in tow. "It will just be me. Russell left early this morning for the airport with some of his buddies. He wanted to check something out on the plane."

The taxi driver wound the car through the streets, and Tina took her last look at the shimmering land and the sea. Somehow the light reflecting off the desert and the water made everything seem magical.

The driver unloaded the bags from the car, and Hunter gave him a tip. "Gracias!" the driver waved.

Tina loved the excitement and uncertainty of an airport. It was like watching a play unfold. She loved the hustle and bustle of people meeting relatives, old friends and lovers reuniting. The stories were endless and Tina was sure that almost all of them represented new adventures with happy endings. Passengers would rush to get to their gate, stand in line to get their tickets or boarding passes, or anxiously await their luggage while the airport employees worked quickly and efficiently, trying to help everyone and take care of their needs. However, this small airport had a section for private planes and Hunter, Tina, and Christina entered through a small, quiet entrance. Tina felt like something was missing; it was almost too quiet. Then the silence was broken by a familiar, but loud, voice.

"This is the wrong amount!" Russell shook the fuel ticket angrily as he leaned toward the customs inspector. The Mexican inspector just shrugged and shook his head. "All the pilots from the convention had been fueling their planes at the same time, and I got charged for two planes! My plane can't hold that much gas!"

"Come on, Russell," Hunter said quietly but firmly. "There's obviously been a mistake and you can dispute this with the credit card company when you get home."

"I'm not paying for two planes," Russell protested.

"Since they aren't cooperating, you're just wasting your time. Let's go, and we can take care of it tomorrow when we can talk to someone who will listen. And, by the way, if you keep arguing, they WILL detain us, and we won't be leaving Mexico today," Hunter said as quietly as possible, hoping the inspector didn't hear him.

The mid-day heat was scorching, and there wasn't a cloud in the topaz colored sky. Beads of perspiration trickled down Russell's cheeks. Having been at the airport since early that morning, Russell was barely enduring the heat's growing intensity.

Finally, everyone boarded the plane. Tina elected to take the same seat with the broken backrest that she had sat in on the way down to Mexico. It was directly behind Hunter. As the planes lined up and idled on the runway, Russell fidgeted and complained of the injustice, as he impatiently waited his turn for takeoff. Planes were taking off every three to five minutes. *Well, the engine didn't seem to have a problem today*, he thought to himself. *We gave it a hell of a workout this morning and it checked out okay. The weather's perfect,* he thought, almost out loud. *I'll get the engines checked tomorrow when I have more time, AFTER I get this fuel thing resolved.*

Shooting the breeze with the other pilots and checking the plane this morning had been better than having some unknown mechanic inspect it. The mechanic might not have found a problem anyway. Russell loved the camaraderie among the pilots. They shared a special love, a special skill that bonded them together in a way that people who had never flown a plane couldn't understand. Russell had run the plane up and down a side runway as fast as he could to make sure there weren't any major problems.

This flight will be a piece of cake compared to the trip from New York to Las Cruces, Russell thought.

Tina noticed that Russell's face was red as he complained for the umpteenth time, "Damn trouble with the gas!"

When Russell and Christina flew into Las Cruces from New York, Tina was impressed that they had even arrived in New Mexico on time. The weather was bad and some pilots would have aborted the trip, but Russell was a skilled pilot and had flown from the East Coast at lower-than-normal altitudes clear across the country as he dodged a storm and made sure that ice didn't accumulate on the wings.

The takeoff was smooth, and Tina sat back, closed her eyes, and reviewed the wonderful, delicious sexy days she had just spent with Hunter. Tina was thinking about the moonlit walks on the beach and the gentle lapping of the waves on the sand in the stillness of the evenings they had spent together. "The almost free condo and the free meals make up for listening to the sales pitch about the ground-floor timeshare opportunities," Hunter said the first morning as they ate breakfast on the patio overlooking the azure Sea of Cortez below. "In fact, let's see how little we can spend on this trip!"

"Okay, tightwad," Tina had teased Hunter, who was usually very generous with his money. Playing that game had made the trip even more fun.

"What's that smell?" Tina asked herself as she thought she detected a light smell of smoke. They had only been in the air for ten minutes, she acknowledged as she glanced at her watch and then at the engines. They were both turning perfectly and there was no sign of smoke or fire outside. In fact, there was no smoke coming from the air vents in the cabin, either, so Tina went back to thinking about the trip. No one said anything, so maybe the smell wasn't as strong as she thought, or it was just her imagination.

Just then, "I smell something burning," Christina said, almost matter-of-factly.

"I smell something burning, too," Hunter, Russell, and Tina said in unison.

Russell radioed the tower. "We need to turn back and land—over."

"Roger—the sky is clear—over," the tower replied.

"You need me to follow you in?" radioed one of Russell's buddies, who had taken off just after them and heard the transmission to the tower over the airwaves.

"I'm turning her around now," Russell replied. "We'll land in a few minutes, so you go on ahead."

Both engines are working, Tina thought calmly. The smell wasn't like fire, but more like a wire touching something. *It will be okay. We'll be back at the airport in a few minutes.*

Tina, still not panicked, glanced out the window again. This time she realized something was wrong—dead wrong!

"The right engine stopped!" she said out loud. "Oh, the left engine is stopping, too!" Tina heard a horn begin blaring through the cabin, and she would never forget that sound.

Christina said, "We know, dear," her voice much too calm. Then she added quickly, "Why don't you lay your head on my lap?"

"Are you going to land?" the radio crackled. Russell didn't answer. A minute or two later, the radio asked for Russell's coordinates, but he didn't give them. As a matter of fact, he never answered the tower again. The tower continued to ask, but he remained silent.

Hunter turned to Tina, his shimmering blue eyes gleaming in the sunlight, contrasting sharply with his grey hair, which only made him look more distinguished. "Is your seat belt tight, babe?" Hunter asked matter-of-factly. Tina nodded the affirmative. She didn't speak—not because she was scared, but because she had been taught not to interfere with a pilot's concentration. The plane was gliding slowly toward the horizon. Tina remembered the conversation with her cousin when she mentioned going down to Baja Del Sol with her friends.

"Are you sure that a small plane is safe?" Tina's cousin Susan had inquired and then added in an anxious, high-pitched voice, "Tina, don't go!"

"It's a TWIN-ENGINE!" Tina had enthused. "If something should go wrong with one engine, there is always the other one." Tina could feel her heart beating, lub-dub, lub-dub. Oddly, she wasn't scared or anxious and thanked God for her life. She knew her children would be comfortable and taken care of, and she also thanked God that she had been able to watch them grow up. Tina wished she could tell people that when you had no choice, it wasn't scary. If she died, it would be okay.

Hunter turned ahead to look out of the cockpit's

windshield again and prayed that Russell could land safely. He had flown planes, and that one engine made this beautiful silver and blue bird particularly difficult to fly, but no engines would make landing very tricky. He knew that the airport they had left just minutes earlier was right ahead. He closed his eyes for a minute and tried to think of something else. What an amazing trip—a free flight, a hotel on the beach, and time with friends, but most of all, he had all the time in the world to shower Tina with his attention and love. She was the best thing that had ever happened to him and he loved her so much. Part of him wanted to get married, and if he had listened to that part of him, they would already be husband and wife.

"Why can't I honestly tell her what she wants to hear—that I can be a faithful spouse for the rest of my life?" he asked himself. He knew his own weakness, and that was saying no to beautiful women, single or married. If they showed an interest in him, everything else flew out the window. It was like he became a different person—a playboy who could be and do what those women wanted, if only for a short time. Tina, whose first husband had hurt her terribly with his philandering, did not need to go through that again. Hunter made up his mind at that moment. *I will be the kind of husband she needs and deserves*, he vowed to himself.

It was at least 90 degrees in the Mexican desert, the kind of weather that Hunter and Tina usually loved. As the plane descended through the air, it hit the ground hard and then skidded on its belly, flattening overgrown shrubs, thistles, bottlebrush, and even saguaro cacti as it left a scar over 100 yards long in its wake. "As soon as this plane stops, I have to get out." Tina told herself calmly.

Somewhere along the ride to the ground, Tina must have blacked out, but when she regained consciousness, the plane was coming to a stop and she knew she had to escape. Russell had told them the plane held 600 gallons of fuel and the tanks were full. She feared that the plane would explode. Tina lifted her head and looked to the right where the window had been. There was no window and no ledge—the plane was open to the ground. She had tried to unbuckle the seat belt, but realized that her right hand didn't work. She used her left hand to free herself and crawled out of the plane. She crawled in an upright position with her arms moving next to her body.

After about two minutes, Tina said, half aloud, "I'm so tired but I should go a little further," but instead, she lay down.

Boom! Half the plane went up in smoke. She heard a second explosion two minutes later and, despite the pain, pushed back up and crawled through the desert a few more yards until she couldn't move another inch. Tina lay down and looked at the agua blue sky. It was an almost perfect sky for this most imperfect day. Tina started to recount in her mind the first few minutes when the plane stopped. She opened her eyes to see the inside of the plane where the windows had been. It was like an old-time sepia picture, reminding her of the Kansas scenes from the *Wizard of Oz*. Dorothy was on her farm surrounded by the people she loved, and then the tornado tore apart everything she knew. The black and white portion of the movie flashed vividly in Tina's mind and mimicked the scenes of the crash that had just occurred. It was as if she was from another place, another time, another life—far away and long ago.

Maybe I'll wake up, like Dorothy, Tina thought, *and everything will be normal.* She must have closed her eyes for just a minute.

"Wait, am I going to die in the desert?" Tina asked herself. As she looked up, she watched large, ugly black birds circle in the blue, cloudless sky far overhead. Looking over at the thick yellow, brown, and black smoke, she remembered pulling herself from the wreckage.

Her left foot and ankle throbbed, and she realized she couldn't straighten herself. "My ribs must be broken," she whispered to herself, and somehow the tiny sound coming out of her mouth was reassuring. She thought she must have blacked out at some point because she didn't know how or when she was injured. Tina thought of Gilligan on the T.V. show, and she knew how he felt—even though he was with his friends, he was still alone, stranded and helpless.

"The vultures won't eat me," she assured herself. Then the ominous birds circled slowly down toward the plane. Tina felt a sick knot in her stomach. The vultures were going after the dead.

"Help, Help!" A deep voice resonated through the air. Tina felt ecstatic for a moment, despite the pain.

"Hunter, Hunter! It's okay! I'm over here!"

"Is anyone there? Please help me!" Hunter's voice was strong and Tina could feel adrenaline racing through her veins.

"Hunter, it's me!" she tried to shout, but her voice was not more than a whisper. There was no answer. Hunter couldn't hear her. She tried to call out again, but it was of no use. Tina tried to get up but the pain was just too great, so she had to lie on the hot, dry, dusty earth. Tina realized that she was too weak for her voice to project. Hunter was alive! That's all that mattered. They were still together! "I love you," Tina smiled. "We'll be fine. If we can survive this, we can survive anything."

"Is anyone out there?" Hunter's voice was growing more urgent, but still sounded strong as he continued to call for help.

Jose Santos wiped his brow as he took a long drink. He sat in the shade of the gazebo where he ate lunch everyday.

Today he had started working at 4 a.m. because he had a load to take to town. This gravel pit, the Brava Sura, served Baja Del Sol and the surrounding area. As the quaint town continued to grow and attract more tourists, the demand for gravel had increased, too. He took one bite of his burrito and almost choked when he heard the explosion. It was deafening.

"BOOM!"

He stopped eating, got up slowly, and looked around. But he didn't see anything. He just heard the continual drone of the conveyor belts moving the rock. As he started to take another bite, another deafening boom sounded again. Orange and black smoke billowed 500 feet into the air from the second explosion, which occurred just two minutes after the first one.

This time, Jose Santos got up from his chair and looked in the opposite direction. He saw the fire and the smoke far in the distance, where he and his family lived on their ranch. He started running toward the plumes of dark smoke. He ran as fast as he could but his progress was impeded by the stark, but dense, terrain covered with bushes, varieties of cacti, trees, and rock. The path was uneven and very narrow. In some places, there was no path at all. "What will I find?" he wondered, as he stopped to catch his breath in the silent desert and then continued on.

"ONE CAN NEVER PAY IN GRATITUDE; ONE CAN ONLY PAY 'IN KIND" SOMEWHERE ELSE IN LIFE."
ANNE MORROW LINDBERGH

CHAPTER TWO

"The heat is really getting to me!" Tina thought, as she saw something move and then blinked. "Probably just a mirage," she told herself. "Maybe I can crawl to the shade of that tree. I am so thirsty." The desert was surprisingly lush, with overgrown bottlebrush trees, green mesquite trees, and Palo Verde trees with lime-green trunks.

Her ankle and foot throbbed more intensely, and she just couldn't move. Tina's leg felt as if ants were crawling all over it and biting, but she couldn't do much. So every few minutes she would wiggle her leg as it lay on the ground. She was so tired that even making that small movement was extremely hard. Lying on her back, Tina thought she should try and elevate her injured leg above her heart. Then she remembered from her years of volunteering in the local hospital, when trauma was involved it was better to be still. Tina lay there thinking of the past, feeling the pain that swept through her body, and she wondered what the future had in store for her.

After what seemed like hours, Tina heard the crunching of footsteps and saw dust in the air. The sound startled her. Then she heard someone speaking to Hunter, and she tried to get up and yell for help. No one could hear the meek whisper that came out. Instead of the usual loud voice that her mother constantly reminded her to lower, Tina said, all too quietly, "I'm here, too!"

The questions the man asked Hunter in Spanish seemed to be endless, and she could hear Hunter's voice answering them as best he could. Finally, the footsteps were close enough that Tina thought she should try and yell again. "Aqui, Aqui, Venga aqui!, I am here!" The man knelt beside her and gently looked into her face. "Gracias, Gracias!" she said. "Hunter…" Tina trailed off weakly.

The stranger with a kind face and soft brown eyes didn't speak English, but nodded. Tina felt elated. This man had found both of them. "Agua," Tina said. The man shook his head. "No agua," he said. He then looked at her foot and a shadow came over his eyes. Tina knew it was bad—maybe even worse than bad, because the constant throbbing pain she felt was excruciating.

"Hunter…," Tina said, even more faintly. "Please…," her eyes pleaded with the stranger. The stranger scooped Tina up carefully. She thought he was taking her to Hunter, but he quickly and gently laid her under a tree. Tina didn't want to let go of his neck. Before the stranger left to get help, he placed his cap gently on her head in an attempt to shield her from the hot sun.

Tina was thankful that the man had found Hunter and had asked him a dozen questions, or so it seemed. *Hunter's fine*, Tina thought. *He has to be. He answered the man's questions. I wouldn't have had the strength. I'm glad he's not hurt like me.*

The stranger went back to Hunter and spoke to him in Spanish. Hunter seemed to acknowledge that he understood when the stranger tried to tell him that he would find medical help. The stranger was concerned because he felt Hunter was less responsive than the woman. His eyes were black and blue and swollen shut, and his chest looked like it had been burned. He had no shirt or shoes on, but he did have a shiny gold bracelet on his wrist.

The stranger hadn't seen too many miracles in his life, but if two people survived the grizzly wreckage next to them, he had just witnessed one today. The stranger moved Hunter away from the wreckage and then hurried off to get help.

"Wait, wait, don't go—stay!" Tina heard Hunter say. His voice continued to assure Tina that Hunter would be fine. They both would be fine, Tina thought with conviction. Then Tina and Hunter waited for what seemed like an eternity.

Why didn't I ask him to move me next to Hunter? Tina asked herself. She could tolerate the pain; she could tolerate anything as long as Hunter was near her. They didn't really have to speak. She was comforted just knowing that he was there. Tina lay there, thirsty, staring at the blue sky, and feeling her body sweat from the intense heat.

"What was that sound?" said Tina turning her head toward the sky. She realized the sound was coming from a small plane overhead. *Why can't they see us? There has to be a mess in the desert between the crash and the fire and the broken trees and bushes*, she thought. A few minutes later, another small plane engine with a higher whine began to circle above, but nobody stopped. They must not have seen the crash site so they flew off. Tina thought again about the episode of *Gilligan's Island* where Gilligan and his friends spotted a plane and ran out waving their hands and jumping up and down, but no one saw them and no one came. Is that how it would be here? What if that kind man couldn't find his way back until dark? Food wasn't a problem; Tina was not at all hungry. Tina's positive side took over and she believed they would be saved, so she concentrated on the present and waited.

As Tina waited on the ground, people at the airport tower and in the air were racing to find the downed plane.

TOWER: Come in.

SEARCH PLANE: Cancel the estimates of the distance. I am already looking for them. The area isn't clear. Looking for the 77Q to see where it landed.

TOWER: In what area did he come apart?
SEARCH PLANE: In the third and fourth.
TOWER: Okay.
SEARCH PLANE: 76V Baja Réal, pilot David Monte,
is trying to call N7777Q. He keeps trying to localize the
place where N7777Q fell. Also, he's trying to locate the
number N20TM and ask for their support to look for the
aircraft. We have to contact the municipality where the
accident was reported.

Tina was restless and the pain in her foot was intense.
She had read somewhere that if you put an injured foot up
so it was above your heart, it would be better for circulation
and pain. She tried to make a platform with her functioning
leg by using that knee as a table and putting her hurt foot
on top of it. Yes, she thought, that felt better. Suddenly, hot
liquid dripped down her unharmed, bent leg. That was not a
good sign.

"Oh, my," Tina said out loud. "That's my blood," as she
quickly put her badly injured leg back on the ground. "So
much for that idea!" and then Tina chuckled. "You are going
through a nightmare of a day and you are laughing. What is
wrong with you?"

Finally, after what seemed like hours, help arrived. Tina
heard the men speaking to Hunter first, and he seemed to be
answering all their questions. Soon a handful of men were
standing over Tina. They asked her the same questions that
they had asked Hunter. Tina's answers were the same. They
had come from Baja Réal and were headed to Las Cruces
and there had been four adults on the plane. Tina asked the
man in the white jacket if he could give her something for
the pain, and he complied and gave her a shot.

Where is Hunter? Where is the ambulance? Tina
wondered. *Where is the stretcher?* The men were circling
around and looking at her. The medic took off his clean,

white, shiny jacket and spoke to the men in Spanish. He motioned to them, and Tina could tell that they were going to make a seat for her and carry her in the jacket. Two men were on each side of her and the four of them each held a corner of the jacket. They moved Tina carefully from her resting place under the palo verde tree.

Tina felt her legs and body being scratched and scraped by thorns and thistles as the four men carried her on and on through the desert. The discomfort and pain were unrelenting. Where was Hunter? Why were the bushes continuously scrubbing her throbbing leg? Why did the men steer her into the bushes as they walked? When would they get her to the ambulance?

She closed her eyes and tried not to think about the pain. She just wanted to see Hunter, to touch him and talk to him. They were both strong and she knew they would make it through this. They would help each other recover, she thought with resolve.

Finally, they emerged into a clearing and the ambulance loomed ahead like a beacon welcoming her broken, scratched body. At last, she would be able to rest. And most importantly, she would finally see, touch, and talk to Hunter.

Finally, Tina saw him. Hunter was lying on the stretcher outside the ambulance. His shirt was off and his chest had a reddish, sunburned cast. His shoes were gone, but Tina also was wearing only one shoe after the crash. His pants were not torn, and his feet and legs looked fine, with no blood apparent. His arms and hands looked fine, too. *Thank God*, Tina thought. *No broken bones*. Hunter's face was black and blue from the nose up and his eyes were swollen shut. On his forehead, there was a bruise the size of a quarter where something must have hit or pierced his forehead, leaving a round puncture. Tina reached out to touch him. He was cold. Hunter did not say anything, and that worried Tina.

Hunter's cold, Tina thought. *That's not good. He's in shock...it's okay. We'll be okay. We will get help soon. The most important thing is that we made it together! They will be able to give Hunter a shot to help him through this state of shock. It will be okay now.*

In the ambulance, Hunter and Tina were placed on raised, spotless stainless steel slabs that lined each side of the vehicle. The center section had a lower floor where the emergency medical personnel could stand and a bar above that they could hold onto.

The bar above each slab reminded Tina of a New York subway car. Everything in the van seemed very clean. *Good, that's good*, Tina thought. "Por Favor," Tina said as she started to speak in both English and Spanish. "Please tie my leg to the top bar," she said as she motioned. "I don't want it to bounce around, and it feels better that way." The attendant complied, which bolstered Tina's confidence that all would be well.

Tina didn't think much about Christina and Russell. But she knew something terrible had happened to them. Right now she just didn't want to know.

Finally, the ambulance started moving fast as it raced down the dirt road, the two attendants bouncing around like marionettes in a puppet show as they tried to steady themselves. The men's arms and legs jerked helplessly as the ambulance continued to speed along on the rough dirt road littered with potholes, rocks, and mounds. Tina felt like laughing. *How comical*, she thought. *They are holding on for dear life and can't even hold on for themselves, so how can they help us?* Eventually the severe bumping eased as the speeding ambulance finally reached a paved road.

One of the attendants placed Hunter's hand in Tina's. She was so grateful! She held his hand in hers. Suddenly one of the attendants was getting ready to pour water from a gallon jug about eight inches away from Hunter's mouth as he lay prone on the slab in the moving, unsteady vehicle. "Stop! No! No, Bueno!" Tina motioned for the men to hold a cloth with water up to Hunter's mouth so he could suck the water from the towel. She sighed when they did as she asked and closed her eyes for a minute, or so it seemed.

All of a sudden, Tina noticed that Hunter's hand was no longer in hers. She looked and the men were doing CPR on him. *What happened? When did I stop holding his hand? Did I close my eyes? Where are the paddles?* Tina wondered.

The men continued performing CPR on Hunter, but he didn't seem to move. Finally, they stopped in front of a small building and carried Tina into the clinic. She was on a raised hospital bed and Hunter was placed on the floor next to her. They were still administering CPR. Lights were above Tina and attendants stood around her. The doctor in charge gave her a shot of something that helped the pain.

Her attention was diverted to Hunter on the floor when the doctor introduced himself. "My name is Miguel Mendosa. I am the doctor here." Tina was so relieved. The doctor spoke English!

"I want a Med-O-Vac airplane to take me to Las Cruces—my home. University Medical Center," she instructed immediately. The doctor left the room, and when he returned he explained to Tina that he had made plans for a plane to arrive for her around 9 p.m.

"We can fly you to Scripps Medical Center in California tonight," Dr. Mendosa told her. The doctor's voice was reassuring. Tina had heard horror stories of people who had accidents in foreign countries and knew she wanted to be treated back in the States, especially if she needed any type of surgery.

"Las Cruces, I would still rather go to Las Cruces," Tina insisted.

"New Mexico," the doctor said to no one in particular. "We'll see what can be done. We will try."

When the doctor came back in the room a second time, he asked if Tina had an American Express Card. Tina shook her head and said it had been in her purse in the plane. The doctor said not to worry and he left the room again. Tina remembered that famous commercial, and saying, "Don't leave home without it!"

When he returned, Dr. Mendosa needed to work quickly to get his patient stabilized and ready to be transported out of the country. He assessed her injuries without an x-ray, sonogram, or any other sophisticated technology. The compound fracture of her foot was quite severe and he needed to set it and keep it free of infection. Several hours had already passed and time was of the essence.

Dr. Mendosa instructed an attendant to disinfect the area. Tina started screaming. She knew it would hurt and it did! When she had worked in the ER, she was sure they used a numbing solution first, but Tina didn't know if they used anything here. Next, Dr. Mendosa started rubbing her skin, and then a sharp, nauseating pain swept through her. The doctor held her foot and to Tina, it seemed like he forced it back in place. In that moment, the excruciating pain was a blinding white light, and Tina screamed.

In a few minutes, Tina actually began to feel some relief after this unbelievable experience. Tina had always been very careful not to injure herself. She was overly cautious and deliberately avoided situations that could cause injury. Now, here she was, in a foreign country and experiencing more pain than she had ever endured in her life.

The doctor then put her foot and leg in a full plaster of paris cast, encasing her leg from the top of her toes to just below her knee. Soon the sensation of burning began radiating from an area on the back of her leg. The burning was constant and it seemed to be related to the cast. It didn't hurt before the cast, but it was hurting now.

"Please, take it off. Take it off!" Tina begged. The heat under the cast was intense. "My leg's on fire!" Tina cried out.

It was time to go. Tina knew she would be flying home. Alone! Hunter was dead.

"SOME PEOPLE ARE ALWAYS GRUMBLING BECAUSE ROSES HAVE THORNS. I AM THANKFUL THAT THORNS HAVE ROSES."
ALPHONSE KARR

CHAPTER THREE

Alone. The word haunted Tina. The ride from the clinic to the airport was quiet. After all, the only occupants in the ambulance were the medical attendant, the driver, and Tina.

"Please take this cast off!" she begged again, but her plea fell on deaf ears as the ambulance drove steadily through the streets. This time there weren't any bumps or potholes and the ride was relatively stable. Tina was more comfortable, and the painkillers that coursed through her body helped dull the memories of the afternoon.

The clinic must not have been too far away and maybe Tina had dozed off for a while, because before she knew it, the medical attendant was preparing to transfer her to the air ambulance. There was this agonizing burning sensation on the back of her leg that seemed to get hotter and hotter by the minute.

Shortly, Tina realized she was being moved into the small plane that was waiting for her. Tina's mind was calm and she didn't think or worry about getting into the plane, even though she was aware that she would be alone on this trip and that Hunter would not be joining her. As a matter of fact, it would probably be a while before his body would be shipped back to the States.

The doctor and the nurse were introduced and they were very attentive to Tina. Immediately, in a low, desperate voice, Tina inquired, "Would you ask the pilot to take me to Las Cruces? Please, please, see what you can do. My son is in Las Cruces and I don't know anyone in California.

I want to go to University Medical Center. I don't want to go to California. Will you please see what you can do?"

"I'll go talk to the pilot," the nurse assured her. "We're still on the ground and have some time before departure, so maybe he can do something."

Tina took a deep breath. She asked the doctor, "Could you please take this cast off my leg? The back of my leg is burning near my knee. I don't know what it is, but the pain medicine isn't helping with the sharp, continual pain. I don't know why this pain doesn't go away, but I think it started when the cast was put on."

The doctor touched the back of her leg and nodded to the nurse, "Yes," the doctor told her. "You won't be moving, so we will remove the cast, and the doctors can do what needs to be done when you get to the hospital."

They cut off the cast, and Tina sighed. It was instant relief! "Thank you, thank you. You can't imagine how much better that feels!"

The nurse gave Tina a shot, but she didn't even feel the injection. She felt relaxed for the first time in over 8 hours. It was almost 9:30 p.m. and the accident had occurred just after 1 p.m. that afternoon.

I am safe, Tina thought. *For the first time since the crash I don't have to worry. I know I will be in good hands.*

Somewhere during the early evening and the start of this ride in the sky, the decision had been made to take Tina to University Medical Center in Las Cruces.

I know I can't change the past, Tina thought. *I know I can't change what happened, and I know I can't bring Hunter back. Our lives changed forever in the blink of an eye. Why am I still here? Why did I survive and not him? Is it fate? Was my grandmother watching over me? Why?*

The doctor interrupted Tina's thoughts, as she excitedly exclaimed, "We're ready to land in Las Cruces! We're going to get you out of the plane and into the ambulance. It will be waiting for you when we land." She pointed toward the window across the aisle from where Tina was laying.

"Thank you," Tina said. *I'm home*, she thought. After Tina was transferred to the ambulance, it moved quickly through the dark, quiet streets. Traffic wasn't a problem at midnight. Out of the window, Tina could see the full moon illuminating the sky. The mountains loomed in dark contrast, as if guarding the moonlit valley below. Even though Tina had moved here from New York many years ago, she felt at home in the desert and glad she was back in familiar surroundings.

"We're going to take you into the Emergency Room for immediate attention," the nurse in the ambulance told her. Tina nodded.

"Jason!" Tina's eyes lit up as they wheeled her through the Emergency entrance of the hospital.

"Everything's going to be fine, Mom," her son said, tears welling up in his eyes. "A man with the Med-o-Vac team called and told me they were bringing you here. He said that the doctor at the clinic in Mexico made the call that started the ball rolling for all the arrangements to be made to get you back to the United States. Grandma and Harry also know what happened; we were all told on a four-way call. They will be coming soon. I'm glad, Tina said quietly. "See you soon," Jason said as she was once again being moved through the hospital.

Tina felt like she was floating out of the sky, totally helpless and surrendering her life to God's hands. She had no control, but was totally at peace. Pain seared through her leg and foot. She blinked, expecting to see the charred, blackened, dismembered plane in a foreign desert, like a baby bird that had fallen from its nest. Tina knew she had broken ribs, her right hand didn't move, and her left ankle was broken, with her foot twisted at an awkward 45 degree angle. She thought back through the day, reliving how she had waited for help and how the rescuers had carried her through the desert. She must have blacked out at some point, though, because she couldn't remember when the injuries occurred.

"Hello, Tina. I'm glad you're awake." The doctor had a warm smile and telling brown eyes. She remembered his face from the ER. "My name is Dr. Adam. I performed the surgery on your foot, leg, and wrist. You're at UMC in Las Cruces."

"I remember coming here in the ambulance," Tina confirmed.

"That's good!" Dr. Adam said. "As I understand it, you are lucky to be alive. We were told there was nothing left of the plane. You have broken ribs, and we put some hardware in your ankle, but you won't have a cast because of the burns. The skin needed to heal from the burns. Your wrist needed the Hoffman, which was named after the man who invented it. These metal spikes go into your hand and arm. The bars are used to adjust and pull the bones apart as you heal. Apparently, your wrist bones were shoved into your arm. The good thing is that you won't need more surgery until it's time to remove the hardware. Best of all, we were able to save your foot, thanks to the quick thinking and actions of the doctor in Mexico. If he wouldn't have casted your foot to prevent infection, well, let's just say things would have turned out much differently."

"Oh..." Tina was at a loss for words. This doctor was her third angel in the past 24 hours. He had literally picked up the broken pieces and put her back together. Somehow, she would survive this and get her life back. She had to, for Hunter and for Russell and Christina, too.

"You get some rest and we'll talk more later. Oh, and

Tina, I'm glad they listened to you. We have a note that you insisted on being flown to the United States in the Med-O-Vac plane. You had a lot of foresight under the circumstances. You probably saved your own life. I'm sorry about the loss of your friends."

A tear rolled down Tina's cheek. "When I was lying in the desert waiting for them to find me, it was so hot, and I felt bugs were crawling on my legs. Then, there were the vultures, circling in the sky and waiting for their lunch. I had plenty of time to think and reflect on my life. My Hunter was calling for help and I didn't even have the strength to go to him. I made a deal with God. I said, 'Dear God, if you get me out of here, I promise that I will lead a good, productive life, and I will never let anyone lie to me, steal from me, or cheat me again.'" Right then and there it seemed important for Tina to take control of her life.

Tina began reflecting on the past two years, prior to the crash, when she had owned a business. She had allowed some people to take advantage of her and other people to steal from her, but she just hadn't cared. She now realized that she must be strong to steer her life along a successful path. Weakness ends up creating more trouble to have to deal with later. Experience had taught her that making poor decisions leads to feeling overwhelmed, and then it takes longer to get back on track. Tina now understood what she had to do.

The rest of Tina's first week in the hospital was a blur. The doctors and her family told her that she had visitors and phone calls, but she didn't remember them. She did remember her sons pushing on the morphine pump and scolding them, telling them she didn't want more. She didn't remember when her sisters flew in from New York and that she asked them to light a candle for Hunter and another for Richard, her late husband who died in November—November 11, nine years ago, to be exact.

Sometimes it seemed like an eternity since his death, and sometimes it seemed like only a minute had passed.

Tina also didn't remember calling her cousin Rita and telling her that she shouldn't worry, that she would be fine in a few weeks and would be able to attend the Bar Mitzvah of Rita's son, Kevin. Rita wasn't quite sure of the information, so when Rita called her Aunt Florence, she was told this would never happen.

Roger, a past boyfriend, visited her in the hospital. Tina had been on Roger's mind ever since she had ended their relationship. She had explained to him that he needed more time to heal from the death of his wife. It was good advice, but Roger missed Tina. He brought her some tapes he had put together, along with a small tape player, so that she could listen to music. Roger remembered that Tina loved music and dancing.

Tina also didn't remember calling her sister Joan and asking her to set up an appointment with her gynecologist because it was time for her yearly appointment. Again, Joan had questioned the unimportance of that request, given Tina's serious condition.

Years later, Joan shared a conversation that she had with a co-worker. Joan's co-worker told her that a close friend had recently lost her parents in a plane crash and that she was devastated by this news because she had practically been raised by the family. She told Joan how very sad she felt. Joan then explained to the co-worker that her sister also had been in a plane crash, and they realized it was the same event that brought sadness to one family and relief to another. It really was a small world.

A week later, Dr. Adam visited Tina to talk about the next stage of her recovery. "You will get better, but it's going to take some time. You were seriously injured, Tina." Dr. Adam's eyes were serious. "When you are stable and strong enough, you will be going to a rehab hospital, where you will be getting initial therapy and using machines that will help you heal."

"When can I play tennis and golf and dance again?"

Dr. Adam hesitated. He hadn't expected that question, at least not today. "Maybe in a year or so," he answered carefully, but Tina noticed a strange look in his eyes. If patients knew they could someday regain the mobility they once had, they often worked harder, but Dr. Adam knew there was a fine line that he couldn't cross. He couldn't give false hope. The truth was, right now he didn't know if Tina would ever walk without a limp.

"You were lucky, Tina. The doctor in Mexico did the right thing, and if you had arrived here at UMC much later, we might not have been able to save your foot. Don't push yourself too hard. God was on your side and you're lucky to be alive. Let's just take it one day at a time."

I'll be dancing in just a few months, Tina thought with more conviction than she actually felt.

The doctor interrupted her thoughts, continuing to talk about her treatment. "There's physical therapy two or three times a week and it will take a lot of perseverance."

"Therapy two or three times a week?" Tina questioned.

"Yes," Dr. Adam confirmed.

"No," Tina shook her head. "If I'm going to get well, I'll go to therapy five times a week." Tina let it all sink in. There would be a lot of time and energy involved, but she would dedicate herself to her recovery.

Tina tried to move. "I need to make some calls to Hunter's family and to the Ericksons's children, too. Can I sit up?" She raised her head ever so slightly and felt defeated when it fell back on to the pillow.

Dr. Adam touched her arm and then her forehead. "Rest

for now. You need to get some of your strength back. Rest now and you can make some calls tomorrow."

Tina shivered involuntarily. Dr. Adam tucked a warm blanket around her, being careful not to move her leg. Before she could thank him, she drifted off. But instead of falling into a deep sleep, she was back in the desert. Why hadn't she tried to do more? What could she have done to save the others and to help Hunter before he went into shock? Could she have signaled for help? What had happened? What had gone wrong?

"Hunter, I love you!" Why, oh why, hadn't she said those words to him when he turned to check on her, to make sure her seat belt was fastened tightly as the engines had ceased to turn and the plane was slowly moving downward? No, not one word had been spoken after she laid her head in Christina's lap. When the man in the desert picked her up and moved her under the tree, why hadn't she asked him to take her to where Hunter was lying? Why had she survived and no one else?

She rolled her head restlessly from side to side, overcome by a guilt that washed over her like the ocean waves she had played in with Hunter just a few days earlier. The dreams—the guilt—the questions—all of it was exhausting. She finally slept and didn't dream at all.

"THERE ARE TWO WAYS OF MEETING DIFFICULTIES; YOU ALTER THE DIFFICULTIES OR YOU ALTER YOURSELF TO MEET THEM."
- PHYLLIS BOTTOME

CHAPTER FOUR

"Mom, I'm here." Tina awoke and saw her son standing next to the bed. "You survived a plane crash! How do you feel?"

Tina's throat felt like sandpaper. She motioned for water. Thinking about all the questions she had before she fell asleep made her feel as if she had just run a race. Her son held the cup with the straw to her lips.

"I'm sore, but I'm here," Tina tried to smile. "It was so amazing that you were at the entrance to the ER when they wheeled me out of the ambulance."

"Mom, you sound great!" Jason, Tina's younger son, was surprised by the strength in her voice. "The doctor down in Mexico knew just who to call to get the show on the road. Everything was perfectly coordinated."

Tina just lay there looking up at her son. "My second angel," Tina said.

"Mom, what?" Jason said, not understanding his mother's reference.

"My second angel," Tina repeated. At this point, Tina was a thousand miles away, thinking about the small-framed man with the compassionate brown eyes and dark hair.

"The doctor stood beside me and helped me through those first few hours after I arrived at the desolate clinic. He knew what to do to save my foot. You know, Jason, it was a miracle that he spoke English, and the immediate critical care and procedures he performed to save my foot achieved the same results as if I was treated by a doctor at one of the finest and most well-equipped hospitals in the United States." She continued, "The first angel found me, the second gave me excellent critical care and had the means to get me to America, and the third angel put me back together again. I am so lucky to have my angels looking over me."

Tina then moved slightly and winced in pain. Her broken ribs were a constant reminder of what she'd been through.

"Here, I'll give you some pain medication." Before Tina could shake her head, Jason had pushed the morphine pump.

"I really don't want it," Tina protested. "It makes my head feel like it weighs a thousand pounds, and I can't think straight."

"You're hurt, mom. You have to rest. The doctor was here. He said he'll talk to you about physical therapy when you are strong enough," Jason said, hesitating. "He also said it could take a long time."

"Oh." Tina hadn't thought about how long she might be in the hospital.

"You're going to have to be patient, since this could take a while. You get some rest. I love you, Mom! I'll be back tomorrow."

"I love you, too." Tina felt a glimmer of hope. She still had her mom and her sons.

As he left, she swallowed hard. The picture of Hunter lying still on the floor near her in that small room at the clinic did not leave Tina's mind. She knew he wasn't in any pain now, but why did he die? *I know he was okay. He was clear in his speech and strong, even though he was in shock. Why?* Tina continued to wonder.

Tina's thoughts then turned to Hunter's son. David was only 14 years old and loved his dad so much. Now he would never see his father again. *I wonder if I will ever see David again?* Tina wondered sadly.

What a wonderful father Hunter had become. It was

another reason Tina had fallen in love with him. He spent hours with David during "their" weeks and weekends. Hunter was making up for lost time—for the father he hadn't always had time to be with his first four children, who were now adults. His love and devotion to his youngest son, who was quickly becoming a man, was genuine, and Tina watched the unique bond between them grow.

Tina felt the tears sting her eyes. She whispered, "Hunter, I'm so sorry. David was lucky to have you in his life; you were able to share so much with David. But what will happen to him now?"

I have a new lease on life, Tina told herself. *I have to make the best of it. Grieving won't help me get stronger. I don't know why I was the only survivor, but for whatever reason, I am still here.*

She thought of Hunter and of all the sweet memories. She would love him forever. Somehow, this loss was almost easier to endure than a relationship that had gone sour. She had loved Hunter completely, but she had been afraid to commit to marriage with him. She felt that she needed more time. With Hunter gone, there was no going back and there was no more time. She had no other choice but to go forward. She knew she could learn from the past, and just knowing Hunter had made her a stronger and better person.

October 20, 1990

"I really need to make some calls," Tina told the nurse when she awoke the next morning.

"We need to check a few things first, and I need to see you eat—even if it's a bite of toast." The nurse was friendly and moved quickly around the room. She changed the IV, took Tina's temperature, checked her blood pressure, and looked at the Hoffman on her wrist and the boot on her leg and foot.

Tina grimaced in pain when she moved. The pain from her broken ribs was unrelenting. Her sides and chest hurt when she took a deep breath, when she turned, and when she tried to sit up or lie down.

"We can get you more pain medication," the nurse assured her.

Tina, who hated taking even an aspirin, felt that the strong pain medication in the pump attached to her body was making her dizzy, and she wanted to think clearly. She also needed to remember what she was doing.

When Tina didn't respond, the nurse went on, "I know it doesn't seem to make sense, but when you have just enough medication to ease the pain, it actually helps you get stronger faster. Your body can heal while you are resting. When you're in pain, you use all your strength trying to fight the pain."

Tina had so many questions, so many things she needed to find out about what happened, but she knew the nurse was right. Her main goal was getting stronger so she could get out of the hospital. She didn't like sitting still. She wanted more than anything to play tennis and dance. If only she could look forward to dancing with Hunter again. She couldn't look backwards! She had to get better for herself. If a little pain medication for a few days would help her get to that point more quickly, she would do it.

Tina turned to the nurse. "I think I do need a little more medication, but only the minimum amount to ease the pain," Tina conceded. "Could I ask you a favor? I need to make these calls first. Could you come back and give me the medication in about an hour?"

"It's actually better to have the medication before you feel so much pain," the nurse answered. "But I know you want to be alert, so I'll be back in an hour. We can talk more then about what will make you comfortable so you can feel better as quickly as possible."

"Thank you so much!" Tina was grateful for her understanding.

As soon as the nurse left her room, Tina called information to get the phone number of the Ericksons's business, since her address book had been in her purse that was on the plane. With the Hoffman on Tina's right hand, she still couldn't write properly, but she could move her fingers and hold the pencil to scribble down the phone number given by the operator. Once that task was completed, Tina picked up the receiver to call Russell Jr. A receptionist answered on second ring.

"This is Tina Morgan. I would like to speak to Russell Erickson."

"Let me see if he's available," the brisk voice answered.

"I was calling to tell him that I'm sorry about the death of his parents," Tina said.

"Oh," the voice softened. "Please wait a minute."

After several minutes, the receptionist returned. "I'll transfer you to Mr. Erickson's office."

"Hello," a deep voice answered.

"Is this Russell?"

"Yes, it is."

"You don't know me, but this is Tina. I was on the flight with your parents when we came back from Baja Del Sol."

"Yes," Russell said slowly. "What do you want?"

"I wanted to tell you that I am sorry." There was silence. "Are you there?" Tina asked.

"Yes, I'm sorry. I still can't believe they're gone. My dad was such a good pilot."

"I just wanted to let you know how sorry I am. I also wanted to tell you that your dad, actually both of your parents, did everything they could. Your mom even had me put my head in her lap," Tina told him. "I just wanted to offer my condolences." Tina could see Christina in her flamboyant clothing and jewelry. She came across as someone who had it all and wanted the world to know, and she also seemed to have a kind heart.

"I don't want to put you through this, but what exactly happened?"

"I wish I could tell you. The engines both quit working, and then we just glided. We were so close to the airport, but we never made it back."

"BOTH engines quit?" Russell asked. Tina could hear the shock in his voice.

"Yes, I don't think there was much your father could do after that."

"Okay, thank you."

Tina hung up. Russell Jr. seemed glad she had called, but he had also been distant and afraid. Why was he in such a hurry to end the conversation? Why did she feel that something wasn't quite right? *Did I do the wrong thing by calling him?* Tina wondered.

The nurse came back an hour later as promised. "Are you ready for that medication?"

"Not really. I'm exhausted and it will make me feel worse."

"It will help you sleep," the nurse said, pressing the button. And it did.

When Tina awoke, the nurse opened the door. "You have a visitor."

"Steve!" Tina practically yelled.

"Hi, Tina," Steve smiled. "It's good to see you."

"Oh, Steve, it's good to see you, too! You drove all the way from Albuquerque?"

"Kim and I can't stop thinking about you and wondering how you survived. After you called the other day, I told Kim what you said—how the plane was on fire, and how you and Dad had to lie in the desert…" Steve's voice choked up.

Steve was Hunter's oldest son. He was a CPA and lived in Albuquerque with his wife, Kim, whom Hunter adored and loved like a daughter.

"I keep thinking about what could have been done differently. When the plane was going down, no one panicked. I think we knew we might die, but we had no control."

"It's amazing you both got out alive! Your guardian angels had to be with you."

"Yes, I thanked God that your dad and I both made it out. Your dad was so brave. He kept calling for help. "I'm sure we would not have been found so quickly if they hadn't heard your dad calling."

Tina thought she remembered that the Mexican man who found them had spoken to Hunter first. Hunter answered all his questions. "I didn't know he was so weak. He was calling for help, loudly and clearly. I heard two planes that seemed to be circling but they never landed. It was the man on the ground who helped us. He walked back through the desert on foot to get the medical help that we needed. That was the only way the authorities knew where we were. He was our angel!"

"That's interesting, Tina," Steve said, "but if Dad was so alert, why did he die?" Tina didn't know the answer so she just shook her head. That was a question she would certainly like to have answered, too. It was a question that kept gnawing at the core of Tina's very existence.

He was hurt. He had a bruise the size of a quarter in the middle of his forehead, and his eyes were swollen shut. Otherwise, I didn't see any blood or anything broken. I'm sorry.

"We'll be leaving for Dad's service in Illinois tomorrow. I just couldn't go without seeing you first." Steve touched her arm.

"Thank you so much for coming."

"Take care, Tina."

Tina was actually glad she and Hunter had never gotten married. It made things less complicated. Hunter's children would get what he left to them, and they wouldn't have to share anything with her. It was really better this way.

She picked up the phone and dialed a florist in Illinois. She ordered a wreath of roses in the shape of a heart for Hunter's service. The card was signed, "All my love, Tina."

Tina was dozing late that afternoon when the phone startled her. She reached for it, but the sharp pull in her midsection reminded her of her bruised and broken ribs.

"Hello?"

"Hi, Tina, this is Brook Grey. I just wanted to tell you how sorry I am and how much Hunter will be missed."

"Thank you. It's nice of you to call." Brook was a developer on the eastside of town where Hunter lived, and Tina had met him when she and Hunter were walking on the golf course. Hunter had met him at one of the homeowners' meetings, but they never socialized together. When they did meet, they would talk about property values and new developments in the area. Brook's voice sounded kind and caring and very sincere as he explained his concern. "I don't know if you've thought about this yet, Tina, but you really need to find a good attorney. You need to figure out how to recoup your medical expenses and see what can be done for your pain and suffering. I know just the right man. He's a pilot, too, which makes working with the insurance company that covered the plane easier. Since he's been around airplanes and airports, maybe he can find out what actually happened down there."

"Well, Brook, I probably do not need an attorney, but I will write down his name."

"It's Cisco Samsel and he is a pilot." Brook spelled the name for her.

"Thank you. I wouldn't have known who to call." Tina hung up the phone.

Hunter trusted Brook, so she trusted his advice, too. She would look up his name in the Martindale-Hubbell Law Directory, just to make sure he was in good standing.

That evening, the hospital was teeming with activity. Ambulances were bringing in a group of volunteer doctors who had been returning from helping the disadvantaged in Mexico when their plane crashed. The ER Critical Care Unit was crowded with diligent health workers and doctors. Many of the usual hospital staff was tending to the seriously injured victims of the medical plane crash.

A different night nurse was on duty and came in to clean the open areas in Tina's wrist and arm where the screws went from the Hoffman into her skin and bones. After the nurse swabbed the first wound with the Q-tip, she then started to use the same Q-tip to clean the second wound.

"What are you doing?" Tina asked as she raised her voice in a loud and angry tone. "You know better!" Tina was incredulous. The care at the hospital had been of the highest quality, and now this? Tina knew that each wound had to be cleaned with a new, sterile swab. The risk of infection in the open wounds was quite high until the wounds healed completely.

The nurse didn't answer but started the cleaning procedure over, this time using a fresh Q-tip at each point of entry.

Tina was furious. She realized that this was the first time she had felt truly angry with the hospital care and believed she had to take charge of her own care. *What does a patient do if she can't speak and protect herself?* Tina wondered.

The nurse left the room without saying good night. What Tina didn't know was that she was standing right outside the door, writing on Tina's chart with a red pen. "Patient is belligerent and uncooperative. She does not want to take directions or assist in her own care."

Tina had been blackballed by a nurse.

"ONE DOES NOT SEE ANYTHING UNTIL ONE SEES ITS BEAUTY."
OSCAR WILDE

CHAPTER FIVE

"Hi, Tina," Sue, the nurse who still treated her with some respect, said as she entered Tina's room. "You'll be going to the rehab hospital tomorrow. Good luck. You're a real trooper!" Since the day Tina had complained about the night nurse not using sanitary procedures to clean her hand wound, the other nurses had treated her differently. They weren't rude, but they weren't friendly, either.

"Really," Tina asked? "I thought Dr. Adam said it would be another week?" Sue was quiet for a moment as she looked at Tina's chart.

"Dr. Adam thinks that you're ready. He's just like the big guy upstairs around here, you know. However, you can talk to him again if you want to, though."

"No, no," Tina answered quickly. "I'm just a bit surprised. Dr. Adam said that the rehab hospital was my next stop, but I would like to stay here a while longer and then go home and start outpatient treatments. I want to recover as quickly as possible."

The nurse sighed as she left the room. Before she closed the file, she read the notations on Tina's chart. The entry immediately following the notation of Tina's exchange with the night nurse about improperly cleaning the wounds around the Hoffman stated: "The patient is still trying to manage her own care and questioning the nursing staff. Move to rehab hospital as soon as possible."

Tina was nervous and excited about leaving UMC. Entering the rehab hospital marked a new chapter in her recovery. She was determined to work harder than she had ever done in her life. *Well, here I am in a bed in a new room in a new hospital on a weekend. UMC didn't waste any time getting me out of there,* she thought. It was very quiet. Tina looked around and said, "I guess not much happens around here on Saturdays, but they said someone would be taking me down to start therapy." Thinking to herself, Tina said, *Let's make a deal, Tina. You are going to work very hard from today on. You are going to surprise Dr. Adam and get well faster than any patient he has ever had. You are going to show them what determination and hard work will achieve.* After the pep talk and promise she made to herself, Tina was ready to start. All she needed...

A strange voice startled her. "I'm here to take you to therapy, Ms. Morgan," an orderly said.

"I'm ready!" Tina answered.

The orderly took Tina in the wheelchair down to the therapy room. When she was face to face with the therapist, Tina saw that Pete had puffy eyes and a red nose. He moved even closer, until he was about a foot in front of her face.

"Let's get started. I'm going to...," he coughed before he could finish his sentence. A sneeze followed and Tina could feel the man's breath on her arm.

"Do you have a cold," Tina asked?

Pete immediately said, "Yes!"

"Excuse me," Tina spoke up. "Would it be possible for me to work with someone who isn't sick?"

"It's just a cold," Pete replied. "Now let me explain what we're going to do."

"Pete, I can't risk getting sick myself. I'm anemic," Tina's voice began to rise. "And my immune system isn't as strong as normal after having surgery and being in the hospital for over two weeks. I don't think sitting this close to someone who has a cold is a good idea."

"I can't believe this!" Pete stood up, sneezing again. "If you don't want to work today, just say so."

"I do want to work today," Tina said. "This isn't personal. I just don't want to become sick. Let me talk to the supervisor. Take me to the supervisor, please," Tina demanded in a voice that was anything but polite. Pete didn't answer. Instead, he strode off, leaving Tina to sit in her wheelchair and contemplate how she could have been more tactful.

"Tina, you are never tactful," her mother always told her. It was as if she was in the room with Tina. "And you're making it worse by raising your voice. How many times do I have to tell you that you get more with honey than vinegar?"

Tina would answer her mother by saying, "When I speak quietly, no one listens. If I don't raise my voice, nothing gets done."

Ten minutes later, the orderly came back. Tina, who was bewildered and shaken, was wheeled up to the person in charge of the hospital on a Saturday.

"What seems to be the problem, Ms. Morgan? Pete has indicated that you don't believe he's competent."

"Not at all! He has a cold, and I'm trying to recover physically. I just don't want to become sick, because then I won't be able to do therapy five or six days a week."

"I don't think the schedule we have for you is quite that rigorous," the assistant chief of staff answered.

"Listen," Tina said as patiently as possible. "I am here to work and get better. That's why I need every ounce of strength I have, and I don't want anything holding me back. Please give me another therapist," Tina demanded.

"It's Saturday," the supervisor said, "and we have no one else. It sounds like you're taking control of your medical care, Ms. Morgan."

"I've found that sometimes it's necessary to take personal responsibility for your life," Tina stated emphatically. She realized that, prior to the accident, she probably would not have stood up to someone in authority, but after what happened in the hospital, she wasn't going to sit quietly when she knew that she could get a serious infection. She had heard of people dying in hospitals because of careless errors, and she certainly wasn't going to become another statistic.

"We're short staffed because it's the start of the cold and flu season. It is taking its toll on our therapists, and Pete said he is feeling better."

"Well, he is not better, and I am not going to sit close to him and end up with pneumonia!" Tina said forcefully. "If you do not have staff who are healthy, then I do not want any treatment today."

"You really aren't being reasonable under the circumstances, Ms. Morgan, but suit yourself," the assistant chief of staff said.

"Thank you," Tina said, relieved. "That will be fine." But Tina was feeling shaken and angry.

The orderly wheeled Tina back to her room, where she once again looked at the four walls. Why did this discussion end up in an argument? What could Tina have done or said differently? Once again, she wondered how patients who are too ill to speak for themselves and don't have family around get the care that they need. Something was wrong with this medical protocol. Where is the patient advocate? Who stands up for the patient? Tina was seething. She closed her eyes for a minute.

"Be calm," she said to herself. "Just breathe and relax. You cannot do any more today." Tina continued to take in deep breaths until she could finally relax and focus on something else.

Tina told herself that she would call Cisco Samsel on Monday after her therapy and discuss medical insurance.

Her insurance carrier refused to cover non-scheduled airline flights, which included private non-commercial aircraft. A man from STA Aviation Insurance Services had made a short visit to Tina when she was in the first hospital almost a week before. At that time, he told her that the plane had $100,000 coverage per seat and $3,000 medical coverage. "That can't be!" Tina had cried. "My car has more insurance coverage then that! Doesn't the FAA have minimum coverage on airplanes?"

"I'm sorry, Ms. Morgan, they don't regulate the insurance limits. These are the limits, and that's what I came to tell you. It would be helpful if you could explain exactly what happened."

"We had this wonderful trip. The flight from Las Cruces to Baja Del Sol was almost uneventful," Tina said, enunciating the word *almost* in three syllables.

The insurance agent picked up on that and asked, "What do you mean by *almost*?"

"Christina Erickson and I were sitting in the backseat and reading our books. Suddenly, Christina raised her head, sat stiffly, looked around, and listened. Then she went back to reading. This body language disturbed me, but I didn't say anything at the time. A few days later when we met at a restaurant for dinner, I asked Christina what her body language meant, but, she did not answer me. Finally, Russell said he had just switched gas tanks, and I was satisfied with that answer and didn't ask any more questions. Thinking about this now, I find the behavior unusual. It's just a feeling. I felt she was holding something back from us and not telling us the truth."

"Then what happened?" the inspector asked.

"The day we were returning, we had planned to pick up Christina and Russell Erickson at their hotel and go to the airport together. When we called Christina to tell her we were on our way, she said that we would be picking her up alone, since Russell had gone to the airport earlier with some friends from the Aerostar Convention to check something out.

When we got to the airport, Russell was upset; he was trying to settle a dispute over the fuel bill, but he never mentioned what he checked out on the plane or why he had gone to the airport early. We boarded the plane and waited our turn to take off. After just a few minutes in flight, I smelled something burning. I looked out the window at the engines, and they appeared to be working perfectly and there was no smoke. About two minutes later, Christina said she smelled something burning, and then we all said we smelled something burning. At that point, Russell called the tower for permission to return to the airport. They gave him permission and asked him where he had come from. Russell was confused and flustered and gave the tower the wrong information, until Hunter corrected him.

"After Russell turned the plane around, I looked out the window and announced that the right engine had stopped. The left engine stopped turning right after that. Mrs. Erickson said, "We know, dear."

"The tower continued asking questions, but Russell didn't answer. His friend used the radio and asked Russell if he should follow us back, but Russell said no."

"'You go on to Las Cruces,' he said. Russell continued to ignore the tower. The loud warning horn and the landing gear lowering were the next things I heard. I thought we were going to die. I thanked God for the good life he had given me and just waited. The plane hit the ground hard and then continued to scrape along the ground until it stopped.

"I lifted my head, unfastened my seatbelt, and crawled out as far as I could. As soon as I laid down, I heard the first explosion and then the second one. I made myself crawl farther away from the plane." Tina said. She was tired of retelling the story.

"Both engines stopped?" the adjuster questioned with a voice that caused Tina to think that this was highly unusual.

"Yes," Tina said. She answered a few more questions and the adjuster left, not seeming to care that he had left her with the worst news she had received since losing Hunter. The inadequate insurance would not pay for her hospital bills.

Tina knew that there would be a lot of problems ahead. She was glad she had Mr. Samsel's name because she needed Russell Erickson's insurance on the plane and whatever else the lawyer could get to help pay for her hospital stay plus the next few months of rehabilitation therapy.

The phone rang early Sunday morning. "Tina?"

"Yes?" Tina recognized the voice, but couldn't immediately identify the speaker.

"This is Dr. Adam." The doctor's voice was gruff.

Tina was surprised he was calling on a Sunday. "Is something wrong, Doctor?"

"That's what I need to ask you. I received a call last night from the assistant chief of staff. You have to understand that we have no other place to put you. There's nothing else that could be done at UMC and you're not ready to go home. I thought I explained this clearly."

"You did, Dr. Adam. I did understand. The therapist was sick, and I just asked if I could work with someone else. I wasn't trying to cause a problem, but I didn't want to get sick myself and then not be able to proceed with the therapy."

"Tina, we are here to help you, but we need your help, too. It's simple, you have to behave while you are at the rehab hospital or no one is going to want to work with you." The doctor's voice sounded like a school principal confronting a rebellious student who had just been sent to his office, not at all like the kind and gentle doctor who had operated on

Tina just over two weeks ago. "This whole situation is very upsetting, Tina."

"I apologize, Dr. Adam. I want to get better and was hoping that I could start therapy right away."

"The staff can only work with who's available, and weekends are tight as it is. With people out sick, they can only do the best they can." Dr. Adam sounded tired. "It will probably be tomorrow when you can have your first therapy session."

Two wasted days! Tina felt helpless but didn't want to argue with Dr. Adam.

"Okay, Dr. Adam."

"I'll talk to you next week, Tina." And he hung up the phone.

Tina had been determined to be optimistic. Sunday in the hospital seemed like the longest day, and now the doctor was upset with her. Tina turned her thoughts to Hunter. He would want her to be strong. Maybe tomorrow would be better.

Monday finally came.

"Hello, there. My name is Emily. We're going to try to reduce that swelling in your ankle and leg. That will help it heal more quickly, and you will feel better. You can't start what I call the 'real therapy' until the bone heals."

"It's nice to meet you. I'm ready," Tina said.

"I'll take the boot off," Emily said, "That steaming water over there will warm up your muscles, and then we'll put your leg in an ice bath. We'll repeat that a few times, and it will help with the swelling."

Tina wasn't quite ready for the shock of the two temperature extremes on her already overly sensitive skin. The ice-cold water covered her foot for several minutes, and Tina experienced a painful, stinging numbness. She wanted to ask if they could quit for the day, but she knew she couldn't give up on her first day of therapy at the rehab hospital. Tina recalled that Emily had said this wasn't even "real therapy." By the end of the session, Tina was exhausted and they hadn't even done anything. How frustrating!

What can I do? Tina thought. *How can I cope and make the pain go away?* Then she recalled a college psychology professor who told the class that a person's mind can, to some extent, control happiness, sadness, anger, or pain. He gave his students the following example: you are on a crowded bus and somebody pushes into you. You turn around angrily, in pain and see a blind person. Immediately, you are not angry anymore. You tell yourself, he couldn't help it. Now let's change the scenario. Say, after you were shoved, you turn around and the person is large and looks tough, with a smirk on his face. You may not say anything aloud, but you still have angry thoughts. Therefore, it is what you tell yourself that can make you feel happy, sad, or angry.

"Okay," Tina said. "I will think of the beach, blue skies, and beautiful waves. I will listen to the surf and feel the sunshine on my back." At the next therapy session it worked! It didn't hurt as much and the time passed more quickly.

"You did great, Tina!" Emily assured her. "Get a good night's rest and I'll be back to see you tomorrow."

Tina glanced at her watch. She was tired and didn't think she was up to speaking with an attorney today. Tomorrow was another day. She could not schedule her appointment at his office until she was released from the rehab hospital anyway. Brook Grey had suggested she visit their law office so she could meet Mr. Baley, Cisco Samsel's partner, who would also be working on her case.

Tina waited in the rehab hospital, but no one came to see her that afternoon. Tina's mother had gone back to New York to make preparations so that she could return and stay with Tina for as long as it would take for her to heal and be on her own.

Tina must have dozed off because, the next thing she knew, the nurse opened her door. "Are you ready for dinner?"

Tina shrugged. "You'd think I'd be hungry after hours of therapy, but I don't have any appetite.

"You've already lost more weight than you need to, Tina. Why don't you just try to eat something?"

"You can leave the tray," Tina said. "I'll try a few bites." The mashed potatoes and pressed turkey didn't look appetizing at all.

She thought of Hunter and remembered how much fun they used to have trying out new restaurants. She closed her eyes so she could picture his face. His blue eyes, silver hair and tall lanky frame, all took her breath away. They had fit together so well. He was her prince, her fairy tale.

She wasn't Cinderella, but he always made her feel like she was special. There was a smile on Tina's face and, before she knew it, the exhaustion of the day overcame her. In her dreams, she was meeting Hunter for the first time.

"I HAVE BUT ONE LAMP BY WHICH MY FEET ARE GUIDED, AND THAT IS THE LAMP OF EXPERIENCE."
PATRICK HENRY

CHAPTER SIX
OCTOBER 1988

Tina's dream took her back to the Saturday morning of the Halloween party. She had just returned from the store, where she had found the perfect leotard and decorations for her costume. Now she needed to get to work. The partial face mask had inspired her idea. It looked like a bird, and the angled eyes and bright colors would keep everyone from recognizing her face. With the right costume, they wouldn't recognize the rest of her, either. She loved Jane's parties, especially the Halloween costume party, which had become an annual event and was the best of all. Everyone dressed in funky, or at least interesting, costumes. People also let their inhibitions go, maybe because they didn't think others knew who they were. Tina worked all afternoon, sewing row upon row of overlapping, colored feathers, so the leotard looked like the body of an ornate, winged creature. She stood up to stretch and admire her creation. "We'll see what this looks like," she said out loud. She pulled on her tights, then the leotard, then her gloves, and finally the mask. She laughed at herself in the mirror as she twirled around and the feathers fluttered with her every movement. She nodded at herself, and then shook her head. She wouldn't even have to talk; she would just nod at the other guests when they spoke to her. Tina went into the kitchen to slip her "special recipe" flan into a serving dish to take to the potluck dinner. People always complimented her on the sweet, delicate dessert that wasn't too heavy and asked how she had the patience to make sure it came out so perfectly every time. Tina always said it was a secret recipe, but the truth was, the flan was a mix she bought in a box. It was almost foolproof and it was quick and easy, too. It had come to her rescue again and had given her time to finish this fabulous costume instead of spending the afternoon in the kitchen.

Tina put everything in the car and drove with her mask on, getting some second looks from passing drivers as she made her way to Jane's house. The street was lined with cars, but she pulled up the long, winding driveway, since she knew she would be one of the last to leave after she helped clean up. Another car pulled in front of hers, and as she made her way up to the grand entrance of Jane's home, dessert in hand, she noticed a tall gentleman getting out of his car. He wasn't in a costume.

Why wear a costume when you're that good looking! Tina thought.

"Good evening," the gentleman said. Tina started to speak, but then remembered that she was an exotic bird. She nodded and hurried into the house ahead of him. She set her flan on the dessert table and started to walk around, admiring the princes and knights and clowns. She hadn't been there more than five minutes when she heard Tasha talking to a group of women in the corner.

"I know who that is!" Tasha told the others. "I would recognize those legs anywhere!"

I didn't fool them for long, Tina thought, but *I'm keeping the mask on.* Everyone was having such a good time, and the food, company, costumes, and Halloween decorations all contributed to a perfect party. Jane's veranda extended the length of the house, and the mountain views were breathtaking. Tina made her way to another group gathered outside near the sparkling pool that reflected the pumpkin lights strung in the trees. The sky was a deep midnight blue and the mountains loomed so close that Tina thought she could reach out and touch them. There was a faint glow over the mountains to the east. As Tina watched the sky, a voice startled her. "I like your costume. You have the perfect figure for that outfit."

As Tina turned to see who the voice belonged to, she realized that she had met the tall, tanned stranger who had parked in front of her. He had silver-black hair, and those twinkling eyes looking at her now were the same ones that mesmerized her at happy hour a few weeks before, when the singles group met. They had just introduced themselves that evening when another woman swooped in to talk to him. Tina didn't like competing for a man's attention, so she had moved on. Tina had met many interesting, fun, and even wealthy men over the years, but she had learned to take things slowly. After being a widow for seven years, she had become very patient. She liked men, but at her age, many of them were not looking for a long-term relationship. They were content to date several women at a time, or one at a time, but only for a few months. Other men preferred marathon relationships that lasted for years but went nowhere. Somehow it was much easier for men to have their cake and eat it too.

Tina was ready for a relationship. She knew just what to do. After all, she had recently finished reading the book *Beyond Cinderella*, by Nita Tucker, and that was the true guide to finding a prince. She was done with relationships that were going nowhere. This party was going to be the perfect venue to interview as many single men as possible and find out if any of them fit the bill. It may have seemed unemotional, but Tina had found that this approach was perfect for her, since she had found herself becoming emotionally attached to someone before she even knew if she and the other person shared enough of the same interests and if he would even consider marriage. She had followed the book exactly—she had made a list of attributes she was looking for in a mate and what values were most important to her. For example, if a man didn't like children, even though her boys were both over 20 years old, he probably wouldn't make them a part of his life. In the past, she had felt she had no control over where a relationship was going, but with this book as her guide, she liked knowing that she could find out so much about a person in a few minutes and not waste a year or complicate the situation with sex. *Here goes*, Tina thought, *Just 10 minutes for this interview and then I'll move on.* "Nice to see you again, I'm Tina."

"Hi, I'm Hunter. Hunter Smith. It's a pleasure to see you again, Tina." He did a mock bow. When he raised his head, his blue eyes looked right at Tina. The corners of his mouth twitched playfully, somewhere between a laugh and a smile. For the first time in a long time, Tina was speechless. She cleared her throat as she looked up at him. He had to be at least 6'2". "Are you from Las Cruces?"

"I moved here years ago from Topeka, Kansas, and I'm still glad I'm not shoveling snow in the winter. In fact, I remember several Halloweens when it was so cold all the kids had to wear their winter coats and you couldn't even see their costumes. I'll take this weather any day!"

"Yes, it's gorgeous out," Tina agreed. "Look, the full moon!" They watched the orange harvest moon climb into the sky and illuminate the mountains and the valley below. *Stay focused*, Tina told herself. She turned back to Hunter. "How do you know Jane?"

"Actually, I met Nancy, who told me to come to the happy hour at Los Amigos. That's where I first saw you and where I met Jane. She invited me to the annual Halloween bash. She said it was fun and that costumes weren't mandatory, so here I am!"

"Do you have any children?" Tina asked.

"Yes, I have five. Four are from my first marriage and then there is David, my love child. I decided to do everything right for him, but since his mother and I split up, I only see him on weekends, school holidays, and summer vacations. Sometimes he stays with me for a few days during the week, but it just isn't enough," Hunter said sadly. "I see David as much as I can. He's really a neat kid. He loves computers and does so well on them. I'm so proud of him."

"That's good," Tina said, putting a mental check mark beside the "Do you like children?" question.

"What do you do?" Tina asked.

"I'm retired," Hunter answered. "I play a lot of backgammon. I love the strategy, and a friend and I have even entered tournaments.

"That's so interesting. My father, grandfather, uncles, and their friends loved backgammon, too! They played most Saturday and Sunday afternoons. It must keep you out of trouble," Tina said, more as a statement than a question.

"I don't have time to get in much trouble. I keep busy," Hunter said. Tina liked that answer, too. He wasn't looking for someone to entertain him. He was sincere and didn't have all the cutesy answers that men often thought were so clever. He was smart but not a smart aleck, know-it-all type. Tina thought of past relationships with those kind of men.

Tina realized her 10 minutes were up. "Well, it was nice talking to you, Hunter. I'm going to see if I can help Jane, even though she seems to have everything under control." Tina walked away and had a hard time not turning around to look at Hunter one more time.

Tina went up to Jane in the living room. "Hi, Jane! I see you've finished another painting. When did you finish it? It's so colorful and the movement in the painting makes me want to reach out and grab the butterflies. You are blessed to be able to express your thoughts and feelings in your paintings. I have no artistic talent at all."

"This one took a little longer than usual," Jane replied, "but I'm happy with the way it turned out. Painting is a stress reliever for me. I'm in another world and become totally absorbed in the paint, the colors, and the image."

"I can relate to that," Tina said. "When I write poetry, I become lost in my own little world, too.

"You are an artist," Jane said, "just a different kind. I see you met Hunter. He seems like a nice guy."

Before Tina could reply, someone rather loudly said, "Jane!" Jane turned her attention to the voice.

Although Tina had planned to use her interviewing skills on more than one male subject tonight, she didn't feel like mingling right now. She slipped out to the backyard where two swings stood tucked away in a corner behind the guesthouse and one side of the pool.

"Hi, Bonnie," Tina greeted her friend, as she sat in the swing next to her. "What are you thinking about out here all by yourself?" Bonnie's son had been in a serious accident and Tina felt sorry for all of her problems.

"It's my son," Bonnie answered, sadly. "I wish he could be like other adults his age, but he never will be. Sometimes it just gets to me. I say 'why me,' but then I feel guilty for feeling that way."

"Listen, Bonnie. You are so good and loving and patient. You devote your life to your son and do everything for him when you're not at work. I admire you so much."

"Thank you," Bonnie said. "Your support and friendship mean a lot."

The two women chatted for awhile. Tina looked up at the full moon. "I'm going to help clean up and then call it a night," Tina told her friend, as she gave her a hug. "See you next week."

As she went around the corner of the guesthouse, a shadow made her jump. "Sorry to scare you," Hunter said. "I'm heading home, but I just wanted to find you and say goodnight. I really enjoyed talking with you."

Hunter leaned down and touched her face so softly that she almost couldn't feel it, until his fingers moved ever so slightly. She closed her eyes. She wasn't expecting it, but when his lips met hers, she didn't back away. He wrapped his strong arm around her back and pulled her close. She opened her eyes and held his gaze.

"I think I had better go," she said, feeling faint.

"I didn't mean to do that."

"You didn't?"

"I didn't mean to scare you away."

"You didn't. I am scared, though. If I don't leave, something might happen that we would both regret."

"I wouldn't regret it. You are really beautiful, Tina."

"I'm flattered, Hunter. But I do need to go tonight. I have a tennis tournament early tomorrow morning."

"Can I see you again?"

"I'd like that, Hunter. I'd like that very much."

This time, Tina kissed him. *I might have found my prince charming,* she thought.

"THEY KNOW ENOUGH WHO KNOW HOW TO LEARN."
HENRY ADAMS

CHAPTER SEVEN

Tina woke up and started to move her arm to rub the sleep from her eyes. She felt the heaviness of the metal spikes and the cross strips of metal that were embedded in her right hand and wrist, so she quickly put her arm down and rubbed her eye with her left hand. She smelled the single red rose before she saw it. "Oh Hunter, what a beautiful dream!" She almost expected to see him standing next to her hospital bed. How she missed him! He had been her prince charming and they had been almost inseparable for the past two years. About a year ago, Hunter took her to dinner and dancing at Crestview Canyon Resort on a Saturday night, as they had done many times before. She had worn a new dress. Hunter loved to see Tina in sexy clothes. Although he wasn't a clotheshorse himself, he never missed a detail in the clothes Tina wore, and he loved to compliment her. She was easy to look at, as he would say. In his eyes, she always had on the perfect outfit. He loved her figure and her hair and the way she walked and the perfume she wore. He simply loved her.

"Tina, will you marry me?" he had asked after a slow romantic dance. He held a box out to Tina, and when he opened it, there was a beautiful diamond ring from her store, Precious Jewelry. It was one of her favorites and he must have gone there when she wasn't in the store. Tina smiled. "I'll pay you for the ring," Hunter said quietly. "I just wanted to make sure this is the one you wanted."

"I love you, Hunter, and I love the ring." *I just don't know if I am ready for marriage*, Tina thought. "I like long engagements," Tina said, trying to sound positive. "We can be engaged, but I think we both need more time."

Hunter kissed her. He wasn't upset that she wanted to wait. He slid the ring on her finger and they danced until the wee hours of the morning. When they got home, Tina put the ring in its velvet box and slid the box in her drawer. She didn't wear it again, and they didn't tell their families they were engaged. They would get married when the time was right. Now that time would never come. "That was then and this is now," Tina thought.

Tina was actually hungry, and she enjoyed the breakfast of fruit and hot cereal. She felt stronger than she had in several days. She thought it was time for her to call the attorney and schedule an appointment. She was going to be in the rehab hospital for another week, so Tina thought the first week of December would be a good time to meet.

"Could I speak with Cisco Samsel?" Tina asked the attorney's receptionist slightly after 9 a.m.

"Just one moment, please."

"This is Cisco Samsel," the attorney answered. "How may I help you?"

Tina suddenly felt nervous. "Hello, this is Tina Morgan. Brook Grey gave me your name. I was in a plane crash in Mexico. Brook called to tell me you were a pilot and that you know a lot about planes. He thought you would be the best attorney to help me since you have your own plane."

"I'm so glad you called. Brook told me about you. If it's not too much to ask, could I come to the hospital sometime today?"

"I'm at the rehab hospital," Tina answered. "I thought I would schedule an appointment at your office after I was released from the hospital. I have therapy this morning, but you can come around 1 p.m. if you would like."

"That will be perfect. I look forward to meeting you, Ms. Morgan."

Tina hung up the phone, feeling relieved. How lucky could she be? A pilot and an attorney all rolled into one. Tina had made some notes for Mr. Samsel. At precisely 1 p.m., there was a knock on the door.

"Come in," Tina called out.

"It is so nice to meet you." Cisco Samsel strode toward her chair. Tina was surprised to see another gentleman enter the room behind him. "Oh, this is Rico Bond. He helps me with investigations from time to time. He's also experienced with cases in Mexico, so I thought he might be of some assistance."

"Brook mentioned that your partner would be working on the case, too," Tina commented.

"Yes, you will be able to meet him later. He's working on another case right now and is out of town."

"It's nice to meet both of you," Tina said. "Thank you for coming. As I mentioned to you, my insurance doesn't cover a non-scheduled flight, and the insurance adjuster with STA told me the limits on the plane were $100,000 per seat and only $3,000 for medical expenses. As I told the adjuster, my car is insured for much more than that! The liability alone is $1 million. It doesn't make sense that a plane can fly and have so little insurance. I definitely need your help."

"Yes, it's hard to believe. How old did you say the pilot was?"

"I don't know," Tina said. "My mother is in her 70s, and I would guess that Russell wasn't much younger. Why does that matter?"

"I'll have to work with the insurance company and find out why the limits weren't higher. In any case, I think we need to sue the Erickson estate."

"Isn't that a little premature? I don't want to sue them," Tina replied. "I just want them to pay my medical bills."

"Well, it looks like there might not be a choice if

you want to get more than the $103,000 quoted by the insurance company. I have a contingency agreement here for 30 percent. If you will sign it, I'll start investigating. We'll need to meet again and iron out more details. I'll need you to tell me about the crash in as much detail as possible."

"My friend brought my mail this morning, and you won't believe what was in it. The doctor in Mexico asked if I had an American Express card, and I received the bill today. It was for the Med-O-Vac plane that flew me from Mexico to UMC, and that bill alone was over $18,000. I know my medical bills will be much higher. I have no experience with any of this, but isn't the 30 percent you're asking for high?"

"It's a typical percent in this sort of case, Ms. Morgan. There's a lot at stake here."

"Would 25 percent of whatever we get after the $103,000 be acceptable?" Tina asked. "I'm sure I'll need every penny of that to pay the bills, and that's really all I'm looking for."

"The problem with that, Ms. Morgan, is that we don't know what that amount will be."

"I'm sorry. I really have to get back to therapy now. Would you be able to come back tomorrow? I'll be here for another week or so. No one tells me much."

"Yes, we can do that. But I really need you to sign this agreement so we can move forward. The quicker we can investigate what happened, the better. Does 1 p.m. tomorrow work for you?"

"That should work," Tina answered. "I'll be right here; I am not going anywhere."

Samsel changed the percentage to 25 percent and handed Tina the agreement for her signature. "We'll see you tomorrow, Ms. Morgan." The men left the room. The elevator door had barely closed, when Bond turned to Samsel. He was grinning from ear to ear.

"Your plan is working perfectly so far, boss!" Bond said, slapping Samsel on the shoulder.

"Yes. I can certainly convince Tina that it's in her best interests for me to go back to Mexico and see what I can dig up there, as long as I'll be going soon anyway. Of course she'll never know that she's the one helping me get down there again sooner than later," Samsel answered.

The next day, Tina was almost too nervous to eat her lunch, even though therapy had dragged on. She was anxious to see what ideas Mr. Samsel had today and to find out what information he needed from her.

Samsel had just gotten off the phone with the insurance company before leaving his office. Bond walked in as he was picking up his briefcase. "A little bird just told me a secret that we don't need to share with Ms. Morgan," Samsel said.

"And what might that be?" Bond said, his head cocked to one side. "There's also $100,000 insurance for the salvage of the plane, but she doesn't need to know that," Samsel replied.

"Hmmmm, that could come in handy," Bond nodded.

"I'm off to the rehab hospital to let her know about the trip to Mexico. See you later." It was a few minutes after 1 p.m. when Samsel knocked on Tina's door.

"Good afternoon, Ms. Morgan. Sorry I'm running a few minutes late. I was trying to get more information from the insurance company."

"That's okay," Tina said. "My therapy session was longer than usual this morning. Hopefully I've had a chance to catch my breath so I can give you the details that you need."

"Why don't you tell me about what happened in the plane? I need to find out as much as possible. Did you know the Ericksons well?"

"Actually, no I didn't. They were Hunter's neighbors in Las Cruces and didn't live there year-round. I was told he was an experienced pilot and they were nice neighbors. They were nice enough. When I mentioned to Christina that it must have been scary flying across the country at lower than normal altitudes to prevent ice from accumulating on the wings, she brushed it off. She seemed almost as confident as her husband around the plane and said she was the co-pilot as they flew from the East Coast to Las Cruces. When the engines shut off, Christina asked me if I wanted to lay my head in her lap. She was very calm and very kind."

"I know this is hard, but could you tell me what happened from the moment the plane took off?"

Tina went through every detail of those first few minutes of the flight again, just as she had told the insurance adjuster from STA.

"When Russell didn't answer the tower or the other pilots, did you hear any other noise in the cabin?" Samsel asked.

"Oh, yes. The cabin horn wouldn't quit blaring. The blaring was loud, but I don't know what made the horn sound. It started about the time the engines stopped, but we also had just smelled a smoldering odor. Russell didn't say what the blaring horn meant."

"That's interesting," Samsel said. "There are actually two cabin horns—one for fire and one for the engine configuration."

"I have to know," Tina said excitedly. "I have to know if the horn I heard was because of a fire or not. If it wasn't the fire horn, why didn't Russell return to the airport after he called the tower and turned the plane around?"

"The best way to determine which one was going off would be to get you back in a plane," Samsel said.

"Can you find an Aerostar so I can hear the sounds?" Tina asked. "I'll never forget that sound."

"The two horns have very distinct sounds," Samsel

explained, "so you will probably be able to recognize the difference immediately."

Samsel expected Tina to be somewhat apprehensive, but she didn't hesitate. "Yes! That would be perfect. I didn't know there were two horns. I do know it was the same sound the entire time," Tina said.

"Okay, that will help. In the meantime, I think we might be able to get more details on what was found at the crash site and any records that were kept in Mexico if I go there while you are still here in the rehab hospital."

"Oh, would you do that?" Tina asked.

"I was planning to go to that area again soon and could combine the trips. I can include it in my bill much later on," Samsel said. "I can fly in my private plane and land at the same airport—retrace some of your steps, if you will."

"Oh, I would really appreciate that. Maybe the men at the airport would remember something, too!" Tina said.

"I think this is a really good idea, Ms. Morgan. It will be much more productive to be there in person. It's almost impossible to get information over the phone from the officials in Mexico, between the poor phone reception and the language barrier."

"Please, call me Tina."

"Okay, Tina, I'll make the arrangements and let you know when I'll be leaving."

Samsel left and Tina felt almost giddy. *He'll be there where it all happened. Maybe there is more to this,* Tina thought. She was certainly ready to find out.

"LAUGHTER IS THE TONIC, THE RELIEF, THE SURCEASE OF PAIN." CHARLIE CHAPLIN

CHAPTER EIGHT

Tina's back hurt from lying in one position. The Hoffman on her arm prevented her from lying on her side. The bones in her hand had been pushed up into her arm when the plane crashed. The Hoffman, the device that would stretch the bones from the hand back out of the area where the wrist bones and hand bones met, would hold the bones in place. Metal spikes and metal bars were used in such an arrangement where they could be adjusted. Even with it on, Tina could somewhat move her fingers, and that felt good.

"Oh, what I'd give to be able to sleep on my side. With the Hoffman on my right wrist and the unwieldy boot on my left leg, I'm stuck on my back, just like a turtle landing on its shell with its legs flailing in the air. What a mess. I can't even dress myself. Now I understand how hard it is for people who have disabilities to manage. They should be given more credit for what they are able to do for themselves, no matter the task. Now, here I am in the same position, and it certainly isn't easy."

Tina tried to stretch. She admonished herself for the pity party she'd just had, even though it was truly how she felt. "I am going to overcome this," she said aloud. "I have to be able to do for myself. I am going to do whatever it takes, and more, to get these broken limbs to work again. Whatever it takes!" Tina said with persistence and resolve.

Once she got up and moved around in her wheelchair, she would feel better. She had almost forgotten what day it was! Her cousin was coming to visit, and her sons, Jason and Harry, would be coming, too. And then there was Roger.

How could she forget that Roger said he'd be back today, too? It would be almost like a celebration. In a few days it would be Thanksgiving, and as long as she showed improvement, Dr. Adam had given his permission for her to go home for the day. Yes, this was a day for celebration and for her to be surrounded by people who supported her and loved her and wanted her to get better.

She spent the next hour trying to get ready. After the aide helped her to the bathroom, Tina washed her face and brushed her hair. She hoped she didn't look as bad as her reflection in the mirror, which reminded her of a scarecrow with matted hair. Nonetheless, Tina thought, *This isn't the movies, and I'm not making a grand entrance for all my friends, who expect to see me made up and dressed to the nines. They will just have to put up with me in my nightgown, but at least it's my own.* Tina thought about Roger, too. He had called her at UMC and she told him she would be moving to the rehab hospital in three days and that she would be there for awhile. A few days after she entered the rehab hospital, he had called and said, "How about a slice of pizza?"

"That sounds great!" Tina said. The pizza had been a real treat after eating nondescript hospital food. What she hadn't quite expected was how much of a treat Roger's visit had been. During her stay at UMC Tina barely remembered any of her visitors, between the medication, fatigue, and trauma of the previous week. It was nice to be able to talk to Roger, and she really enjoyed his visit.

Roger's wife had passed away more than three years ago, and Tina had met him at the singles' club. He was one of the sweetest, kindest, and most gentle men she had ever met. He was friendly and helpful, too. Many of the women at the club also noticed his wonderful qualities, and he had plenty of invitations. When Tina had met Roger he had been a widow for only 6 months. Between going out with all the women and his work, Roger was busy, but he still found time to call Tina once a week. They would go out for dinner or meet for a drink and talk. For six months, Tina didn't date anyone else.

She remembered the last Thursday night Roger had called. "Would you like to go to dinner on Saturday night, Tina? I was thinking maybe we could start seeing each other more than once a week."

Tina had taken a deep breath. "You are a great guy, Roger, but I have been a widow for seven years. We're at different points in our lives. You need to date and spread your wings. You need time to heal and not rush into anything. I'm ready for something more. When I meet the right guy, I want to settle down again and get married. I wish you the best, but I don't think we should see each other anymore."

"Tina...?" She could tell that Roger wanted to say more.

"No," Tina said.

"I really like you and respect you. I wish you the best. Good luck." Tina could hear a hint of disappointment in Roger's voice when he answered her.

Tina had started seeing Hunter a few weeks before having this conversation with Roger. Hunter, as it turned out, had been single for many years and hadn't married the woman who was the mother of his son. Tina wanted to see where this relationship could go, and she knew that Roger needed time and space to recover from his loss. Tina thought that now there would be time to get to know Hunter. From that point on, it had been a mutually exclusive relationship for both of them. The next two years had been everything Tina could have hoped for. There had been two marriage proposals along the way but, at the time, there didn't seem to be any rush. Tina had just wanted to feel sure that Hunter was ready for the same commitment she was ready to make.

The door to her room opened, startling Tina and bringing her back to reality.

"Hi, Tina!" Susan, her cousin from California, said in a loud, jolly, voice as she whisked into the room and gave Tina a hug. Susan was thankful that Tina was alive. She had begged her cousin not to take the small plane to Mexico. She didn't have a good feeling about it, and the worst had happened.

"It's so good to see you," Susan said. "You really look great. Jason is coming, right? It's strange seeing you without Hunter," Susan said.

"He was such a gem. I miss him, too," Tina said.

"He was so special!" said Susan. "When he took all of us out to dinner, he was not only charming and generous, but he had an understated way of making everyone feel welcome and at home with him."

"That's how my boys felt, too, Susan. They really loved him, and now they feel another father is gone. It is really hard for them. I was surprised how great the impact of his death had on them. I have dated a few other men, and when I quit dating them, my sons were relieved. Kids know the phony men from the good guys. And if you ever want the real truth, just ask a kid!"

Just at that moment, Harry came into the room and gave his mom a kiss. The three of them chatted for awhile. Ten minutes later, Jason came through the door, and it was lunchtime.

"Are you tired of staring at these walls?" Susan asked. "We could go down to the cafeteria and get some lunch."

"That sounds wonderful," Tina said.

Harry started wheeling Tina to the cafeteria, but in the "Harry fashion," which meant running down the halls with the wheelchair, weaving in and out. He was so much like his father, it was almost scary! The menu was set, so they would get what was offered that day, but no one complained. It was good to spend time together. The conversation turned to Hunter and the crash. Beloved Hunter would be missed by all.

"Remember the day Hunter took us all to his club for 'formal dining' and it was lobster night?" Jason reminisced. Tina did remember. Part of the family was there, including Hunter's son and daughter-in-law, his sons Dan and David, and Jason and Tina. "We had that lobster-eating contest to see who could eat the most lobster and, of course, I won the contest, eating six of those things!"

"Yuk!" Tina and Susan said at the same time, and they all started laughing. Tina found herself feeling more like her old self.

"It looks like you are all having too much fun!" a familiar voice said. Tina turned in her wheelchair to greet Roger. She introduced him to Susan, Harry, and Jason. Roger sat down with them, and they all talked some more.

As they ate their lunch, Susan, out of the blue, said in a serious, quiet voice, "I just want to warn you, Roger. Tina is bad luck! Any man who decides to hang around her doesn't have a chance. She has killed two men already. Men are unlucky around her. You'd better run while you have a chance."

There was truth in Susan's statement, so nobody laughed or thought it was funny. Tina wasn't sure whether she wanted to laugh or cry, but it was so true. Her first husband had died after trying to avoid a tractor trailer on the freeway, and she had waited for the perfect guy after years of being alone. She thought she would be with Hunter forever, and now he was gone. Susan continued by saying, "She's like the black widow. She is just plain bad luck!"

As the others continued to talk, Tina thought, *The truth is, I don't want another man! I married my high school*

*sweetheart and he gave me my boys, and then I had my
prince charming. I have had it all.*

"I need to get going," Roger said.

"We should let your mother rest," Susan said to her
cousins.

"I am a little tired," Tina admitted, breaking away from
her thoughts.

Everyone said their good-byes.

The next morning, Tina was overjoyed. It was
Thanksgiving Day and she could finally go home. She would
return to the rehab hospital that night, but being with her
family and being out of the hospital for the first time was the
best gift she could have asked for. Susan and her sons, Harry
and Jason, were at the rehab hospital promptly at 11 a.m.

"Are you ready to go home?" Harry asked.

"I am more than ready!" Tina answered. "Let's get out
of here!"

The attendant wheeled her out the front of the building,
where Jason was waiting with the car. It was a warm
November day, and Tina's entire body soaked in the sun's
rays. She looked up at the blue sky and the mountains.

Once in the car, Tina turned to look at both Harry and
Jason. Spontaneously, she said, "I love both of you so much.
Thank you for being here and supporting me."

"I love you, too, Mom," the boys said in unison. "You
seem really happy today."

"I am. It will be strange to have Thanksgiving without
Hunter, but I am so blessed to have you and Jason," Tina told
her sons. "And then of course, my favorite cousin, Susan,
who begged me not to fly in that small plane."

"I was so scared that I was going to lose you when the call
came in that you were in a plane crash. It was so scary! I'm still
just a kid, and I didn't want to lose my mom! You're the best,"
said Harry. Susan looked on, content and pleased that her

cousins were so happy. *Harry is right!* Susan thought. *It was really close.*

As they drove toward home, Harry said, "Look, pizza!" There was a small, pizza restaurant just a few blocks from home.

"We aren't eating until later this afternoon," Susan said. "Let's stop. What do you say?"

"That sounds so good! Let's do it! It's amazing how much you appreciate something when you don't have it—family, pizza, turkey, the beautiful sky and the mountains; it's all here for me to enjoy again," Tina said.

The true spirit of Thanksgiving was in Tina's heart as she spent the day savoring her family, the sights, the sounds, and the smells.

Life can be bittersweet. Here I am enjoying the day at home, but without Hunter," Tina thought. *I will miss him always, especially on holidays.*

By the time they had finished the turkey dinner, Tina was so tired she could barely sit up. In fact, she was exhausted, and she hadn't been able to enjoy the day quite as much as she had anticipated. It was a big step, though, to leave the hospital and be back in familiar surroundings. It was a tiring step, as she found out, but more than worth it. Yesterday she thought she would dread the ride back to the hospital, but now she was actually looked forward to returning. She was too tired to talk, so she let the others carry on the conversation. Harry knew his mother was strong, but she looked so pale and frail due to all the weight she had lost. It had been a long day for Tina.

Tina silently greeted the hospital as an old friend when Harry, Susan, and Jason brought her back to her room. After all, she knew her days here were numbered, and she still had a lot of work to do.

"Thanks for everything, you guys," Tina said, giving her sons and Susan big hugs and kisses.

"It was so great to see you," Harry said. "I have to go home and back to work tomorrow. I am catching an early plane. Mom, I know you'll be out of here soon."

"I know. There's still a lot of work to be done so I can walk and use my arm and hand again," Tina said.

"If anyone can do it, Mom, you can. I'll see you soon," Harry said. "I'm proud of you."

"Have a safe trip and call me when you get back. Love you!" Tina smiled up at her son. They all said good-bye as the attendant brought the wheelchair out to the car. Tina got ready for bed and then, as her head hit the pillow, she sighed. "We can do this!" she said to the walls, as she started to drift off to sleep. She felt as if Hunter were right next to her, cheering her on.

"ALL GLORY COMES FROM DARING TO BEGIN."
EUGENE F. WARE

CHAPTER NINE

J ust a few days after Thanksgiving, Tina was going home for good. She was disappointed that she hadn't accomplished more at the rehab hospital, but she remembered what Emily, the physical therapist had said: "I know you are impatient, Tina, but actually little can be done until the Hoffman is off your hand and wrist and your wounds have healed. The doctor may take some of the hardware out of your ankle, too, so you must be patient." Patience was not one of Tina's virtues, but, at this point, there was nothing she could do.

Just two days before she was to be released, on December 1, there was a knock on her door.

"Hi, Sunshine," Roger smiled.

"Hi!" Tina said, surprised, but happy to see him. Apparently, Susan's stories of the black widow hadn't been enough to scare Roger away.

"I woke up in the middle of the night thinking about you," Roger said.

"Oh, really?"

"Well, I was trying to think of the best way for your mom to get you home. You will also need transportation when you start therapy," he explained.

"You must have ESP!" Tina said. "I was thinking about the same thing early this morning. There is a big problem. My BMW has a manual transmission, and I don't think now is the time for Mom to learn how to drive a stick shift. When I was 12 and we moved to the suburbs in New York, the first car our family ever owned had an automatic transmission!"

"Here's my idea," Roger went on. "If you trust me with

your "Beemer," we could swap cars until you are mobile and able to drive again. I kept my wife's big boat; it's a four-door Chrysler automatic, with very easy access to the backseat. I think it would be perfect for your wheelchair and walker."

"And my mom would feel safe and comfortable driving it, too!" Tina beamed. "I can't believe this! It's almost too good to be true."

"It's a deal then?" Roger asked.

"It's a deal!" Tina said. "I just don't know if I'll be able to ever repay you, Roger. And remember what Susan told you—I'm bad luck."

"Tina, I'm not looking for repayment. Actually I think you're quite amazing, and if you don't mind me being around, I can help out, too. If your mom needs a break or you need me to run an errand, I'd be happy to do it."

"Thank you, Roger. I can't tell you how much I appreciate this. I feel like the damsel in distress in a fairy tale, except that I've been rescued now more than once!"

"I'll go get the car ready," Roger said. "If you want to let your mom know about the plan, I will get the car to her later this afternoon. What time are they letting you out of here on Wednesday?"

"I should be checked out and ready to go by 11 a.m.," Tina answered.

"I will drive over in your car and meet you here. I can help your mom load up your things, and then we'll get you in the car. How does that sound?"

"That sounds so wonderful! This is really the beginning of a new life, a different life for sure, but I know I need to get strong and make the best of it. I'll see you Wednesday. Thanks again, Roger."

Roger left and Tina still couldn't believe how things were working out. She wasn't sure why Roger was there to support her, but they had been friends. They had very much enjoyed each other's company during their six months of sporadic dating. As Tina had told him, before she had gotten more serious with Hunter, the timing hadn't been right for either one of them a couple of years ago.

Wednesday morning dawned bright and clear. Tina felt like a child getting ready for her first day of school. She absolutely couldn't wait to get out of the rehab hospital. The morning seemed to drag on. She was too excited to eat breakfast. Finally, she called the front desk to request the paperwork that she would need to complete before her release. That kept her busy for a while.

"Are you ready to go home, Tina?" her mom asked.

"I'm glad you're here, Mom. Yes, I am definitely ready. Is Roger's car okay for you to drive?"

"Oh, Tina, we couldn't have asked for a car that would work better for you. It has a roomy trunk and a big backseat. It's easy to drive, too."

"That's great. It was really nice of Roger to offer to trade cars until I can drive again."

"Yes, it was," her mom agreed.

Both women turned when they heard someone walking into the room. "Did I just hear my name?" Roger asked.

"Were your ears burning?" Tina laughed. "Mom was just saying how great the car is going to work out."

"What are we waiting for?" Roger asked. "Let's get this show on the road."

Tina felt helpless as Roger and her mom started carrying things to the car. She took a deep breath. In addition to working hard to recuperate, she also had to remind herself to be patient. She had no doubt that she would walk again and that she would once again dance and play tennis and golf. Her challenge was to not get frustrated during the recovery process. Tina was a very self-disciplined, organized person, and when she didn't have complete control over a situation, she felt lost. "Stay positive," she told herself. She knew that the negative feelings caused by feeling overwhelmed and frustrated were counterproductive.

When Roger and her mom came back to walk with the attendant who was pushing Tina's wheelchair to the car, Tina said, "I just want to tell you that I'm going to work as hard as I possibly can and get better in record time. You'll see!"

Both her mom and Roger smiled. They had no doubt that she would do whatever she set her mind to.

Tina had been home for a week and she was happy to be home. Doctor Adam had ordered a CPM machine for Tina to use to exercise her foot. *CPM* stands for "continuous passive motion," She would lay her foot in it and the machine would raise Tina's foot up and down. She used the machine for 30 minutes to an hour three or four times a day while watching TV or reading. This helped to pass the time. She couldn't do much, but at least she was home.

Thanks to Roger, her mother could take her out, wheelchair and all. Tina and her mom could play bridge at the bridge club. They went Christmas and Chanukah shopping in the mall, and Tina felt like an animal that was let out of her cage.

In the mall, everything was alive as people rushed around and shopped. At one point, a young boy of about 14 came up to Tina's wheelchair and said, "I had one of those," as he pointed to her wrist. "I was thrown off a horse and put out my hand to stop the fall. Look! See, I can move my hand halfway around."

"How long ago was your accident," Tina asked?

The young boy answered, "I've been out of the Hoffman for over eight months now."

"That's great!" Tina said. "I wish you lots of luck and a full recovery."

Wow, Tina thought as her mom wheeled her in and out of

the specialty stores. *That's not good. His range of motion is only about 60 percent. I won't be able to play tennis or golf with that kind of range of motion. I'll have to work harder if I want to get my life back together.* Tina decided that she would schedule her outpatient therapy and follow-up doctor appointments as soon as possible.

The next day, while she and her mother were eating breakfast, the phone rang. "Hi, Susan!" Tina said. "It's great to hear from you." Tina's mom listened to the one-sided conversation. "Well, I'll have to ask my mom. Yes, I would really like that. Let me see if it will work out. I'll call you back later this morning."

"What was that all about?" her mom asked.

"Susan asked if I could come out to California over Christmas break. She has a couple of weeks off, and she mentioned that it would give you time to go back to New York and be with the twins during the holidays." Tina's sisters, who were three years her junior, would enjoy having their mom home for the holidays. "I wish I could tell you when you could go home for good, Mom, but I just don't know when I will be able to do things on my own."

"I don't want you to push yourself too hard, Tina. Are you sure you're up for a trip?"

"I actually think a change of scenery would be really good for me, and I can't start the outpatient therapy until January. I don't want you to disrupt your life too much and I will be fine with my cousins. Just being at Susan's house will be nice, and I'll feel more independent, being able to go somewhere."

"I can stay as long as you need me," her mom said. "Going to New York would give me a chance to tie up a few loose ends, make sure some mail is sent here... things like that. If you're sure, Tina."

"Thank you, Mom. I am sure, and I think this will be good for both of us."

Tina called Susan and told her the good news. She felt like a teenager going to visit her cousin for a holiday. She remembered those visits when the girls would stay up until all hours talking about various businesses, future plans, and careers. It seemed like only yesterday.

That evening, Tina's cousin Rita called to talk and to tell her she had a friend, Bonnie Prudden, who had written many books on exercise, health, and pain easement. She said Bonnie had done the research and written the report on the comparative fitness of European and American children. President Eisenhower created the President's Council on Physical Fitness and Sports based on her findings. "She has been so successful with her treatment of pain that you must speak to her," said Rita. "Promise me you will."

"I will, I promise. No one wants to get well more than I do. I know I have to take on the responsibility of my treatment. I will work hard. I will do whatever it takes."

Dr. Adam had scheduled outpatient surgery for removal of the Hoffman from Tina's right wrist. She was happy that she didn't have to spend another night at the hospital.

When December 18 arrived, Tina and her mom were at the hospital early. "Are you ready?" Dr. Adam asked.

"You bet," Tina said. "I've been waiting for this day for a long time." As the medication in the IV dripped into her veins, she started to relax. This time there was a grin on her face and she felt total peace because this would be the next step toward her total recovery. "Now I will really have time to catch up on things at home, spend time with Mom, and just get back on my feet." *I am so lucky*, she thought, as she drifted off.

When Tina woke, she had a cast on her wrist. "What is this, Dr. Adam? You said I wouldn't need a cast."

"Well Tina, I did this as a precaution."

"Oh, please, take it off. It's restricting my movement. I'll be careful. Please, I don't want a cast now after not wearing one all these weeks."

Dr. Adam thought for a minute and agreed to remove the cast the next day if Tina still wanted it removed. He said she had to get fitted with a removable wrist splint as soon as possible. He filled out a prescription for it.

"I want you to go to occupational therapy two days a week for your wrist and three days for your ankle. I want to recommend an aggressive therapy program for both," Dr. Adam said.

"Doctor, I want to go five days a week. I want to get better fast."

"Well, let's not get too aggressive. How about three days on your wrist and four days on your ankle?"

"Okay, Dr. Adam, that will work for me. One other issue, Doctor. I told you about Myotherapy, a procedure done by a therapist on trigger points that are causing pain. By applying pressure to the trigger points, the blood flows better to the muscle and the pain eases. When an injury occurs, trigger points cause pain that keeps the patient from doing other kinds of therapy that will help the patient recover. Here is a copy of *PAIN ERASURE: The Bonnie Prudden Way*. It explains the wonders of 'trigger point therapy.' I spoke with Bonnie, the author. She is a friend of my cousin Rita in New York. Rita called to tell me I needed to look into Bonnie's therapy. If Myotherapy reduces or gets rid of the pain, I can concentrate on therapy and get better much faster. Bonnie sent me her book, and I want you to look at it. I feel that this method, along with everything you want me to do, will help me get well. I spoke to a myotherapist in Albuquerque, but he said I need a letter from you before he will treat me."

"After I remove the cast tomorrow, I will see you on December 27, Tina," Dr. Adam said. "I will let you know then."

Tina went home with a whole host of instructions, a boot on her left leg, and a wrist that didn't move much but would be free tomorrow. This cast was coming off! Oh, what a day!

A few evenings later, Tina's mom said, "Things are really moving along. I haven't told you this, but I'm proud of you, Tina. You have an underlying strength that just won't quit."

The doorbell interrupted their conversation. Her mom went to open the door.

"Roger! It's so good to see you," her mom said.

"Sorry I dropped by unannounced. I was just thinking about the holidays and wondered what everyone's plans were. I thought maybe we could have dinner together."

As they entered the den, Tina looked up at them and said, "I just made plans to go to California to see Susan. Look at my wrist! My Hoffman was removed yesterday," Tina said with excitement in her voice.

"Well, look at you. Pretty proud of yourself, aren't you?" Roger said with a chuckle. "What's this about California?"

"Mom's going back to New York, and I'm going by myself," Tina announced.

"Well, I'm not going anywhere, so I'll play chauffeur and make sure two of my favorite ladies get to the airport."

"Roger, you really don't have to," Tina began.

"I don't think a cab is very practical, do you?" Roger asked. They all burst into laughter, as if they all pictured a cab driver pulling up, looking at the stuff Tina had to take in addition to her suitcase, shaking his head, and driving away.

"At least you know what you're getting yourself into," Tina agreed.

Tina spent the next few days getting ready for the trip. She also made a calendar of the outpatient therapy schedule that she would start after seeing Dr. Adam at the end of the month.

The day she left for California, Roger came as promised and loaded everything into the Chrysler, including her. He was so polite and positive. They joked about how she would set off all the bells when she went through security with the screws and plates in her ankle.

"Thanks, Roger. I'll see you when I get back."

"I'll be at the gate at 3 p.m. sharp on December 26. Merry Christmas, Tina!"

When Tina was settled in her seat in the front of the plane, she leaned back and closed her eyes. Roger was a prince of a man, a knight in shining armor. She realized how much help he had been and how much time he had spent lately with her and her mom. He was so busy with work, but he found time to help them. *He must not have much of a social life right now*, she thought. Maybe he had gotten to the same point she had been over two years earlier when she needed a break and didn't date for awhile. Roger was a good guy and someone to grow old with. *Another time, another life*, she thought. *At one time I may have been interested, but not now. I don't have time for a man in my life. I have too much to do. So much work ahead of me.*

What she didn't know was that Roger was thinking of her as he drove home. He had hoped to spend this Christmas with her, but if his feelings continued to grow for this beautiful, resilient woman, there would be many more Christmases. *The last thing she's thinking about right now is a man in her life*, Roger told himself firmly. *I am a patient man; I can wait.*

Before the plane departed, a little boy sat down next to Tina. He was about seven or eight years old and he was traveling alone.

"Hi," Tina said.

"Hi," he answered quickly, wanting to ask the question that was on the tip of his tongue. He kept looking at Tina's leg in the boot. "What happened to you?" he asked.

"You don't want to know," Tina told him.

"Yes, I do."

"You really don't," Tina said. They were both quiet for awhile.

"I do want to know," the little boy said again with persistence.

Tina thought for a minute. "Okay, I'll tell you, but I don't want you to be scared. I was in a plane crash."

The little boy's eyes became as big as saucers. "Really?" he said quietly, in a questioning tone.

"Yes, but I'm not afraid to be on this plane, and I don't want you to be either. It was a much different kind of plane. Something happened, and we landed in the desert in Mexico. Some men saved me. See, I told you that you didn't want to know."

The little boy looked at Tina like she was a hero. He had so many questions to ask her. They spent much of the short trip talking.

What did go wrong? Tina asked herself. *When Cisco has time, he will go to Mexico. Maybe then we'll have more information. I have to go back into another Aerostar plane. I have to see the plane again and hear those alarms.*

Tina tried to rest, but Christina's voice haunted her. "We know, dear."

*"NOTHING GIVES ONE PERSON SO MUCH ADVANTAGE OVER
ANOTHER AS TO REMAIN ALWAYS COOL AND UNRUFFLED UNDER
ALL CIRCUMSTANCES." THOMAS JEFFERSON*

CHAPTER TEN

Just as he'd promised, Roger was waiting at the gate when Tina deplaned in Las Cruces after her visit to California. Being with her cousin Susan and the family had been exactly what Tina needed. Even though she was there for only a few days, it had been the perfect holiday, with time to relax, play games, and talk and laugh together.

They had even taken Tina to the beach for a couple of hours. The waves crashing on the sand soothed Tina's mind and rejuvenated her soul. The ocean's power and beauty were contrasts that Tina could relate to now more than ever. As a child, she had experienced the dangerous strength of riptides and had respected the sea's unpredictable ebb and flow ever since. Tina had been taught by a friend, who was a strong swimmer and lifeguard, to remain calm and focused. If she swam parallel to the current, she would be able to get out of the water's strong pull and swim back to shore. That's how she was going to confront her recovery, with a calculated approach that would allow her to be in control, even though she knew the odds might seem insurmountable at times.

"How was your trip?" Roger asked.

"I feel so refreshed and even a little stronger. I'm anxious to see Dr. Adam tomorrow and find out if he'll sign off on the Myotherapy treatment that Rita suggested," Tina answered. "I've read some more about it, and I can't wait to try it."

"I have to work tomorrow, or I would be glad to take you to your appointment. I can pick you up in the afternoon and we can go to the airport to pick up your mom," Roger said.

"Thank you, but I have already taken care of that. Jack drives a cab, and I asked him to pick me up and take me to my appointment. I will call him when I am ready to be picked up. Mom is not returning until the end of the week; she is staying a few more days. Jack will be there when she arrives. Thank you anyway, Roger. I'll never be able to repay you as it is," Tina smiled.

Roger helped Tina get settled and, before he left, her friend Jane came to stay with her. "I'll see you tomorrow," Roger said. "Have a fun evening!"

Tina and Jane had fun catching up. "I just thought of something," Tina said. "If Hunter and I hadn't gone on that trip, we would have been at your Halloween party, just like last year, and the year before. And Hunter would still…"

"Hey, no 'what ifs,'" Jane said gently. "What ifs and if only's can't change what happened. They can make you feel really bad, though."

"You're right, Jane," Tina told her friend. "I can't help but feel guilty. What did I do to deserve to live? And why did he die? I keep thinking that I should have done more. I should have looked around the plane before leaving. I should have called out to Hunter. I should have crawled over to where I heard his voice instead of just staying where I was. I try not to think negatively, but it does seem worse when I'm tired."

"Tina, stop. You were injured. You couldn't do anything, and it was a miracle you crawled out, considering how severe your injuries were. It still hasn't been very long, Tina," Jane said, putting everything into perspective. "You are an intrepid soul, my friend. You should get some rest."

"Intrepid?" Tina teased. "That's a big word."

"Well, you're more than brave. I really admire you," Jane said.

"Because I look so stunning? This boot could make a great Halloween costume."

"Come on, I'll help you get ready for bed," Jane offered.

Tina didn't realize how tired she was until her head hit the pillow. What happened to feeling totally rejuvenated earlier today? There it was again, that ebb and flow, just like the ocean.

She slept almost better than she had since before the accident.

DECEMBER 27, 1990

Today, Tina would find out if the occupational and physical therapy she had discussed with Dr. Adam were set to proceed as she hoped. Jack drove her to UMC and said he'd be back when she called. She was on a first-name basis with the nurses. Suddenly Tina was very nervous. What if her bones weren't healing properly? What if she had reached a plateau? The longer she waited, the more nervous she got.

Finally, there was a knock on the door. "Hello, Tina, good to see you." Dr. Adam's calm, knowing demeanor made her feel better. "We're going to take a few pictures and see how everything's healing. I'll send a report over so the occupational and physical therapists will know at what level you are progressing."

"Okay," Tina said. "I'm ready for the camera!"

Dr. Adam came back in the room with the x-rays in his hand. "Both your leg and wrist are healing nicely. Now let's check your range of motion." Dr. Adam's hands were cool on Tina's ankle and foot. It didn't hurt when he moved her foot slightly, but her ankle wouldn't bend very far.

"Any pain in your ankle or foot?" he asked.

"My ankle aches," Tina said, "and look how swollen it is."

"You have about 30 percent flexion in your ankle right now. I will ask that your therapists work with you so that you progress to full-weight bearing with the cast boot on. The physical therapist will work with you on lateral ankle strengthening. If you are comfortable, you can transition from the boot to high-top tennis shoes for the next couple of months. One of the fractures is continuing to heal slightly faster than the other. There's some movement in one of the fracture lines, but it's still fixated and not separating, which is a good sign."

"That's great," Tina said. "It will be nice to have the boot off."

"Now let's take a look at the wrist. Are you having any pain in your wrist?"

"Not much, if I don't move my wrist. But it is stiff and doesn't do what I want as far as turning." When Dr. Adam tried to rotate it, her wrist rotated about 30 percent. Tina's wrist wasn't swollen or deformed, like her ankle, and she had little pain when her arm hung by her side.

"Is that bad?" Tina asked when they discovered she had limited rotation of her wrist.

"Occupational therapy for your hand and wrist range of motion will really help. We'll work on strengthening your forearm, too. It's had quite a rest! We'll get you into a splint for your wrist," Dr. Adam explained.

"What do you think about my trying Myotherapy as well?" Tina asked. She felt as if she were holding her breath, knowing that some doctors didn't agree with alternative medical treatments.

"From what I've read, it can't hurt," Dr. Adam replied. "Your muscles are definitely going to be sore for a while, and the Myotherapy might help with that. We don't want the stiffness and soreness slowing down your other therapy sessions. You'll be busy, so I won't need to see you until March, unless something changes."

"Thank you for everything, Dr. Adam. I'm going to have my old life back because of you."

"I may have pointed you in the right direction, Tina, but now it's up to you." Dr. Adam patted her good hand. "If anyone can make a full recovery, you can."

"I'll be playing tennis and golf again. You just wait and see!" Tina looked at the doctor with tears in her eyes.

"You've made quite a name for yourself around here, Tina. Take care."

With that, Dr. Adam left and the nurse walked with Tina back to the waiting area.

"Look, I'm sorry if I caused any trouble or problems for anyone," Tina said in a quiet voice as she left the office.

Tina threw herself into her therapy. She was also anxious to start seeing the Myotherapist from Albuquerque. Those sessions would be on weekends and would start in a couple of weeks. The days flew by.

During the week, Tina was at UMC getting therapy. They used hot wax on her wrist and then started to twist the hand slightly upward. The wrist didn't move much. Tina couldn't even hook her bra in the back, since that would require turning her wrist, so she had to get bras that hooked in the front. But she kept trying. When Tina was home, there was her mom, the slave driver, who would say, "Tina, let's practice," or "Tina, let me work your wrist a little more." And so the days went by, and Tina's wrist and ankle got stronger.

"Stand up straight," the therapist working on Tina's ankle and posture would say. "Chin up, back straight, and walk." Tina looked at all the work as a job.

"This is my job, and I am going to do the best I can do. I will put in overtime, if necessary, and I will work every day." The only problem with this approach is that most people who worked jobs had a day or two off, but not Tina. There were no holidays and no breaks, and it was all very tiring, but Tina forged ahead and didn't complain.

In mid-January, Cisco Samsel called. "Hello, Tina. I was wondering if I could stop by to talk to you. I have located an Aerostar out at Parker field. It's the same model that you flew in. I also want to take some pictures of your injuries to add to the pictures I took when you had the Hoffman and the boot. I'm also getting ready to go to Mexico next week and see what I can find out. I don't know if you're feeling up to going to look at the plane now, or if you want to wait until I get back."

"Thanks for calling, Mr. Samsel. You don't even need to come by to talk, unless it's to pick me up and take me to that plane. I can put weight on my foot and I am wearing a high-topped tennis shoe, so it will be easier to get in the plane. You can take your pictures at that time."

"Could I pick you up tomorrow morning around 10?" Samsel asked.

"Perfect!" Tina said.

Tina's mom helped her get ready the next morning. She was doing more and more on her own each day. "Do you want me to come with you?" her mom asked.

"I'll be fine," Tina said. "If I need a boost to look at something, I'm sure Mr. Samsel can help."

Samsel arrived right on time, and they headed toward the small airport that housed private planes. "Like I said earlier," Samsel said, "I'll see what I can find out in Mexico. As you know from being there, that could be easier said than done. If I can find somebody who was around when the crash happened, we might get more information.

"Their media coverage on things like this is different than it is here in the United States. We can't just ask for a copy of a tape that aired on the news the next day."

"I understand," Tina responded. "I do appreciate your

checking it out. If you go to the airport, someone there will probably know something. The air traffic controller spoke English and might be able to help."

They drove right up to the hangar where the Aerostar was parked. Tina's heart lurched for a moment. It was not as pretty as Erickson's plane, which was striking with colors of silver and teal blue, but, on the other hand, it would be the same inside.

Samsel came around, opened the passenger door for her, and helped her out of the car. Tina wobbled getting out of the car. "Are you okay?" Samsel asked.

"Just got dizzy for a second," Tina answered, holding onto the car door. She took a deep breath. "Let's have a look."

They walked over to the plane with its call letters displayed proudly on the tail. Samsel opened the single door on the pilot's side and they got in. This time, Tina was sitting in Hunter's seat. "I'm going to set off both alarms," he said. "You tell me which alarm you heard. The first alarm went off and it was loud, incessant, and high pitched.

"That's it!" Tina said, in an excited and loud voice. "That is the one."

"Okay, Tina, now let's listen to the other horn, to be sure." The other horn was a lower, deeper sounding horn and equally loud.

"That's not the one," Tina said. "Now, tell me what does the horn I heard indicate? Don't hold me in suspense. I've waited a long time to know this."

Samsel turned off both horns and calmly said, "The sound you heard in the cabin was the engine alarm."

"That's the only one that ever sounded. There was never a fire. That alarm never went off," Tina confirmed. "I knew it! I knew it all along," Tina said excitedly. "You don't have to be a pilot. My observations about the engines had always been correct."

"There's one mystery solved," Samsel said.

Tina had an urge to stay and look at the intact plane with its shiny instruments and perfect wings. When she shut her eyes for a minute, she could picture the burnt, dismembered wreckage lying in the desert. Tina slowly and quietly got out of the plane and walked toward the car with Samsel. She didn't look back.

"If there was no fire, why did the engines stop? What do you think that means?" Tina asked.

"There wasn't a fire," Samsel said. "The sound you heard was the airplane telling the pilot that it cannot fly in that configuration when the engines are turned off."

"So you are saying that Russell had to manually turn off both engines?" Tina asked.

"Let's see what I can learn when I am in Mexico."

"Have a safe trip," Tina said, after Samsel delivered her to her mom and took the pictures he wanted.

"I'll call you when I get back," he answered.

More questions crowded Tina's mind. *Why hadn't Russell answered the other airplane, or the tower for that matter? Why did both engines turn off? Why didn't he tell Hunter and Tina what he was looking for before he went to the airport early that day, and why, oh why, didn't I ask? I am usually so perceptive.* In the restaurant, Christina actually avoided my questions about her behavior and body language in the cabin of the plane when I asked why she stiffened up and looked around before continuing to read her novel when we were flying to Baja Del Sol.

Tina didn't have the answers. Her father had always told her never to speak ill of the dead. Tina had defended the Ericksons when anyone even hinted that maybe something could have been done to land safely. "He tried to do everything he could," Tina would say. Now, she wasn't so sure. There were so many unanswered questions. Thinking back, Russell didn't even answer the tower or give them the plane's coordinates.

She prayed that Samsel would find some missing pieces to the puzzle in Mexico.

"THE SETTING OF A GREAT HOPE IS LIKE THE SETTING OF THE SUN. THE BRIGHTNESS OF OUR LIFE IS GONE."
HENRY WADSWORTH LONGFELLOW

CHAPTER ELEVEN

Tina went to occupational and physical therapy like clockwork. She continued to believe that therapy, to her, was like a job, and she always put her heart and soul into it. This temporary work was challenging, difficult, and rewarding all at the same time. In fact, she heard the therapists comment among themselves that her dedication was amazing. The therapy was painful, as Dr. Adam had warned her it would be, but she ignored or tolerated the pain as much as possible, because she knew that quitting early each day would add up to hours or even days over the months ahead. While she worked her body hard, sometimes harder than she should, her mind was a million miles away. She missed her Hunter, and nothing would ever change that, but she was finding herself becoming attached to Roger. He was kind, and he was fun in a laid back, casual sort of way. He wasn't boisterous or outspoken, and he showed through his action and words that he always thought of others. There was plenty of time to find out what "attached" meant.

One day, following therapy on her hand and wrist, Tina returned home and was feeling pain in her forearm. As she walked past the phone, it rang.

"Hello?"

"Ms. Morgan? This is Jeremy Bell. I am the Myotherapist in Albuquerque. I'm calling to confirm your appointment for Friday morning. Will the day and time still work for you? I will meet you at your home, and I will bring my folding table. As I mentioned before, I alternate weekends in

Albuquerque and Las Cruces because I have six patients in Las Cruces. Since I already come down from Albuquerque, I won't charge you extra for the treatment. We'll have one-hour sessions three days in a row, twice a month at your home. You can come up to Albuquerque one weekend a month or on the alternating weekends."

"That works out fine, Jeremy. I look forward to meeting you. Driving to Albuquerque won't be a problem. Maybe, as I get better, some shopping at that new mall just built in Albuquerque could be good therapy, too," Tina laughed.

On Friday, Jeremy set up his table in Tina's living room. He helped Tina up on the table and had her lie down. "The Myotherapy, or trigger-point therapy, will be administered while you're lying on the table," Jeremy explained. "What are you working on now in your occupational and physical therapy?"

"I'm working on range of motion, strength, flexibility, and flexion in both the wrist and ankle. I've put full weight on my foot and ankle for a couple of weeks. One thing I don't understand is that when I've been working on my hand and wrist, I often have the most pain in my forearm when I'm done."

"That's the interesting part about trigger points," Jeremy explained. "So many parts of our body affect other parts that we don't even realize. If you're tense or tired, for example, doing Myotherapy on trigger points on your head, neck, and shoulders could make your back and legs feels better. After I work on you, I'll show you some exercises you can do yourself. This crook will help." Jeremy handed Tina a silver curved rod with rubber tips on each end. It looked like a shepherd's crook. "If you hold it like this," Jeremy said, placing Tina's hand on the straight shaft, "you can reach a knot in your back way back here." Tina felt the rubber tip against her back muscle and Jeremy pulled just a little as the tip of the crook applied pressure. "Believe it or not, the goal of Myotherapy is to learn to treat yourself so you don't need me. Your case is different. With a broken wrist, that won't be possible for a long time, but someday you can do it yourself. Learning what trigger points affect which areas of the body is the key."

Tina lay on the table while Jeremy worked on trigger points in her shoulder muscles, at the base of her neck, and around her arms and shoulder blades. "This should ease some of the pain in your forearm," Jeremy told her. As he worked, he gradually increased the pressure. "On a scale of one to ten, with ten being the most pain, tell me how this feels," Jeremy said, as he pressed on her lower back with his elbow.

"Five," Tina said. Jeremy moved to the right and applied more pressure. "Eight," Tina said. She had always had a high tolerance for pain. "So far, it feels like a deep massage in one spot." The next trigger point almost sent her off the table. "Nine! Nine!" Tina said, louder than she meant to. Jeremy eased up.

"We'll come back to that spot. Trigger points on your back can affect the pain in your leg and ankle," Jeremy said.

"Great!" Tina tried to make light of the situation.

"You might be a little sore after the first couple of sessions," Jeremy said.

"Wait, I thought this was supposed to make me less sore," Tina replied.

"It will ease the pain once your body is used to having the trigger points worked on," he explained.

Jeremy was very thorough. He worked slowly and carefully on Tina's back, legs, thighs, feet, ankles, buttocks, calves, neck, and base of the head. Then he worked on her arms, wrists, fingers, and the tops of her arms and shoulders. When Tina thought she was finished, he turned her over and started the process all over again. Tina felt like a baked potato that had been turned so it was completely done on both sides. In one sense, the therapy was like a very thorough massage. On the other hand, it was pure torture when Jeremy worked on the muscles above and below the broken ankle and the wrist.

Later that night, her back and shoulders felt like someone had used her as a punching bag. The next day, the treatment started all over again. Sunday was no different, but Tina knew her body could rest the following week. However, Jeremy had left the crook for her to use on the pressure points and more information about muscle therapy and erasing pain using trigger points. *That was a miracle*, Tina thought. Before the treatment, her ankle was swollen to the size of her thigh. Once the treatment started, the swelling reduced to an extent that was clearly visible to the naked eye. Tina continued to exercise until her next appointment. She also continued her physical therapy at the hospital.

Within a few weeks, she was feeling better than ever, thanks to the Myotherapy. She was using the crook with her left arm and hand like a pro. Jeremy had cautioned her that many patients didn't get the results they expected because they didn't take the time or put the effort into doing the exercises and trigger-point therapy at home. *That's not a problem for me*, Tina thought. *My mother, the slave driver, is at home, and we have all the time in the world. I am going to use every minute I can so I can have my life back.*

Tina was glad she was mobile and, with her mother's help, she could even go to the store or mall, but she was itching to do something more active, something where she could burn a few calories and maybe work up a sweat. Tina had started moving and swaying to music on the radio at home, but she hoped that, before long, she and maybe Roger could go dancing. That would be a day to celebrate!

Sooner than expected, Cisco Samsel returned from Mexico. He called Tina to ask when they could get together. "I was able to bring some things back for you," he told Tina. She was eager to meet with him, and they agreed to meet the next afternoon.

Tina and her mom headed for Samsel's office around 1:00 p.m. the next day. They felt excitement and hope that maybe Tina's theory of what happened in the airplane was correct. When the secretary called them, Samsel motioned for them to sit at a small, round table. He handed Tina a packet.

"What's all this?" Tina asked.

"There are some newspaper articles from the Mexican newspapers, and I got you a copy of the transcript from the tower. I was able to get part of it translated, and it does confirm what you remember. From what I can gather by just glancing at the transcript, Russell made no attempt to communicate with the tower or other planes after the engines stopped, just like you said. The newspaper article appeared in the local La Rosa newspaper in South Baja. The authorities gave me pictures for you from the crash site."

Tina looked at the headlines but the text was in Spanish so Samsel translated for her and basically it said: "A Small Plane Crashed in Floridas; 3 died—A lady jumped and saved her life. She's in delicate condition. Only ashes remain of the small plane Piper Aerostar. They were traveling from Las Baja to Las Cruces when the apparatus failed..."

"They thought I jumped," Tina said. "Why would they think that?"

"Because the article goes on to say that only ashes and twisted iron were left," Samsel said. "Remember, you were a lot farther from the plane than the others."

"They definitely tell it like it is," Tina commented.

"No sugar coating here." Samsel continued to interpret the article for Tina.

"After a bare thirteen minutes of flight and having left the International Airport of Baja Réal, the Aerostar plummeted to the earth, because of unknown causes at this time, at the place known as 'La Mesa del Llano,' the Plateau of the Plains, about 15 miles to the northeast of the airport."

"You definitely weren't far away," Samsel commented.

"Thirteen minutes and 15 miles…only 15 miles to the airport, not 25?" Tina repeated slowly. "I almost can't believe we didn't make it. I just know we could have made it back." Again in Tina's mind, she saw the engines were turning properly and there was no smoke. The question, did the engines stop by themselves or did Russell turn them off?"

The rest of the article described the workers at the Brava Sura Company being the first witnesses and also the first to report the accident.

Tina smiled when she read about her Hunter. And she couldn't keep the tears from welling up when she read: "Hunter Smith was transported to the hospital and moments after his arrival died from cardiac arrest, in spite of all the futile efforts to save his life." Yes, they had certainly made efforts. *If only…*, Tina stopped her thought as soon as it started, as if her friend Jane was standing next to her. *I know, if only's can't change what happened*, she thought.

The end of the article stated that the rescue was made on Tuesday under the supervision of the state police, Red Cross helpers, and the secretary of the Department of Health and Assistance. "All of this was certified by Pablo Tomas Romarez, an agent of the local Public Ministry. The burned cadavers of Christina and Russell Erickson were recovered. The Americans' possessions were also burned except the gold chains and bracelets that they were wearing. Until now, the causes of the accident remain unknown. It is up to the Civil Aeronautics Authorities to clarify these causes."

Other pages described the doctor's description of Tina's injuries and also that workers arrived before the plane hit the ground. It also stated that some of them stayed at the scene. Even though Tina was in shock and delirious with pain, she knew these statements weren't true. The men heard the explosion and ran on foot through the desert, and they all left to get help after attending to Hunter and laying Tina under the tree.

The last page in the packet was a map of the area, and Tina gently laid her finger on the spot where Hunter had died.

The wreckage was so vivid in Tina's mind that every time there was coverage of a plane crash in the newspapers or on TV, she was back in the desert with Hunter. She thought about her angels and the man that saved her. She thought about the doctor, his warm brown eyes and his knowledge and skill, which saved her foot from infection and gave her the time she needed to get additional medical attention. This time, Tina considered going back there someday.

Samsel interrupted Tina's thoughts. "I still don't have all the answers. I'm sorry I can't tell you more. The air traffic controller does not have any idea why Russell didn't respond when he made contact with the Aerostar. They could hear the static in the radio, so it wasn't dead."

"I could hear the air traffic controllers trying to get a response," Tina said. "Russell chose not to answer. I thought maybe he had a good reason, but I don't know."

"There's something else I need to tell you," Samsel said. His voice was gentle and he appeared to be interested and concerned. "The authorities are investigating. One engine was less damaged than the other. The investigators might be able to tell us much more when the findings are released in a few months. I asked them to call me, and I'll have a copy of the report sent overnight. The Erickson family requested that both engines be shipped to California and inspected for manufacturer defects and malfunctions. Of course, the family stands to collect more money if the inspection proves it was the fault of the manufacturer. Even if that isn't the case, we'll get information from the report."

Tina knew she would keep reading the newspaper articles over the next few days, so she drew them close to her, folded them, and put them in her folder. "Mr. Samsel, are you saying if the report confirms there was no mechanical problem, then Russell purposely shut down both engines?"

"That's what it would confirm, Tina. That would also explain why you didn't hear the alarm until after the engines stopped. The smoldering smell you described wasn't a fire, so that alarm never sounded as you confirmed that day we went to the airport."

"But why?" Tina asked. "Why didn't he try to at least land on the dirt road or in the giant wash, which you reported to me were both right there?"

"My friend who owns the plane we looked at told me that the Aerostar is very difficult to fly with one engine; it pitches and yaws and is very hard to control. I don't know why he didn't try to communicate what was going on? We need to wait for the report before we assume anything else," Samsel told her.

There had to be something wrong with the plane that didn't get fixed, Tina thought.

She could feel anger and resentment welling up in her gut. "Dad, I'm sorry," she said softly to herself, "but this dead man was one selfish bastard. He killed his wife and an innocent man, my fiancé!" Tina could usually keep her emotions in check, but right now she was downright mad. "Russell was too busy partying to have the plane checked out and get to the root of the problem! Why didn't they tell us? And why did we go back with them?"

"THERE IS NO SUCH THING AS CAN'T, ONLY WON'T. IF YOU'RE QUALIFIED, ALL IT TAKES IS A BURNING DESIRE TO ACCOMPLISH, TO MAKE A CHANGE." JAN ASHFORD

CHAPTER TWELVE
MARCH 1991

Mr. Samsel said it could take months to get the report on what caused the engine failure; I can't question him about it yet, Tina reminded herself. Most of the time, she was too busy to think about the investigation that was taking place, but sometimes it was hard to wait patiently for the answers.

Tina's mom was preparing to move back to New York, and Tina was taking her out to lunch. Tina wanted to spend the day expressing her appreciation to her mom for all she had done; she was fully aware that her mom had given up her own life to come to New Mexico and spend day in and day out with her daughter until Tina was well enough to be back on her own. It was the beginning of March, and Tina was self-sufficient once again. She could drive by herself and now her mom could go home, at least two to three months sooner than anyone could have predicted.

In addition to the ongoing occupational and physical therapy, Tina continued her Myotherapy treatments as well, and she was looking forward to dancing in public again. Tina still felt uncomfortable when there were too many people around because she felt someone might bump into her or accidentally push her. As her ankle healed and she regained her strength, Tina knew she would be tearing up the dance floor again before long.

"Isn't it a beautiful day?" Tina asked as they drove to the restaurant for lunch.

As Tina slowed down for a stop sign, her mom said, "Please don't try to overdo it too much when I leave. If something doesn't get done one day, there's always tomorrow. It's not worth wearing yourself out."

"As long as I can get back to doing the sports I enjoy—like playing tennis and golf—and dancing, I'll be fine," Tina answered. "Even dancing slowly, like I've been doing at home, gives me an energy boost, and I'm just having so much fun that it doesn't even feel like exercise. I can't wait to do everything again."

"It has definitely helped with your stamina, and I can see that you are truly happy, Tina. When the accident first happened, I read a couple of books about severe injuries that said patients often become depressed. You have put your heart and soul into your therapy, and you haven't looked back..." her mom began.

Tina interrupted, "Mom, death is so final. Someone in my position doesn't really have a choice. There's no going back. There is only one direction and that is forward."

"You are right, Tina, and that is what you have done. You'll be dancing to all kinds of music again soon. And you're strong enough mentally, too. But please, please call me, even if you just want to talk."

"How can I ever thank you for all of the care and support you've given me, Mom? You have given me over three months of your life. You pushed me when I wanted to give up; I just didn't say it out loud. And I can't say I haven't looked back. I have probably thought too much about what happened, and I hope to find out more about why it happened as soon as Mr. Samsel gets more information. To this day, the hardest thing for me is knowing that I will never see Hunter again and wondering, as I replay all the events of that morning, what could have been done to avoid the accident. I keep blaming myself for not crawling next to Hunter when we were waiting in the desert. Why didn't I press the Ericksons for more information when Russell went to the airport early? My intuition is usually sharp, so why didn't I tell Hunter that we would take a scheduled airliner home? I miss him, Mom. I don't think I can ever get married again. I'm done with men."

"Never say never, Tina," her mother said. "You are a strong, beautiful woman, and you have more confidence than ever."

"Mom," Tina said, "I'm attractive, but not beautiful. Remember when I was young? I always felt like the ugly duckling—too heavy, too awkward, and too clumsy. I was the worse ballerina in dance class when I was in 6th grade."

"Maybe it's just that I have more fight, Mom. If I hadn't taken charge of my care at the hospital or at the Rehab Institute, I could have gotten an infection or a cold and then I wouldn't have been able to recover as quickly. I guess I have learned not to sit back, unaware of what is going on around me."

Tina and her mom enjoyed a scrumptious lunch in the Foothills. It was one of those early spring days when sitting on the outdoor patio, with views of the city below and the mountains all around, was the perfect place to be.

"Guess what I'm going to try this weekend?" Tina said as they waited for the check.

"Do I really want to know?" her mom asked.

"I'm going dancing! The country western music will be great therapy. My ankle's so much stronger and my balance is almost back to normal."

"Isn't that music usually fast? Just watching it makes me think of tripping over my own feet. Please be careful, Tina. I know I can't talk you out of it."

"I will be careful, Mom. Dancing after the accident will certainly be different and offer a new challenge."

Tina drove her mom to the airport and they said their good-byes. "I go back to see Dr. Adam in 10 days. I'll let you know what he says. Call me when you get home, Mom."

"Take care, Tina. I love you!"

"Love you, too, Mom. Have a safe flight."

After her mom boarded the plane, Tina sat in her car near the gate, watching the planes taxi and take off. She watched planes land, too. Where were all the passengers going? Were the travelers going on happy trips, or were they going to visit a friend or relative in the hospital? Finally, the plane leaving for New York backed away from the gate and idled in position. Tina watched it taxi out of sight. The plane turned around at the end of the runway and rose into the sky right in front of her. "Be safe, Mom," Tina said silently. "Please be safe."

On the solo drive home, Tina felt exhilarated. Of course, she would miss her mom, but this was a graduation of sorts. Tina's total independence marked another chapter in the road to her regaining her old life.

Tina went dancing that day and continued dancing for two hours, four times a week. Tina wasn't usually one to make the first move, but she wanted to go out Saturday night. She called Roger. "Would you be interested in being a dance partner for a recovering invalid?" she asked.

"I would definitely be interested, but from what I've seen lately, anyone who doesn't know you would never guess that you are recovering from anything," Roger said.

"Okay, it's a date. I'll even pick you up!"

On Saturday night, Tina was floating on a cloud. The line dance started, and she crossed one foot over the other. Oh, it hurt some, but Tina would not give in to that pain. She continued to bend her foot and dance for a few hours.

"You look particularly radiant, this evening, Ms. Morgan," Roger said as he extended his arm to her so they could take a break and get a drink. Tina was breathless and smiling.

"Thank you, kind sir! I'm having the time of my life!"

They took a breather and talked about anything and everything. The band started playing a slow country western number. "Will you join me?" Roger asked.

"I'd love to," Tina said.

Tina was glad the lights were low because, for some reason, she felt herself blush. For the first time, she felt like they were on a real date instead of Roger just helping out.

Tina closed her eyes and moved to the music. She didn't even think about tripping or falling, with Roger's arms around her. Was this really happening? She was dancing—fast, slow. and everything in between. Roger had been a helpmate and friend; could there ever be more? She had just told her mom that she would never be seriously involved with another man. *Slow down, Tina. Dance and be happy. That's enough for now*, she told herself.

Tina had spoken with her mom every day since she had returned to New York. On the morning of her appointment with Dr. Adam, her mom called. "I just wanted to let you know that I'm thinking about you today, Tina. And tell Dr. Adam hello from me."

"I will, Mom. Thanks for calling. I'll call you back with the full report."

"Tina Morgan," the nurse called from the doorway.

Tina had been reading and was startled for a moment. She was anxious to see Dr. Adam.

She greeted the nurse and waited for Dr. Adam in the examination room. When he knocked on the door, Dr. Adam poked his head in for a moment before he opened it. "Hi, Tina, it's great to see you again. I want you to know that I shared your case with some interns and and they are here to listen to our discussion and assessment of your recovery today?"

"Oh, okay," Tina said with a smile "I don't mind at all, Dr. Adam."

He opened the door and the students filed in. "Let's look at your ankle first and then we'll take a look at your wrist.

"Do you feel any pain?" Dr. Adam asked as he moved her ankle from side to side.

"Yes, there is pain, but I can handle it. It isn't my old ankle, but I can handle the discomfort," Tina said.

"Can you flex your foot as far as possible? Remember," he said, turning to the interns, "Ms. Morgan's flexion was 30 percent in January." Tina pointed her toe and then flexed it back toward her leg.

"Oh!" and "Wow!" exclaimed several of the interns.

"I'll echo that," Dr. Adam said. "That's amazing, Tina. I certainly didn't expect that much improvement by now."

"I will continue Myotherapy treatments when I think I need them, Dr. Adam. I told you I would be just fine. I've started dancing again, and it's really helping me. I'm stronger. My wrist seems to have healed more than my ankle has. I don't have as much discomfort in my wrist. Look how good it looks next to my other one." Tina held out both arms so her wrists were side by side. "You can't tell it was injured, except for the nice scars where the spikes held the Hoffman in place. My ankle is still a problem, but I have to be grateful. I can manage the discomfort. Most of the time, the real discomfort is when I am lying in bed at night; the side of my ankle and leg where you put the screws and plate is really sore. It just doesn't seem to heal. I use vitamin E on my scars, and they look as if they are healing nicely, including the burns on the back of my leg."

Dr. Adam rotated her wrist in his hand. "Can you spread your fingers and flex your hand backward?"

Tina smiled as she moved her hand. "You are witnessing

the work of an incredible surgeon. You are lucky to have him for an instructor," Tina told the students.

They nodded and smiled.

"This is one of those cases," Dr. Adam said, looking right at Tina, and then back at his students, "that defies what medically we would have predicted to be less than a full recovery. I knew you would be mobile again and, with your determination, walk and do some light form of exercise. You have my permission to resume your golf and tennis again, but just take it slowly. This is nothing short of a miracle."

"Thanks to you, Dr. Adam, I have made a full recovery."

"I don't think I've ever seen anyone work quite as hard at this as you have, Tina. I'm proud to have been part of it, but please give yourself credit for your recovery."

The interns started to applaud quietly. Tina felt slightly embarrassed. "I don't think I deserve this," she said. "You put me back together and you deserve a gold star."

"Dr. Adam told us you might have a hard time with what he had to tell you today. With all the therapy you've had, if you were flexing only at 50 percent for example, that might have been as good as it would get," a young intern explained. "Instead of disappointment, we get to share in your good news."

"Oh, I see," Tina said. "Thank you for everything, Dr. Adam. I've been driving on my own for a couple of weeks, and my mom went back to New York. She said to tell you hello, by the way. I am certainly blessed to have made it back to Las Cruces for the surgeries. I was so lucky that you were my surgeon. If it weren't for you, I would not have recovered so quickly. It was you who made this happen, Dr. Adam."

"No, Tina. It was your hard work."

"Dr. Adam, in rehab I saw other patients with Hoffmans, and they were in pain and had much less flexibility.

Their doctors weren't as good as you, and that is the bottom line."

"Thank you for giving me all the credit, but you made your own recovery possible. Take care, Tina. We won't be seeing you around here again for quite a while."

Tina left the building humming and thought about jumping in the air. "Golf, tennis, here I come!"

She called her mom and then Roger. "Guess what?" she said excitedly during both conversations. "I've beaten the odds and made an almost full recovery!"

A few months later, Tina was feeling great, except for the fact that she still had tenderness in her left ankle. She felt something wasn't quite right and finally called Dr. Adam.

When the nurse heard who it was, she put Tina through immediately.

"Hi, Tina, is everything okay?" Dr. Adam asked.

"I'm doing very well and can do just about anything I want, but the tenderness in my ankle when I lie down hasn't improved at all. If anything, my ankle is even more tender, and it's most tender in the same place where you put the screws and plate. Could I ask what kind of metal you used?"

"The plates and screw are all made of surgical steel," Dr. Adam replied.

"Oh," Tina said. "I'm allergic to surgical steel. That explains why it's so tender in that area."

"Tina, I'm sorry," Dr. Adam continued. "I had no way of knowing. I didn't have all your medical history when you came in as an emergency patient."

"Oh, I'm not blaming you, Dr. Adam. How could you have possibly known? I found out a few years ago, when I pierced my ears for the second time, that I react differently to gold versus surgical steel. Years ago, I used a 14K yellow gold hoop; it never bothered me. Years later, when I wanted a second hole, I went to an earring store in the mall. A saleslady there pierced my ears and put in surgical steel studs. My ears never healed and were always sore and infected. After about two months, I took the studs out, and my ears finally healed. Can you take the hardware out, Dr. Adam?"

"Yes, Tina, that can certainly be done. I want to take one more set of x-rays, just to make sure the bones will be okay once we take everything out." *Dr. Adams wasn't the type of Doctor who wouldn't listen to his patients. He certainly was the best of the best,* Tina thought.

Later that week, Dr. Adam scheduled surgery.

After the surgery, when Tina came back for a checkup, she turned to Dr. Adam as he walked into the room and said, "Dr. Adam, you've performed another miracle. The tenderness is gone!" Tina knew she had really recovered. For now, it was as good as it would get. It wasn't perfect, and she would never wear high heel shoes again, but, considering the severity of the injury, she would not walk with a limp.

"I THINK A HERO IS AN ORDINARY INDIVIDUAL WHO FINDS STRENGTH TO PERSEVERE AND ENDURE IN SPITE OF OVERWHELMING OBSTACLES." CHRISTOPHER REEVE

CHAPTER THIRTEEN

The ringing phone seemed louder than usual. Tina took a deep breath, as if instinctively bracing herself, before she answered.

"Hello?" Tina said.

"Hi, Tina," her sister answered in a subdued, almost monotone voice.

"What's wrong?"

"Grandmother died during the night."

Tina swallowed hard and tried to speak, but no sound would come. Of course she knew her grandmother's death was inevitable one day in the not-too-distant future. The whole family knew her grandmother's health was declining. After all, she had had round-the-clock nursing care for the past two-and-a-half years. Tina was visiting her family in New York when her grandmother had a major stroke. Prior to that, she had had several mini-strokes, sometimes so small that the changes they caused were almost imperceptible. But Tina knew that the mini-strokes took their toll, even when she had the first one. She was talking with her on the phone one Sunday, and Tina noticed her grandmother's slurred speech. Tina called her mother immediately. When her mom called to check on her, her grandmother was speaking normally and had no symptoms. Grandmother was in her mid-nineties, or so the family guessed since many older people blurred the truth about their age. The doctors mentioned cleaning out the carotid artery, but Tina's grandmother didn't want it. Her grandmother didn't like doctors and, more importantly, she didn't trust what could happen in a hospital. So nothing was done. Tina's mother had told her about this just the other day, and Tina knew that her mother would never tell her grandmother what to do. The strokes continued over a period of time until the last one changed Grandmother's life forever. After that, she couldn't walk, talk, or care for herself. The doctors said she wasn't aware of what was going on, but when Tina visited, she knew that wasn't true. When Tina was there, sometimes Grandmother would cry.

"Squeeze my hand or blink," Tina would gently urge her. And very weakly her grandmother would.

"I'm here, Grandmother. I love you." Tina knew her grandmother understood.

"I'll call you back when we have made the funeral arrangements," Tina's sister said. Her voice brought Tina back to the present.

"Okay. Thanks for calling right away."

Tina hung up, feeling totally drained. She knew that Grandmother was in a better place, no longer trapped as a prisoner in her own body. But, despite knowing it was Grandmother's time to go and it was really for the best, Tina sobbed. Weakness and helplessness washed over Tina, feelings that were foreign to her, even after everything she'd been through in the past months. "First, I lost Hunter and now Grandmother," Tina sobbed. This loss was almost more than she could bear. She closed her eyes and her life with Grandmother washed over her like the gates of a damn breaking. Tina had always given her grandmother credit for much of who she was. Her grandmother had shaped and influenced Tina's life in countless ways.

Tina's grandparents had always lived very near them. After Tina was six months old, her dad and grandfather had walked the carriage from 187th Street to 95th Street to the apartment building where they would live. "You see, your carriage was quite large and, at that time, no one had a car," her dad explained when she was older. "The buses and taxis wouldn't do, since they didn't have room for a large baby carriage, so walking was our only choice." Shortly thereafter, Tina's grandparents moved to the same building, in a one-bedroom apartment on the second floor, with Tina's uncle and great grandmother. Tina recalled that her family had the best seats for the annual Veterans Day Parade, hanging out the windows and waving to all the soldiers as they walked by. Later they moved to a bigger apartment on the ninth floor.

A few years later, Tina's twin sisters were born, and the second bedroom would be for the twins and their nanny. Six of them shared that two-bedroom apartment, so Tina stayed in a crib in her parents' room until she was 5. Then she was delegated to a cot in the dining room, adjacent to the kitchen. It was a spacious, two-bedroom corner apartment on the twelfth floor, and it had the most incredible views of the Hudson River and the Palisades in New Jersey. The apartment building was quite fancy, with a doorman and men operating the spacious, mirrored elevators. New Yorkers didn't need a lot of room; they made do with what they had. Everyone had small spaces and Tina never heard anyone complain. The funniest part was that no one ever moved. They stayed in one apartment building forever, and if they did move, it was just to a larger apartment or maybe to a building just down the block.

To this day, Tina thought, *when I go back to visit my cousins and other relatives, they are still in the same apartment that their families lived in when I was a kid. Other relatives, too, are still living in the apartments they moved into in the 70s. Some things never change.* Tina cherished fond memories of New York and her family. Remembering her childhood brought back other thoughts, and she grabbed a notebook and started to write. Tina had discovered over the years that one of the best stress relievers for her was writing a poem or jotting down notes in her journal.

Tina recalled: *As I got older, Leona, a special friend from kindergarten and elementary school would visit, and we would play in the apartment for hours. One of our favorite games was "jacks," a game with little metal pieces and a small rubber ball the size of a quarter. We would bounce the ball and pick up one jack at a time, bouncing the ball again and again while holding each jack we picked up. My friend and I played together for hours, and we were inseparable.*

Tina wanted to talk, so she called her friend Leona. They had been friends for years, and Leona had known Tina's grandmother. Leona lived on the fifth floor of the same apartment building as Tina. Leona answered the phone and expressed her sorrow that Tina's grandmother had died. Leona knew, though, that Tina's grandmother had not been able to enjoy her life for the past two years.

"Tina, remember what you told me when my grandmother died?"

"I don't remember," Tina said.

"You told me that she will always live in my heart and in my mind. Your grandmother was a great inspiration for you and you will never forget her."

There were a few minutes of silence and Tina said, "You are right! I am so grateful that she was in my life for all these years."

"It's like you and me," Leona said, "we will be friends forever! Hey, remember when we would play outside and our toys included a jump rope, chalk for hopscotch, and roller skates that fit on the bottom of our shoes and gripped the sides, holding the skates in place?"

"Yes. And when Halloween came, we didn't even have to leave the building," Tina said. "Remember, there were eighteen floors, and we could visit both sides of the buildings."

"Yes!" Leona excitedly interrupted, reminiscing about their carefree days, "There were very few children living in the building and many of the tenants didn't have Halloween candy. They would give us unopened boxes of assorted candy or lots of coins and even an occausional dollar bill. What could be better? All we had to do was go door to door. What Fun!"

"No wonder I always loved Halloween," Tina said. They reminisced a while longer and then Tina promised to visit the next time she was in New York. After they hung up, Tina continued to sit, staring at the phone and remembering sixth grade and her grandmother.

Her grandmother taught Tina how to buy fruits and vegetables. When Tina was old enough to visit the fruit stand by herself, her grandmother said, "Run over to Broadway and buy some tomatoes." Tina trudged up the hill. The fruit man watched her pick up the tomatoes and place them in the brown paper bag. She paid for them and hurried home, knowing that her grandmother would be proud of her for going alone.

"Here, Grandmother," Tina said breathlessly, as she handed her the bag. "It was fine. I can go again for you anytime you like."

"Thank you, Tina. Let's see here," her grandmother said as she removed the first tomato from the bag. She clicked her tongue. "Tsk, Tsk, Tsk. These will never do, Tina. Look, they're too soft. Remember what I told you about checking to see if they're too ripe?" Tina nodded silently. "Did you check these before you bought them?"

"No, Grandmother. He was watching me. I didn't want to make him mad."

"He'll be madder when you take these back," Grandmother said.

"Take them back?" Tina asked, not wanting to believe what she just heard.

"We aren't paying for something we can't use," Grandmother explained.

Tina knew better than to talk back, so she didn't try to argue.

"Do you remember how to push on them gently to make sure they're firm?"

"Yes, Grandmother."

"Okay, then. When you show him these tomatoes and tell him that I sent you, he'll take them back."

"Okay," Tina said grudgingly as she walked out the door. She marched up the hill to the Broadway fruit and vegetable stand.

"Here, sir," Tina said holding out the bag.

He took the bag from her. Tina turned around and softly squeezed two other big tomatoes on the stand.

"Hey, kid! What do you think you're doing?" the man yelled. "Don't damage my tomatoes!"

"Please, sir. I got the wrong ones. They're too soft and my grandmother sent me back."

"I'll let you get away with it this time, but you'd better not bring anything back again! Ever again! Is that clear?"

"Yes, sir!" Tina answered. *I'm squeezing them first*, she thought. She didn't want to face the wrath of her grandmother OR of the fruit man. From then on, she always tried to do things right the first time so she didn't have to re-do something.

Tina and her grandmother walked everywhere. They thought nothing of going from 95th Street and Riverside Drive down to 34th Street and 6th Avenue. This was about five miles, but it went quickly because there was always so much to see. They could always hop on the bus to get back home. Tina's grandmother would return things if they weren't just right and would search for bargains, buying the sale items that were the best value.

"There is no reason to pay full price if you don't have to," her grandmother would tell her.

To this day, I almost always buy things when they are on sale, Tina smiled to herself.

When Tina's family moved to Long Island, her grandparents moved to Long Island, too. They had spent years together and now one of the greatest influences in Tina's life was gone.

Tina was too restless to sleep that night, but she finally dozed off on the couch for a couple of hours. When she awoke, she was still in the clothes she had worn all day. The moonlight streamed in the window, lighting a path on the floor. The house was so quiet, and Tina tiptoed across the room, trying not to break the silence. She opened her desk drawer and took out the poem she had written about her grandmother during one of her visits.

It would still be a day or two until the funeral. Tina knew that in the Jewish faith, they buried their dead within 24 to 48 hours. This custom went on for centuries because, in the early days, there was no way to preserve the body, so the burials were done quickly. Since Tina's family was not orthodox, they might stretch that time frame a few more days to accommodate relatives traveling from out of town to attend the funeral.

Tina didn't go to her grandmother's funeral in New York, but the memories of her grandmother would always be with her. Tina's sister had put together a book of their grandmother's life. Tina had written the poem after her grandmother's stroke, when she was unable to speak and move on her own. Her sister, Joani, included the poem in the book and read it during the eulogy she composed for their grandmother.

GRANDMOTHER

My Grandmother was Great, when I was Eight
She came from a Foreign Land and could tell you every Detail

My Grandmother was Great, when I was sixteen
She could tell you all the Birthdates of our
one hundred Cousins, Aunts, and Uncles
Without so much as a slip of paper to remind her

My Grandmother was Great, when I was Twenty-One
She could recite poetry by heart of
Annabelle Lee and Gunga Din,
and Poems that went on forever

My Grandmother was Great, when I was Twenty-Eight
She could spend hours reciting to my children all the
Nursery Rhymes and Stories
without needing a book, or, a record for a prop

My Grandmother was Great, When I was forty
and she was Eighty-Seven
She sent birthday cards to all our family members and
Knew the names of the children,
of the one hundred Cousins, Aunts and Uncles

My Grandmother is Great, now that I am Forty-Eight
She still looks the same, but age is taking her memory away
and the records she kept so long and knew so well are fading fast
as if one is using an eraser on the pages of a book and
there isn't even time, to hold on to the page

And when I call her today, will she remember me?

On the day of the funeral, Tina stayed home and thought about her grandmother. She read the poem again and looked at some keepsakes her grandmother had given her. Tina's appreciation for antiques and fine jewelry had been fueled by Grandmother's love of old, beautiful, and rare objects. That evening, Tina's sister called. "I just wanted to let you know that I read your poem at the funeral. Everyone commented about how alive it made Grandmother seem, almost as if she were right there with us. They also said to tell you hello and that their thoughts and prayers have been with you. I miss you, Tina."

"I miss you, too," Tina told her sister. "And I miss Grandmother."

"ALL GLORY COMES FROM DARING TO BEGIN."
EUGENE F. WARE

CHAPTER FOURTEEN
SEPTEMBER 1992

Tina drove to Cisco Samsel's office. He had information he needed to share with her. She hadn't thought much about the court proceedings, since she was continuing to focus on her recovery, but now that he had called she was ready to move forward. She wanted to pay the hospital, medical, and therapy bills with the money. Then she wanted to thank Mr. Samsel for his help, and be done with this chapter of her life.

Tina parked, put coins in the meter, and walked into the Law Offices of Samsel & Baley in the Barrio district. The office was small and tidy. In addition to the fact that Cisco was a pilot, the size of the firm had helped her make her final decision to retain him as her attorney. *His fees would be reasonable*, she thought, *since the partners didn't have the expenses of a large office staff and high-priced rent on a multistory building.* The two partners and their office, in a historic district on the edge of downtown, had seemed the perfect fit—unassuming and down to earth. It was hard to choose an attorney when she had never before needed one and even harder to pay for one since there was little insurance money. Any expenses would have to come from Tina's savings.

The bio information that Samsel had given Tina with her copy of the contingent fee agreement stated that aviation was one of their specialized areas of practice. The firm had represented commercial clients, including Southwest Helicopter and Solo Aero, a fixed base operation. In addition, individual clients had retained the firm in cases directly related to personal injury. Tina definitely wanted the two attorneys to represent her in this case.

Tina parked and opened the door to the small, sparsely decorated office. The receptionist was sitting at her desk and Samsel was just getting up to get a cup of coffee. "How are you, Tina?" he asked.

"I'm getting stronger every day, thank you. How are you? You said you had some news?"

"Yes, yes. Please come in and sit down. I didn't mention it earlier, because I didn't know if it would make a difference, but a few months ago, I entered a Notice to Creditors declaring that you had been appointed the personal representative of the Ericksons's estate.

I asked that all claims be submitted either to you or this law office, but Russell Erickson Jr. filed an opposing Notice when he found out about it. He notified Judge Lockman that he would like to settle after the first of the year. So far, Judge Lockman hasn't signed the petition I submitted requesting that Letters of Personal Representative and Acceptance be issued in your name. I just found out yesterday that the judge denied this request."

"What does that mean?" Tina asked. "I don't understand what you are talking about."

"I filed a motion to make you the personal representative of Russell Erickson's estate, which means they have to inform you when any action is taken. We would have more control over what bills are being submitted through the estate and would be able to keep track of what's going on. The purpose was to make sure the settlement would cover all of your outstanding obligations and more for your pain and suffering, of course."

"As I've told you before, I want to pay the medical expenses and have some left for ongoing therapy.

My intent is not to drag this on forever," Tina said. "Has the insurance company given you any more information about the engines?"

"No, their investigation has been delayed. If you remember, my friend, Mr. Sussman, the investigator that I selected, was trying to arrange for the engine teardown. I had planned to be there, too, but Mr. Sussman just notified me that Mr. Markman from STA, the company that insured the plane, is not cooperating at all."

Tina sighed and interrupted him. "What are we going to do?"

"Sussman said this is a 180-degree turnaround from what was previously agreed upon."

"What changed? Why isn't he cooperating?" Tina was frustrated. "We really need to know what those findings reveal."

"I can't imagine what happened," Samsel answered softly and calmly, as he thought to himself, *After all, there is no need to tell her that Markman stated in a letter to Sussman that relations between his office and ours have deteriorated.*

"I did file a complaint with the court asking that Russell Erickson Jr. be served with a summons requesting a judgment in your favor," Samsel continued. "With the Ericksons's personal property, as well as moving to Las Cruces and being away from the business in New York, I'm sure we can prove that they had an income and assets to support a high-class lifestyle."

"That's possible," Tina said, "but as I told you, the Ericksons wintered in Las Cruces to escape the New York winters. We don't know the mortgage amounts on their properties, especially the one that is being sold in Las Cruces, or any other outstanding debts for that matter."

Samsel cleared his throat and pulled on his collar. Tina could tell he was agitated.

"Mr. Samsel?"

"I am your attorney, do you understand? I need you to say what I tell you, when I tell you. 'Moving' to Las Cruces will have a different impact on the judge than 'wintering' in Las Cruces!" Samsel spouted. "Do you understand what I'm saying? You are to say exactly what I tell you to say. They are moving from New York." His tone was even stronger, and there was a threatening undertone in what he was saying.

"I don't know that," Tina said.

"You do now," Samsel said curtly with a raised edge to his voice.

Tina was taken aback. "I don't think all of these idiosyncrasies are for us to decide. We need the facts, Mr. Samsel. As your client, I would think that you would want to do what is in my best interest, and as I have patiently and quietly asked before, I want a jury trial. Nothing is getting accomplished and I just want to pay my bills. Now I am demanding a jury trial, and I would like for you to proceed with the legalities of making that happen."

Samsel straightened in his chair and took a drink of water. "I will see where we stand with all of this and get back to you on the money issues. A couple of other things I should let you know. I just heard from a representative yesterday that two of the men who were at the Aerostar convention are being called as witnesses, Mr. Monte and Mr. Hubble."

"Oh," Tina said surprised. "Mr. and Mrs. Monte came to the clinic in Mexico right after the crash. Mr. Monte was the one who was trying to talk to Russell on the radio and asked if he should follow us back to the airport," Tina said, remembering having seen the familiar faces and asking the couple if they knew what happened. "I called Mr. Monte after I got home from the hospital, but since you were my attorney he wouldn't talk to me.

"Mr. Monte's attitude toward me had definitely changed,

and he wouldn't give me any information or have anything to say to me. He was very distant and cold. I just wanted to know why Russell and a few of his buddies had gone to the airport early on the morning we were leaving. I asked Mr. Monte if he knew what they were looking for, and he plainly said he wouldn't talk to me. I found that quite strange and I really felt that he was covering up something, that there was something more, something more important that they don't want me to know."

Samsel didn't answer Tina and just continued to tell her more bad news.

"I wanted to let you know that Judge Lockman filed a minute entry approving the Ericksons's attorney's request that all the legal fees be paid out of the escrow account."

Again, Tina tried to clarify the words she was hearing. "If one judge put the money, deeds, and other assets in a special account so that the money was protected until more information was available, why did Judge Lockman allow the money to be used by the attorneys and give none to the victim to pay her bills, caused by the injuries she received in the Erickson plane? What kind of a Judge is Lockman? Is he just plain evil or sadistic? What is his plan for me? Where will the money come from for my bills if it isn't protected in the escrow account?" Tina's voice rose and she became more agitated. She didn't even wait for an answer but continued to ask, "What about the ancillary estate that was established in New Mexico when Judge Sally Cross approved it last April?"

"That's what I was getting to," Samsel said. "Once Judge Lockman took over, all monies were transferred to the escrow account."

"So are you saying that their attorneys are guaranteed payment, and we can't touch any of it? Are you saying

I can't pay my bills but they can pay their attorneys?" Tina interrupted.

"Exactly," Samsel answered.

"What about the $3,000 check you are holding?" Tina asked.

"I don't want to give that to you yet, or it will let the insurance company know that we have settled. We're not at that point yet. I don't know how much more we can get, so my 25% will have to be paid out of the $100,000."

"Mr. Samsel, that is not what we agreed upon," Tina said. She felt her neck turning red.

"I just don't know what else there is to collect, so that's why we need more information on the Ericksons's estate."

"Mr. Samsel, I am extremely disappointed that you would even suggest that. I retained your services to ensure that I was given fair and just treatment. Just look at my injuries! They are real. Look at my scars," Tina said, as she held up her foot. "And look at my hospital bills. They are real, too! I don't get it, Mr. Samsel. People sue over nothing, like the lady who spilled coffee in her lap when she was in her car. She had just purchased the coffee from a fast food restaurant; she got hundreds of thousands of dollars. Remember, this wouldn't even be an issue if the insurance limits for the passengers on the plane would have been higher. Higher medical insurance coverage on the passengers would have covered injuries that occurred in the plane crash." Tina went on and on, spilling out her frustrations.

As if he hadn't heard her, Samsel said, "We should settle this sooner than later. It would be in everyone's best interest."

"Everyone?" Tina asked. "What about Hunter's family? Aren't they plaintiffs for the Erickson estate, too?"

"I'm sure I'll be hearing from their attorney in Illinois. I think he's working with the case pending in New York."

"New York?" Tina asked. "I thought the case was opened

in New Mexico because they had property here, instead of in New York?"

"Russell had businesses and property in New York, too," Samsel said. "Multiple cases in different states aren't unusual."

"Why didn't you immediately tell me to hire New York attorneys? Why did you wait so long to tell me?" Tina took a deep breath and tried to calm down. "I would like you to give me the information on the New York case, then. Maybe that's where we need to be focusing our attention."

"If you want to be a plaintiff in New York, too, this could go on for months, even years," Samsel said. "Is that what you want?"

"I want what's right. You are my attorney, Mr. Samsel, and that's why I hired you."

"Then trust me and let me do my job!" Now Samsel's face turned red. He stood up, signaling the end of the meeting. "I'll be in touch when I have more information."

"Mr. Samsel, I just want to remind you that I am your client and the victim here. I want justice and to find out the truth. I am not looking for a quick fix, especially if we find out negligence was involved."

Again, Samsel didn't even acknowledge Tina's comments.

"I would like details on the medical provider liens until we are able to pay them, so I know where I stand. I'm concerned about my credit, too," Tina told him.

"I will get that information for you. Good day, Ms. Morgan."

"Good day, Mr. Samsel."

Tina left the office, shaky and unnerved. Something wasn't quite right. *Why was Samsel trying to hurry things along when he could be in a position to get something out of this also?* she wondered. Tina started to play back the conversation with Samsel in her mind.

After he took me to the airport and we listened to the horns in another Aerostar, he explained that the engines would not have stopped working in flight, like they had done before we crashed, unless they were feathered, which means they were shut off manually. He explained that if the engines had stopped functioning, they would have kept turning very slowly and would have continued to turn for some time. Once I explained that the warning horn I heard was the one associated with the shutting down of the engines and not the horn signifying fire, Samsel asked aloud why Russell didn't land in a wash or on the dirt road that was ahead? Samsel also explained that pilots will shut the engines down and then go through a checklist and restart them, but Russell never did that. Russell just panicked. *So now I really don't get it,* Tina thought.

What was really starting to puzzle Tina was why wouldn't Samsel want to follow this case through to the end, if he was so sure we could win? Samsel already had a feeling there was negligence and something wasn't right.

After mentioning Hunter's family to Samsel, Tina couldn't stop thinking about Hunter's children as she drove home. She called Hunter's son, Steve, as soon as she walked in the door. "Hi, Steve, I just met with my attorney and have been thinking about you. How is everything going?"

"Hi, Tina, you know these law firms. Everything seems to take much longer than it should."

"Steve, I'm concerned. I want a jury trial and my attorney seems to be side-stepping the issue. Today he said that we should settle this as soon as possible. I had a wonderful woman judge for a while, but now she's off the case, and everyone's tune seems to have changed. This newly appointed judge is totally against me. I have very good instincts, and

I strongly believe that this judge is not going to be fair or give me justice. That could be a coincidence, but it's all very frustrating."

"Tina, I should have mentioned this earlier, but I know lawyers have opinions of each other that may or may not be factual. After Burt Martin, one of my attorneys from the firm in Chicago, flew to Las Cruces a couple of months ago to meet with Mr. Samsel, he told me he had some concerns."

"He met with Samsel here in Las Cruces? Samsel never told me. What else is he hiding from me?" Tina wondered aloud.

"Well, when Mr. Martin returned, he called me. He told me that Samsel was a bit shady. My attorney doesn't trust him. I didn't want to alarm you when things seemed to be moving along for you, but I guess it's something you should be aware of. The firm in Chicago is highly respected and has a reputation for honesty and integrity, so I do trust them."

"Okay, Steve. I'll be careful. I knew from my meeting today that I will have to be more forceful to make sure Samsel carries through with what I'm asking for, but I'll be sure to be on the alert and take matters into my own hands if something is really wrong."

"Take care, Tina. Keep in touch."

"Thanks, Steve. I do appreciate you letting me know what you heard." After Tina hung up the phone, things became clearer. *So that's why the Smith family is not joining forces with us against the Ericksons. They don't trust Samsel*, she realized.

I thought I had to take control of my care in the hospital, but now I have a feeling that was nothing compared to the ride ahead through this legal system.

"JUSTICE DELAYED IS JUSTICE DENIED."
WILLIAM GLADSTONE

CHAPTER FIFTEEN
SEPTEMBER 28, 1991

Tina's work was definitely cut out for her. She had spent most of the morning drafting a letter to Cisco Samsel. They had played phone tag for more than a week, beginning after she received a note from him requesting her approval for him to authorize healthcare provider liens. Tina had decided that documenting what she wanted to say to him would not only be the quickest form of communication, but would also serve as hard evidence of her requests, if she encountered problems with him representing her again. She re-read the letter before signing it.

Dear Mr. Samsel:
Tuesday afternoon, I was assured by your partner, Mr. Baley that you would call me first thing on Wednesday morning. I didn't receive a call from you, but at 2:10 p.m. I did receive a call from your secretary to set up an appointment for Wednesday, October 14, as this was the first available chance we could talk. Three weeks is too long to wait on the issue of payment to the creditors, so I would appreciate you sending me the form to sign, as well as an explanation of what it means.

When I spoke with Joy earlier in the morning, I said I would be by to pick up the book of photographs. When I arrived at 11:30 a.m., I was told I couldn't have them because you were afraid they would get lost. This explanation was contrary to your statements in the past when you had offered the pictures freely and told me not to worry as you had all of the negatives. When I returned Joy's 2:10 p.m. phone call at 4 p.m., I told her I would be happy to have someone from your office go to the nearest copy shop with me and wait the ten minutes it would take to make copies. Then I could return the originals to your office. However, I was told again in a very nice way, that this wasn't possible. In the same letter, please address the matter of the photographs and the matter of the releases for the insurance carrier you had me sign in blank that I did not want to sign. These releases should be torn up and returned to me and rewritten at a later date when they will be used. As I have expressed before, I do not like my signature on forms that are sitting in a file to be pulled out and used at a later date.

Also, please let me know where we stand on obtaining information regarding the Ericksons's property. Please explain why the insurance company hired a lawyer on behalf of the Ericksons to handle this case, when the insurance company confirmed pilot error?

The insurance company paid the Ericksons $100,000 for the death of Christina Erickson by her husband.

I would appreciate your immediate reply to these matters, since we have been unable to talk by phone.

Sincerely,
Tina Morgan

Tina signed the letter and addressed the envelope. She noticed that her hands were shaking as she inserted the letter in the envelope before sealing it. Here was not one but several more examples of her attorney not doing what he said he would do. Not being able to get copies of the photographs from Mexico bothered her most of all. She had been in the crash, and she had a right to the photos of the site and the remnants of the plane.

He also had photos of what the Mexican Red Cross had recovered from the site in the days following the crash, including the burnt torsos of the Ericksons. Tina wasn't trying to be morbid, but those photos belonged to her. She had always been thankful that even though Hunter hadn't survived, at least his body had been intact and could be returned to his family for a proper burial.

That night after a candlelight dinner, Tina finally felt more relaxed. "Roger, I just don't understand what Samsel is up to? He's an attorney, and I don't understand why he doesn't want to win this case. He's certain Russell was negligent, and the Mexican government even confirmed pilot error. If this is confirmed once the engines have been inspected, we can present concrete, scientific findings to the judge. I don't know what Samsel has to lose. And now he's refusing to give me the photos of the site."

"It doesn't make sense, Tina," Roger agreed. "You should definitely have access to the photos, especially when he told you not long ago that it wouldn't be an issue. There's still a long road ahead, and I just want you to know that I'm here for you. I know this is stressful, but you have to try not to be consumed by all of this. It will wear you down, and you're still getting your strength back."

"You're right, Roger. I needed a diversion, and this dinner is perfect. We should talk about something else. Thank you for listening. I would really be going crazy if I didn't have you to talk to about all of this. I don't want to bother my mom or sisters with all the details because this is all so complicated, and quite frankly, I can't even explain my own attorney's behavior."

"Maybe we should get away for a few days, just the two of us," Roger suggested.

"I would love that, Roger. I just don't think I'd be the best company right now, considering everything that is going on with the case. I couldn't promise you that I wouldn't be wondering if Samsel finally sent a response, or if he actually called when he said he would, or if he finally changed his mind about the pictures. I do need to think about other things, including you, but right now this case is really all-consuming. I don't trust him, and if I don't stay on top of it, things could really go wrong."

"I understand, Tina. I just don't want it to affect your health when you have made such a remarkable recovery. Too much stress could undo what you have worked so hard for. There will be time for us to travel later."

"I said you were like a prince who had come along to give me another chance when I was in the hospital, and here you are, still holding me up and standing beside me. Remember how I said I could never repay you? I still can't, but I can keep thanking you."

"I'm the lucky one, Tina. You told me the time wasn't right once, and I respected you for that, but I'm not going to let you get away again. I love you, Tina."

After dinner, they took a short walk and the cool night air refreshed Tina. That night, Tina let Roger's strong arms hold her as she fell asleep. She could feel them giving her the strength to face tomorrow.

OCTOBER 23, 1991

Mr. Samsel had advised Tina that his partner, Mr. Baley, would be handling her case since he felt they had reached a stalemate. "He can call it what he wants," Tina told Roger, "but he doesn't know how to do his job. His only concern was that if I hired a different attorney, he would get nothing. That's why he's being so insistent on being paid 25% of the $103,000."

"Maybe Mr. Baley will do a better job and focus on your

case. That's what needs to …." The ringing phone interrupted Roger in mid-sentence. Roger answered it. "Yes, she's here. Of course, Mr. Baley, I'm sure there are a lot of hoops to jump through."

He handed the phone to Tina and smiled, giving her courage to hear the latest development.

"Hello, Mr. Baley. I hope you have some good news."

"Well, Tina, as I was telling Roger, sometimes I feel like we're chasing our tails with these attorneys in New York. Let me fill you in. Mr. Delgoto, the Ericksons's attorney with the law firm in Staten Island, New York, actually hung up on me. I explained to him that Russell's estate honored Christina's claim seeking $100,000 for her death, which occurred in the exact same incident upon which your claim, as my client, is based. I have also requested from Mr. Delgoto that we be provided with a complete and accurate inventory listing of all properties owned by the Ericksons, as well as the respective appraisal for each property.

"Since he has failed to provide this information so far, I just informed him that his further lack of cooperation will be construed as an acknowledgement on his behalf that his client is liable to you. I still don't know why he hung up the phone, but the good news is that a court will certainly want to see a valid and true inventory of properties."

"Why would they not provide a list of properties?" Tina asked. "Do you think they are trying to hide something?"

"I'm not sure if they're hiding some vital information or just stalling."

"What do we do now?" Tina asked.

"We'll see if Attorney Delgoto replies to the request for the inventory. In the meantime, I filed a memorandum with the court stating that Christina Erickson made a claim of negligence against Russell Erickson for purposes of enriching her separate estate and then turned around and denied the negligence to preserve her resources. The bottom line is there either has to be a claim or denial of negligence. They can't have it both ways. I also let the court know that neither the Ericksons nor the insurance company have provided a copy of the insurance policy. Christina Erickson is not able to deny the allegations of negligence in response to the complaints I filed for you against both of their estates in mid-September. If you remember, the complaints stated that Russell owed a duty to you to maintain and operate his airplane in such a manner as to not cause a crash. Whether by negligence, inattention, or otherwise, he breached that contract."

"So Russell Jr., acting on Christina's behalf, claimed negligence so his father's estate could pay his mother's estate?" Tina wanted to make sure she understood everything Baley was telling her.

"Exactly. And there's more. The insurance company has also paid Erickson Aircraft Corporation owned solely by Russell, $99,000.

"In addition to the $100,000? What for?"

Baley explained, "The $100,000 is the same per-seat liability payment that you are seeking, and the $99,000 is for the salvage of the plane."

"I'm not trying to be greedy, Mr. Baley, but because of my injuries, medical expenses, and pain and suffering, shouldn't that money be held or frozen by the courts until this is settled?"

"That would be the ideal situation, but since that hasn't happened and we know what Russell Jr. has received so far, we will seek a settlement from him."

"Mr. Baley, I feel like the ball is in the Erickson family's court and we have no way to get it back." Tina couldn't think straight. "I am the victim and I don't see how our court system is helping me at all."

"Don't worry," Mr. Baley told her. "We're not going to give up now. I wanted to thank you for getting the interrogatories that you were asked to answer back to me in a timely manner. All of the answers you gave should help, but some of them the judge hasn't been made aware of yet. The fact that you retired and closed your business, Precious Jewelry, because you were planning to marry Hunter Smith and travel with him is a tragedy. The fact that your health insurance didn't cover you on a non-scheduled airline is another legitimate reason to seek the highest amount of damages possible. Even after you fully recover, you have no immediate source of income. Also, the judge is aware of your physical injuries, but the insomnia, nightmares, and mental stress of seeing detailed pictures of what happened over and over again in your mind will be important points. I'm sure it was hard to answer all of these questions, Tina, but you were very thorough and that should be on our side."

"I hope you're right, Mr. Baley. I hope you're right."

"JUSTICE CONSISTS NOT IN BEING NEUTRAL BETWEEN RIGHT AND WRONG, BUT IN FINDING OUT THE RIGHT AND UPHOLDING IT, WHEREVER FOUND, AGAINST THE WRONG."
THEODORE ROOSEVELT

CHAPTER SIXTEEN
NOVEMBER 25, 1991

"I absolutely can't believe that our legal system allows this back-and-forth bantering. First there's an order, then an appeal, then a reply. After that, a summary judgment is filed, and then of course there has to be a reply to that! The hours and hours spent by both sides—it reminds me of a tennis match, but no one is scoring a point, except for the attorneys who are making all the money. This is costing a fortune," Tina told Roger after getting off the phone with Mr. Baley.

"What is the standoff over now?" Roger asked.

"It seems that Vicobi & Valenzuela, the Ericksons's attorneys here in Las Cruces, are trying to prove that Christina's estate shouldn't be part of the litigation at all. Mr. Baley said they are trying to prove that New Mexico was Russell and Christina's winter home only, and the fact that New Mexico is a community property state has no bearing in this case since they lived, paid taxes, owned a business and worked in New York. He also said that Russell Erickson Jr. filed a summary judgment on behalf of Christina, stating that because of these facts, Christina's estate should basically be off limits and, even though they were married, she is not responsible for her husband's actions."

"Can Samsel and Baley object?" Roger asked.

"Yes, Mr. Baley said that he and Samsel have submitted background facts to substantiate the claim. The bad news is Samsel is asking me to lie and say I lived next door to the Ericksons at the address in the Country Club where they were "domiciled at the time of their deaths." First of all, their winter home was next to Hunter, and I wasn't living there on a permanent or even part-time basis. Secondly, he told me that I knew them very well, since that is what he said in his memo to Judge Lockman. It's true that Christina told me that she had Parkinson's disease, which Samsel put in writing too, but he stated that I had many conversations with them, and Christina was settling in Las Cruces where they would have family visit for holidays from then on, since the climate was better for her health."

"It seems like something's not quite right," Roger said. "He should not be asking you to admit to things that aren't true."

"This is the second time he's said to me, "I'm your attorney and I'll tell you what to do. Last time Samsel's exact words were 'I'll tell you what to say,'" Tina lamented.

"It seems to get more complicated," Roger commented. "What about your request for a jury trial? They seem to keep ignoring that request. Then the judge and jury could look at all of this so-called evidence and make an unbiased, informed decision. That's what our legal system's supposed to be all about."

"Don't get me started on the jury trial. Sometimes I think that's why this game is never ending. If the Ericksons's attorneys keep playing it, maybe they think they can keep from going to trial, where the jury would hear the truth," Tina said, trying not to let her emotions get to her. "I think they're also trying to wear me down. At some point, they probably think I'll just give up. But I can't, Roger. I can't give up. We still don't have all the facts, and I am just not going to throw my hands up in the air and walk away.

"Remember my promise? I promised God that I would not let anyone steal, cheat, or lie to me again."

"You're right, Tina. Some people probably don't feel like being dragged over the coals by ruthless attorneys, so they do give up. The Erickson family and their attorneys just don't know who they're up against." Roger smiled at her. "I know you can hang in there. We can hang in there! I would think the judge would also be getting tired of the altercations. Maybe he'll set a trial date soon."

"That's all I want, Roger. At least I would know we tried and justice was served."

"It would just be nice to know that you had an attorney who was backing you all the way," Roger said.

"Yes, it would," Tina agreed.

DECEMBER 4, 1991

Tina had been poring over more medical and insurance forms and needed a break. She went for a walk, and the fresh air and brilliant blue sky cleared her mind and lifted her spirits. Before she went back inside, she stopped to get the mail and rifled through a stack of bills, ads for holiday sales, and vacation fliers. She walked into the kitchen and almost tossed the stack on the counter when an envelope caught her eye. It was from the Law Offices of Samsel and Baley. She tore the envelope open, almost holding her breath to see what news her attorneys had for her now.

Tina first saw Samsel's familiar scrawl at the bottom. Her eyes went back to the top of the page and she read the first sentence.

Dear Tina

A number of motions were heard by Judge Lockman on December 1, 1991, which relate directly to your case and the Erickson estate.

"Good, good," Tina thought. "Maybe now we're getting somewhere." She couldn't wait to read more.

The Judge has ruled that Mrs. Erickson's separate estate is not liable for any damages that you have sustained as a result of the aviation disaster. Since the ruling of the court generally tracks New Mexico law, I believe that the ruling is correct both factually and legally. You do have the right to appeal and I'd be happy to consider the same; however, it is my recommendation that you do not do so.

What? Is this guy for real? Tina thought. She kept reading, but had a hard time focusing. The last sentence in the first paragraph stated that if she wanted to appeal the ruling, it had to be done within 10 days. The second paragraph didn't get any better.

In addition, the court has ruled that it does not have the authority to order the personal representative to produce inventory of New York property in the state of New Mexico. Accordingly, in order to protect your rights in this matter, you must take immediate steps to retain New York counsel to enter an appearance for you in the New York estate.

Attorney Samsel went on to say that he was willing to make recommendations of attorneys in New York, but he knew from past conversations with Tina that she also knew attorneys in New York. *Yeah, I bet you'd love to recommend someone to help me, just like you have,* Tina thought sarcastically.

An unfamiliar feeling of bitterness welled up inside her. She wasn't just upset anymore. Tina was mad, angry and desperate, all at the same time. She rubbed her temples and tears welled up in her eyes just as Roger walked into the room.

"What is it, honey? What's wrong?" Roger asked gently.

"I can't believe it," Tina cried. "It's like starting over. I have to get an attorney in New York. What did I ever do to Judge Lockman? I could appeal, but Samsel doesn't support it, so I don't know where that would get me. Here!" She handed him the letter.

Roger quickly read the letter.

"You have to meet with Samsel and Baley," Roger said.

"Oh, I didn't even get that far. I was too stunned by everything else," Tina replied.

"Make an appointment," Roger said, "and I'm going with you."

Tina took a deep breath and made the call to schedule the meeting with Samsel and Baley. The receptionist answered and confirmed a date and time to meet the following week. "Just a minute," the receptionist said. Tina could hear her covering the mouthpiece. "Do you have a moment to speak with Mr. Samsel?" she asked.

"Yes," Tina answered, really not wanting to speak to him at all.

"Hello, Tina. I take it you received the letter?"

"Yes, I did, Mr. Samsel, and I can't tell you how distraught I am over these rulings."

"I can understand that, Tina, but as I said, the judge's decision is bound by the New Mexico laws. I do have a copy of Russell Erickson Jr's answers to interrogatories, and one of the questions asked was whether he or anyone acting on the plaintiff's behalf had spoken with you, the defendant. Both Erickson Jr. and Mr. Markman from STA Aviation, the insurance company, stated that you spoke very highly of the Ericksons and their conduct in the aircraft prior to the crash. Erickson Jr. said that you told him that his father tried to land on a paved road, but apparently just couldn't reach it and how brave and comforting his mother had been. He stated that your tone was one of 'gratitude and obvious deep feeling towards both Mr. and Mrs. Erickson.' He also said, in his words, 'She expressed how grateful she was to Erickson Sr., who she felt had saved her life, and how calm and controlled he was during the last few minutes prior to the crash'."

"What? How can they turn what I said into a complete lie? I'm sure that impressed Judge Lockman!" Tina was incredulous.

"The judge was going by the facts, but yes, since this was a sworn statement, it was one of the facts," Mr. Samsel said. "I just thought you should know."

"Why didn't the judge believe my affidavit? It was a sworn statement too," Tina screamed. Then more calmly, Tina said, "Wait a minute. My father always told me, 'Never speak ill of the dead because they cannot defend themselves.' When I called Russell Erickson Jr, a few days after the plane crash, I told him how calm everyone was and how kind his mother had been. That was before I knew that the engines were deliberately turned off. I had thought they had just stopped, but that was not the case. What I did not know at that time was that Russell could have chosen to land on a dirt road or in a great big open wash. Instead, as you know, he landed on the desert floor, after the rainy season, with all of the large green trees, overgrown shrubs, and mighty cacti in the way. With your help, I now know that there was no fire in the plane and that the warning horn was blowing because he shut down the engines. He wasn't a hero. He should have had the engines looked at after we landed in Baja Réal. We now know that his friends said the right engine was losing power. He just partied and didn't have the engines checked!" Tina was fuming and couldn't believe that her kind words had been used against her. "I will see you next week, Mr. Samsel," Tina slammed the phone on its cradle.

"What did he have to say?" Roger asked.

Tina relayed her conversation with the attorney.

"I think he's trying to put the blame on someone else, turn this over to the New York attorney or an attorney of your choice, and be done with it," Roger said. "I still don't know why, though."

Tina spent the next several days drafting a letter to Samsel, outlining her frustrations with his law firm, the judge's decision, and the terms of the insurance payments to her, as well as the payment Samsel and Baley were demanding from her.

On December 18, Tina received his reply. He addressed her points, all right, but he also blatantly threatened her. She read the third paragraph. *"In view of your refusal to authorize and pay for a teardown of the engines, I must advise you that you are jeopardizing your case and you may lose on the issue of liability and be held responsible to pay the costs incurred in defense of this action to the Erickson estate."*

"Roger, listen to this. Samsel had said an inspection and teardown of the engines was part of the overall investigation. He never told me that I would be responsible for paying for it. In fact, he said the insurance company would require the teardown. The Erickson estate needs the results just as much as we do. I get the feeling that Mr. Markman, with STA Aviation Insurance, doesn't get along too well with Mr. Samsel either."

"I think Mr. Samsel alienates people, and they don't want to deal with him. It is just easier to ignore his antics, but not necessarily the right thing to do."

By now, Tina was really raising her voice, as she said, "He isn't a defense attorney. He's a spineless attorney. I want to terminate my relationship with his office. As much as I don't want to start from square one, I'll find an attorney in New York and work with the courts up there, since Judge Lockman and 'jellyfish' man aren't giving me any other choice."

"Tina, Stop!" Roger said, raising his voice so he would be heard above Tina's yelling. "Look at this from Samsel and Baley's point of view. Right now, they can get 25% of $103,000 because you signed the agreement, even though you verbally said it's after the $103,000. Why should they continue to drag this case out any longer and go to trial if it will cut into their profits? They don't honestly think they can get any money from this case in Las Cruces."

"Roger, are you saying they will never take this case to trial?" Tina asked.

"Tina, I don't want to pop your bubble, but it looks that way. Don't hold me to it, but it is just a gut feeling."

"THERE ARE TWO KINDS OF WEAKNESS: THAT WHICH BREAKS AND THAT WHICH BENDS." JAMES RUSSELL LOWELL

CHAPTER SEVENTEEN
JANUARY 1992

Tina usually loved the holiday season: the decorating, planning, and entertaining that were all part of it. But this year, she just hadn't been in the mood. The pending court case loomed before her like an insurmountable mountain, and she felt as if she were carrying a weight on her shoulders that she couldn't put down.

Tina had sent her letter to Samsel and Baley in December, and she and Roger never met with the attorneys. The first two weeks of January had been quiet, depressingly quiet, and Tina had been researching attorneys in New York. On January 13, Tina received a letter from Samsel and Baley stating that her deposition had been scheduled for January 26. She was instructed to call their secretary to set up a meeting prior to that date to discuss the deposition.

Tina sighed. *I guess I'm not quite done with Samsel yet,* she thought.

January 26 was changed to February 2, but finally it was time to give her deposition. She hadn't expected to be nervous, but when she walked into the room, she felt claustrophobic. Tina hoped some fresh air would blow into the room soon, but as she looked around, she doubted that it would. A court reporter was present, and Samsel explained that everything she said would be recorded verbatim. Graham Lennar, the attorney for Russell Erickson Sr.'s estate in Las Cruces, would be asking the questions.

Coincidentally, he worked for a prestigious firm in town that had represented Tina and her husband, when a customer had sued her business, Precious Jewelry, back in the early 80s.

Her attorney had done an excellent job, and she didn't have to pay the legal fees associated with the jury trial. When people asked about law firms, Tina never hesitated to mention Chambers, Thomas, Ubanks and Reed, but right now, with Mr. Lennar hovering like one of the vultures that had circled above her that fateful day in the desert, she wasn't feeling quite so complimentary. Samsel was there, too, and had told her he probably wouldn't even speak, unless Attorney Lennar pushed on an issue that he didn't think she should answer. He had also told Tina to keep her answers short and to the point.

In a rather twisted way, Tina actually found it somewhat comforting that Samsel was there. Even though she didn't trust him one iota, he was the only person present that could possibly steer her in the right direction if the questioning got off track.

Before the court reporter had typed even two pages, Attorney Lennar had admonished Tina for nodding or shaking her head, instead of saying "yes" or "no." Tina knew one of her own weaknesses was working against her. Whenever she knew what someone was going to say, Tina had a habit of interrupting. It was a New York thing, and it allowed people there to talk even faster, but she knew it could be annoying. It obviously aggravated Attorney Lennar, especially since he had to make sure his question or statement was recorded in its entirety in the deposition. He asked more about Tina's background than she had expected, including the automobile accident that was the cause of her first husband's death. He also asked if she had ever been injured in an accident. He asked about the long years of migraines after she chipped a bone in her neck in a car accident years before. In a short time, all the memories came flooding back. Attorney Lennar asked which vertebrae had been injured. She simply replied, "I don't remember," but wanted to say, "that's the least of my worries right now, and what in the world does it matter?"

A couple of times, Tina thought she should just grab the man by the shoulders and shake him. "Can't you understand what I'm telling you?" she wanted to shout. Lennar would re-word and re-ask some of the same questions three or four times. She had already referred to Hunter as "Mr. H." several times, but when he questioned her about what happened at the airport in Baja Réal before the plane took off, he asked "Mr. H, who?"

Tina tried to stay calm. Was he just trying to catch her saying something that could be used against her, or was he actually trying to get her so confused that she would say something wrong? Or was he just trying to be as annoying as possible so Tina would let her temper show? Tina was trying to explain to Lennar that Russell did not do an instrument check or let the cabin cool off before they took off from Baja Réal. Lennar didn't come right out and say it, but Tina could tell by his questions that he doubted her explanation.

"I'm not a pilot." Tina said, "Russell did not check the gauges and the cabin temperature after we boarded the plane, before we left Baja Réal." Lennar also tried to pin her down on their exact location, altitude, and coordinates when Russell turned the plane around immediately preceding the crash. "I thought we were at about 6,000 to 7,000 feet," Tina said, "but I have no real reason to know that."

"What happened next?" Attorney Lennar asked.

"We crashed!" Tina wanted to shout. Instead, she remembered Russell's words before he quit talking. "Russell said, 'I hate this place. I will never come back to Mexico again!'" she repeated. Tina could imagine Russell's red face and the veins in his neck. Maybe he had been so angry and worked up that he couldn't even think straight.

"We also had to tell Russell that we were going back to Baja Réal to the airport when the tower asked," Tina told Attorney Lennar. "Russell was very confused about where we had come from or where we were going. He mumbled about La Rosa and Mazatlan, and Cancun so we told him Baja Réal."

"The tower couldn't understand your location and they were confused?" Lennar asked.

Tina remained calm. "No," she said, glancing at the court reporter to make sure she got that down. "No, Russell was confused." Tina considered that possibly he was so angry and confused that he had caused the crash, or maybe he felt guilty and distraught because he didn't get the plane checked more thoroughly.

"Can I get up?" Tina asked. She started to get out of her chair before she even had an answer. "My foot fell asleep."

"Sure. Want to take a break?" Attorney Lennar asked.

Tina knew they weren't even half through the deposition, but she couldn't sit in that room one more minute. "Sorry," she said, as she walked out of the room and down the hall. Walking helped lessen the feel of pins and needles in her foot and leg.

I wish I could give you some pins and needles, Mr. Lennar, Tina thought and smiled to herself. She returned a few minutes later, willing herself to get through the rest of the questioning.

"Okay, where were we before the break?" Tina asked.

"We were talking about what happened at the airport and the ride after you took off," Lennar said when they reconvened. "What else was said?"

"Nothing, the tower kept talking to us, but Russell didn't answer," Tina said. "When I said, 'the right engine has stopped,' Christina said, 'We know, dear,' but other than that no one spoke."

Tina could still hear Christina saying those three words, over and over "We know, dear, we know, dear, we know, dear…" those haunting words. At the time, Tina didn't know the exact meaning of those words. She closed her eyes, as she pictured the next scene.

"The tower kept asking Russell questions, but he just held onto the wheel and didn't answer. The plane kept going down lower and lower. I put my head on Christina's lap. Hunter asked if my seat belt was tight, and I nodded yes. We weren't talking after that, but the noise from an alert horn of some kind was deafening."

Attorney Lennar's questioning about how Tina got out of the plane, what the men who found the crash site said to Hunter, and the other questions of when Hunter died seemed to go on and on. When Lennar asked if Hunter was alive when he was on the floor of the clinic, Tina almost lost it. She hadn't expected to feel so overwhelmed, but the questions were so repetitive and insistent.

"No, for all purposes, Hunter died in the ambulance, but they kept working on him anyway. If he had a pulse, by the time we got to the clinic, it was very low." She could see Hunter lying on the stretcher, and remembered thinking that they would both make it. He didn't seem to have broken bones, so they would be there for one another as they recovered from this ordeal. Tina knew she could use his help through the long recovery that was ahead of her. It was a sure thing they would help each other through this nightmare.

Attorney Lennar questioned her about the burning smell and the right engine stopping.

"I thought you started to say something about, 'Well, he shut the right engine down.' Do you know, did it stop on its own or did he stop it or…?"

"At the time, I just looked out the window; the engine was dead stopped. I did not see Russell at that time push the control, but the engine was stopped. It wasn't turning slowly, it was... That's a picture that I can never get out of my head, it's there with me all the time. It stopped," Tina said her mind back in the plane.

"Did he say anything about that?"

"I told you, I told you. No, no!" Tina wanted to shout. "He never said anything," she answered in a voice that was much calmer than she felt.

"Do you know why it stopped?"

"Do I know now?"

"Yes," Attorney Lennar said.

"I know why it stopped. He turned it off."

"What was that?"

You heard me, Tina wanted to say. She definitely knew she was talking clearly enough. She certainly didn't want the court reporter to miss this part.

"He turned the engine off," Tina repeated, a little too loudly.

"Why do you know that?"

"I was told that an engine, when it's feathered, will stop. When it shuts down by itself or when it's malfunctioning, it will continue to rotate, but once you feather it, it will stop dead."

"Who told you that?"

"A pilot, a couple of pilots, a bunch of pilots," Tina tried to lower her voice.

"Who are they?"

"I have friends who are pilots," she answered. "I asked them."

"Can you tell me their names?"

"No, I don't know."

Attorney Lennar went on to ask how Tina knew about feathering and if someone had demonstrated it to her.

"I was back in a plane, but not..."

145

"What airplane were you in?"

Hadn't Attorney Lennar lectured her about letting him finish his questions? How about letting her finish her answers?

"I wasn't flying in another Aerostar, but I was in one."

"Who took you?"

"I believe it was Cisco Samsel."

"So he took you into an Aerostar to show you how to feather an engine?"

Boy, could this guy ever put words in her mouth! "No, I wanted to know what the noise was that I heard."

"And did you figure out what that was?"

"Yes, when you take an engine and you shut it down, the plane's alert system sounds, warning you that you can't fly in that configuration; if you don't raise the throttle you're going to crash."

"So what was the noise that you heard?" Lennar asked.

"I heard a loud, deep noise, the warning horn."

"And Cisco Samsel reproduced that same noise?"

"Yes," Tina said.

"Were the engines running? How did he do that?"

"I don't know. It was upsetting and I didn't watch every little thing he turned."

"You don't recall if the airplane was running or not?"

"No. It was traumatic to get back in an Aerostar at the time, but I had to know what the noise was."

"What else did he show you about the plane?"

"I don't remember. I was only interested in knowing about the noise."

"How long was this after the accident?"

"I don't know, three or four months."

"Had you already retained Cisco Samsel as your attorney?"

Tina's radar went up. What did that have to do with

anything? Was Lennar implying that Samsel shouldn't have been the one to show her the plane? Was it a conflict of interest? He definitely couldn't let this line of questioning go.

Samsel came to the rescue. "I'm going to instruct her not to answer. There's no relevance, and the fact of retention is privileged."

"If you weren't her lawyer, there isn't any privilege," Lennar retorted.

"All communication in anticipation of retention is privileged," Samsel said.

"I don't think so," Lennar said.

"I think it is, and I'll challenge you." Samsel stuck to his guns.

The men continued to argue and Tina just wanted this interrogation to stop. Tina really didn't know if one of them could put an end to it, but finally Samsel said, "You can go on to another topic. If I'm wrong, I'm wrong."

Attorney Lennar couldn't let it drop that easily. He turned to Tina. "We're probably going to court, and this is really a simple matter. Are you going to follow your attorney's instructions and not answer the questions about when you sought legal counsel in this case?"

"At this point in time," Tina answered.

The man just didn't give up. "At what point in time will you?"

"I don't know," Tina said. "At this point in time I'm not answering the question."

"Did anyone in the plane say why the engine stopped?" Lennar went on.

"Christina Erickson said, 'We know, dear.' Remember? We know, dear. We know, dear." *Was the man deaf?* Tina thought angrily.

Attorney Lennar finally finished his questioning about

the crash itself and went on to ask about her injuries and the pain in her wrist and ankle. He also questioned her about what activities caused the pain to return. Did she catch a hint of him implying that she shouldn't be trying to play tennis, a sport she dearly loved, if she was in pain?

"Does the foot hurt all the time when you're playing tennis?" he asked.

"I don't... I don't pay attention. In other words, I want to play tennis. It can hurt and I'm still going to play," Tina answered. "Then afterwards, it still hurts."

"This is in your ankle that it hurts?"

Tina wanted to say, "Of course it's in my ankle, you knucklehead. You're the one that just asked me to stick to the pain in the ankle and not talk about my wrist right now." But instead she said, "Well, it's in the ankle but it goes up, travels up the ankle."

"How high does it travel up?"

"The foot itself hurts and the ankle," she said. "I have lots of pain and swelling." Tina thought, *And it really isn't going away. Dr. Adam told me that the most trouble would be with my wrist, but it's truly my ankle. I am always on my feet so I am really always in pain, but I try to stand up straight, hold my head up, and go on. What else can I do? Feel sorry for myself?*

"How often do you play tennis now?"

Hadn't she just told him that she was just trying to play again? This guy was really dense. "I haven't... I haven't played, but I plan on playing. I played maybe one time in two months, but I want to play again, and I'm going to play, try to play." *No, I'm going to play*, Tina said to herself. Why was Lennar making her doubt herself?

"Have you tried any of the other things you mentioned, like racquetball, hiking, or ice skating?"

"My doctors advised me against those. And hiking, I'm just petrified."

"What have you done in the last three months for exercise?"

"Nothing, I've just gone for therapy." Tina realized how lame that sounded. Did this man know how grueling, how painful, how exhausting therapy could be?

Attorney Lennar went through the same type of questions about her wrist and finally asked how long it took for the pain to go away.

"I have no idea, probably three, four months. I don't know. I just told you it still hurts and is stiff if I do something like painting, which I did yesterday, or if I bump it."

"Would the same thing be true for your ankle?"

"I still have pain in my ankle."

"Even when you're not using it, Lennar asked?"

Hadn't they just been through all of this? Tina was about to use it on him. "Yes, if I move it a certain way. It hurts if I point my toes and move it to the left."

"Okay, what about when you just walk?" Lennar asked. "Do you have pain when you walk around a room?"

Just walk? Did he know how badly she had wanted to "just walk" when she was in the hospital? "If I wear...if I don't wear these high top sneakers, I have pain."

Attorney Lennar continued on for several more minutes about her broken ribs, the number of bones in her wrist and ankle that were broken, and the burns and scars on her leg and right arm.

"I need to see the scars," Lennar said. "Maybe we can set up a time in Cisco's office, and you could wear shorts and a tank top. Its part of what I've got to do. I'm not trying to embarrass you."

Luckily, Samsel interjected. "We'll give you an answer on that."

Like a year from now, Tina thought.

After several more minutes of questioning about the scars and burns, Attorney Lennar moved on to the therapy. When Tina explained her physical therapy versus Myotherapy, Lennar had the nerve to imply that Bonnie Prudden wasn't even qualified to do therapy. "Does she actually write books or is she doing the therapy, or is she too busy writing books?"

The only reason I mentioned that she writes books, Tina thought, *was to give her credibility when you kept asking what kind of a therapist she is, and is she a physical therapist. I said "Myotherapist" and then explained what it was.*

"Any other doctors you're going to for your injuries?" Attorney Lennar asked.

"I see Carmen Lopez. She's a psychologist."

"What is she doing for you?"

Why did he care? Tina thought. "Grief and loss." Tina said aloud.

"I assume that's because of the loss of Hunter, is that right?"

"I feel the loss of a lot of my life. The loss, the images I can't get out of my head. That's what she's helping me with."

"Did someone direct you to her?"

No, I took control of my own life, once again. Thank heaven for that. Just like in the hospital, just like with you lawyers. "I felt I needed help. I felt that I couldn't... I wanted to get rid of the images of the engines in my head, and the cockpit and the plane, and I just couldn't seem to get rid of it on my own."

"Are you doing better now with her help?"

"Yes, a little better."

"Anybody else you're seeing as a result of this accident?"

"Not right at this minute, no."

"That makes me think you've got plans to see somebody else," Attorney Lennar said.

"No, just right now, there's nobody else," she answered.

Attorney Lennar finished by asking questions about the medical bills and insurance.

"We'll read and sign. Send the signature page to me," Samsel said.

The whole thing had taken a little over two hours, but to Tina, it had seemed like two days.

"TRUTH IS TRUTH TO THE END OF RECKONING."
WILLIAM SHAKESPEARE

CHAPTER EIGHTEEN

Three days after giving her deposition, Tina was trying to relax and read, but she could not help but relive that frightening experience. During the deposition, she repeated almost everything she had said before—whether it was to the insurance adjusters, her attorneys, family members, or friends. What was different, she realized, was that she had told bits and pieces of the story each time, but the questioning by Mr. Lennar, the attorney for the Ericksons's estate, had extracted each minute, intricate detail in just over two hours. This type of questioning had been more emotionally draining than she could have imagined. Some of his questions had made her reexamine the actual events and even caused her to second guess herself. When the attorney continued to ask the same question twice or in three different ways, or put words in her mouth, Tina had to restate the facts to make sure they weren't being twisted or misinterpreted. It seemed the opposing attorney's tactic was to wear Tina down and catch her off guard. Most unsettling was that Tina didn't necessarily have a good feeling about the way the deposition had gone. Those nightmares she had told Lennar about had been worse the past couple of nights, and even during the day, the guilt she felt for not having done something differently gnawed at her. Of everyone in the crash, she was the only one who was in any shape to have acted. Christina and Russell were dead, and Hunter had obviously been injured far worse than she was. Sometimes she thought that if she could have crawled back in the direction of Hunter's voice, despite the crippling pain of her broken ribs, she might have been able to save him. Or, if she could have talked to the nice man who placed the baseball cap on her head and somehow insisted that he take her to Hunter, she might have been able to save his life. Or maybe, Tina felt, she should have just tried harder… Tina couldn't concentrate on the book she was reading. Why had she been the only one to survive? What was the reason? Just then the phone rang.

"Hi, Tina, Mr. Baley here. I wanted you to know that I filed an opposition regarding the approval to pay their attorney's fees out of the escrow account. I stated in the document that the estates were opened in the first place because of your efforts in an attempt to protect yourself, not for the estate to pay their attorney's fees. The net proceeds from the sale of one of the properties are in conflict: the original estimate was almost $20,000 and the opposing counsel now discloses that the net cash available is less than $7,500. In light of that, and their lack of response to our continued requests, I also stated that you demand an accounting breakdown of the escrow account."

"Well, Mr. Baley, I have to thank you for going to bat for me. Maybe we'll at least see what's in the account."

"You have a legal right to that information, so at some point they have to give it to us."

"Is it up to Judge Lockman to get a response, then?" Tina asked.

"Yes, I hand delivered the opposition to his courtroom, so we'll see what happens."

"Thank you again, Mr. Baley. I'll talk to you soon."

"Oh, one more thing, Tina, Mr. Samsel informed Mr. Lennar that he is calling Carmen Lopez and Bonnie Prudden as witnesses."

"Thank you, Mr. Baley. They definitely know the extent of both my mental and physical injuries."

"Have a good day, Tina."

"You too, Mr. Baley." *Maybe at least one of my two attorneys is on my side*, Tina thought.

A week later, Tina and Roger were enjoying breakfast on a beautiful morning. Tina was feeling less stressed and was hopeful about what might be transpiring on her case. The phone rang, and Tina considered not answering it. She didn't want to break the tranquility of spending some quality time with Roger. When she saw that it was Cisco, she changed her mind.

"Good morning, Mr. Samsel."

"Hello, Tina. I'm afraid I'm the bearer of bad news this morning. Before Judge Lockman had a chance to reply, Mr. Vicobi, the attorney for Christina's estate, filed a memo to the judge in support of the attorney's fees being paid out of the escrow account. He presented the argument that unpaid administrative fees are the number one priority and should be paid first. Also, the man I hired to help oversee the teardown of the engines, Mr. Sussman is requiring a $2,000 deposit before he will travel to California for the engine teardown. As I've mentioned before, if Mr. Sussman isn't present at the teardown, it is my opinion that you will lose this case on the issue of liability."

"I don't understand, Mr. Samsel. The teardown needs to be done."

"Yes, but if Mr. Sussman isn't there, we might not get all of the facts."

"This seems like an expense that isn't needed, Mr. Samsel. I am extremely frustrated with the way this whole engine teardown issue has been handled."

"So you are refusing to pay Sussman's travel expenses?"

"I don't see why this is my responsibility. I know the Erickson family would want to have the engines checked so that they could sue if the engines were defective. However, I really don't think I should pay for their teardown!" Tina

retorted. What she wanted to say was, "Is this another angle to get more money, Mr. Samsel?" but she bit her tongue. "I will talk to Roger and get back to you."

"We have a pretrial settlement conference scheduled for March 1 at 10 a.m."

"What is a pretrial conference? I don't want a conference. I want to go to trial. We've discussed this countless times and I want a jury trial. I don't want a conference. Who is involved? Judge Lockman has never ruled in my favor so why would I want another delay and conference? What is going on?" Tina demanded.

"Tina, calm down. We have to do things in a logical order, and the pretrial conference is part of the sequence of events. It doesn't necessarily mean..." Samsel hesitated and rephrased his explanation. "It doesn't mean that you won't have a jury trial."

"Thank you, Mr. Samsel. I will talk to you soon."

"I can't take much more of this man's shenanigans," Tina told Roger.

"Maybe the pretrial conference will have a good outcome," Roger said. "Russell Erickson Jr. has to be aware that he isn't going to get out of this without paying your bills."

MARCH 1, 1992

The pretrial conference was the straw that broke the proverbial camel's, or in this case Tina's, back. Tina noticed in the first few minutes of the meeting that no court reporter was present, which she thought was strange. Tina had spoken with Mr. Samsel earlier and said that she wanted the judgment backed by collateral. The judge was seated on his bench, and Tina and Roger, along with Mr. Samsel, were seated in the courtroom. There were other cases to be seen that morning so the courtroom was full.

Judge Lockman said, "This is a pretrial/settlement conference. A judgment is entered in favor of the plaintiff, Tina Morgan, and against the Estate of Russell Erickson Sr., in the amount of $425,000 plus taxable costs accrued."

Everyone knew how Tina felt. This judgment was not acceptable without collateral backing it. After Judge Lockman's statement, the room was silent. Tina kept waiting for her attorney to say something, but Cisco said nothing. Finally, out of desperation, Tina said in a low, timid voice, "Excuse me, Your Honor, I do not accept this judgment if it is not backed by collateral." Tina's voice was meek, as she did not want to be held in contempt of court for yelling or speaking too loudly. The judge completely ignored her and instead asked the attorneys from both sides to step up to the front.

What should I do? Tina wondered. *Why isn't my attorney saying anything? What is going on? Judge Lockman is totally ignoring me. Why? Should I fire Cisco? Should I speak up and tell the judge that I will absolutely not accept this offer? What happens? What should I do? I feel trapped. I don't know what to do.* Tina did nothing. She had lost her confidence and her nerve.

Tina looked at Roger, and she knew she had to do something. "I refuse this offer," Tina said boldly, "unless it is backed by collateral. I still don't know what assets or property make up the Erickson estate."

Attorney Lennar immediatly and boldly replied, "The estate of Russell Erickson Sr., accepts the offer of Judgment." What he then put in writing to the court was this: "This acceptance is merely a means to put an end to the litigation at hand. It is not to be used as an admission that the defendant is liable in this action."

Judge Lockman dismissed them. *Why was this allowed?* Tina wondered. *Where was Cisco? Why didn't he protect me?*

Tina practically ran into the hall. "Roger, what just happened in there? We still don't have an inventory of the Ericksons's assets. With the trial just a few weeks away, how does this judgment affect what the jury is going to be told?"

"I don't know, Tina," Roger admitted, "but we need to find out." Roger turned to find Cisco Samsel walking the other way. "Mr. Samsel," Roger said loudly enough for several people ahead of Cisco Samsel to turn around, but the attorney kept walking. "Tina and I need a few questions answered," Roger continued, as he and Tina walked closer to their attorney. Samsel quickened his stride. Tina was almost running to keep up.

Samsel had to slow down to open the door leading to the wide steps on the outside of the building. He turned to look at Roger and Tina as he opened the door.

"Could we have a few minutes of your time?" Roger said patiently.

Samsel said, "I don't have time right now," and without saying another word, he let the door close before Roger could reach for it, and sprinted down the steps toward the street.

"What is going on here?" Tina asked. "I didn't even sign the offer before it was submitted. There could be stipulations or amendments on it that are just fine with Judge Lockman and the attorneys but that we haven't even seen."

"I think the only thing we can do is go home while this is still fresh on our minds, and draft a letter from you to Mr. Samsel."

"Yes," Tina agreed. "About a month ago, when Samsel went over what would happen, he said there were two options: to go to trial or to settle. He explained that the disadvantage of continuing on to trial was that we couldn't predict the outcome, and collecting after the trial can be very difficult. He also said that since I am a successful woman, the jury would not side with me. He said I had made a good living when I had my store and didn't lack immediate money, so the jury would likely not rule in my favor. He explained that submitting an acceptable offer would mean I would be paid and the whole matter would be finished."

"Perfect," Roger said. "State those exact points in the letter, but also ask what the settlement means as far as total monies paid and how they will be disbursed and when."

"Okay," Tina said. "I'm going to get it in the mail first thing tomorrow so we can get some answers. The judge totally ignored me when I said I would accept the judgment only if it was backed by collateral."

"Yes, he did," Roger agreed. "I'm surprised he didn't give you a copy of the judgment today."

As soon as they got home, Tina started writing. She laid out everything precisely as she and Roger had discussed, so it was all documented.

Within a couple of days, Tina received her attorney's written response. His first concern was that his 25% would be first, with the net proceeds going to Tina. He stated that the insurance checks would be issued right away, but he didn't even mention the $425,000 or how that sum would be collected. He said that money could come from properties in New Mexico first and then from those in New York.

The very same week, Hunter's son, Steve, in Illinois, called Tina. "Mr. Blackman, the attorney for Dad's estate, just sent me a copy of the results of the engine teardown. I know a copy will be sent to your attorney too."

"So they finally did the inspection!" Tina almost couldn't believe what she was hearing.

"Yes, they did," Steve confirmed. "And Tina, you've been right all along. "There's a detailed report that refers to the different parts of the engines, and the left one was much more severely damaged by the fire. But the bottom line is that there was no evidence of engine malfunction."

"I guess that leaves pilot error," Tina said. She had thought she would be more excited when she heard this news. As the months went by, Tina had become more certain that the plane crash was caused by pilot error. Now it was a sobering reality.

"Yes, it does, Tina. I'm sorry this has taken so long, but now we know. This will close the claim we have open for Dad's estate, but I know things aren't wrapped up yet for you. Are you still going to trial?"

"That's the plan and what I keep fighting for," Tina replied. "We had a pretrial conference, but after a letter from my attorney this week, I'm still unclear where we are with the trial. As usual, I have more questions that need to be answered."

"Good luck, Tina, and keep in touch."

"Thanks so much for the news, Steve," Tina said. "I really appreciate it."

"Guess what?" Tina said to Roger after she hung up the phone. "The engines didn't malfunction."

"You could be a detective," Roger smiled warmly at her. "You did your own investigation, went back in an Aerostar with Samsel, and that's what you've been saying ever since."

"You're right, but for some reason, I don't feel as good about getting it officially confirmed as I thought I would," Tina said. "I also don't know if it means that anything is going to change on this case."

"I guess that's another question for the infamous Mr. Samsel," Roger said. "It's been a long few days. How about I take my favorite lady to dinner this evening?"

"Oh, Roger, I don't know."

"Come on, Tina. Walk away from your desk and this

case, just for tonight."

"I think I'll take a bath and get dressed up!" Tina said, changing her tone. "Thanks for going to court with me, Roger. Sometimes I feel like I'm going crazy and Mr. Samsel isn't seeing or hearing what I'm telling him, and I feel the same about Judge Lockman. But at least you are there to see and hear what is going on. With you to back me up, I don't feel like I'm totally going insane."

Roger thought for a moment, and then said, "I haven't been around lawyers or judges that much, but this case has certainly had its twists and turns, and I agree with you, Tina. There's more going on here than meets the eye."

"IN THE DEPTH OF WINTER, I FINALLY LEARNED THAT WITHIN ME THERE LAY AN INVINCIBLE SUMMER." ALBERT CAMUS

CHAPTER NINETEEN

By April, Cisco Samsel seemed to have disappeared from Tina's case, and even from the law firm in which he was a partner. When Tina called, she was told he wasn't in, and she would eventually get a call back from Mr. Baley.

"Tina, I let Judge Lockman know that Mr. Vicobi, the attorney for Christina's estate, is out of line. You clearly stated to the judge that the judgment must be backed by collateral, and now both Vicobi and Lennar, the attorney for Russell Erickson's estate, are stating that there is no community property in New Mexico."

"But, Mr. Baley, the Ericksons did own property here. In fact, I thought one property had already been sold," Tina protested.

"That's true, Tina. How the court is defining community property is the issue. Since the Ericksons died simultaneously, the attorneys for their estates are pointing out to Judge Lockman that the property would be divided between the two estates, and Christina's estate can't even be considered in the equation."

"Once again, Mr. Baley, I have to ask what that means."

"Well, Tina, as you know, Russell's estate, represented by Russell Jr., accepted the Judgment. Now, his attorney is placing conditions on it, which basically means they are rejecting it. My theory is that they signed the Judgment merely for the sake of saving the defendant the costs of defense during a trial. In other words, Russell Erickson Jr. signed the Judgment knowing he could not be held to it.

As the plaintiff, you should not be denied a fair trial just to save expenses for the defendant."

"Have you gotten any reaction from Judge Lockman?" Tina was almost afraid to ask.

"Unfortunately, we're pushing the judge and he doesn't like to be pushed. To be honest, Cisco has worked with Judge Lockman several times in the past. This is only my second encounter with Lockman, but I can tell that his patience is growing thin. Mr. Vicobi and Mr. Lennar know how to push all the right buttons, which, in our case, happen to be the wrong buttons. I also told Judge Lockman that if the Judgment isn't immediately collectable against Russell Sr.'s property in New Mexico, and if there is any chance at all that some legal challenge will be raised to the Judgment, then you are being deprived of a fair trial. Therefore, I have asked the court to amend the Judgment. My other concern is that the estates for the Ericksons have claimed that there is no community property, but they have also claimed there is. These issues are what frustrate Judge Lockman. Because of this, I pointed out that you shouldn't have to begin collections proceedings in New York, only to be told that you haven't collected from all available community property."

"I appreciate what you're doing, Mr. Baley, but frankly, I feel like we are just spinning around in circles."

"Believe me, Tina, I understand how you feel. Writing all of this to submit to the judge makes me feel like I am chasing my tail also. It's in your best interest to put it in writing." Mr. Baley went on to say that the defense is trying to force Tina's lawyers to clarify the discrepancies, since first one thing is said and then another. I know you feel there is an issue about the various spellings of Russell's name and which name really belongs to which man, but to be honest, I think Russell Jr. and his attorneys hope we will just throw our hands up in the air and give up because we've had enough."

"I certainly hope that's not what you feel, Mr. Baley. I've come too far to do that, and I want my medical expenses paid. I know there is something going on with the names, since the original papers showed the father as Russell A. Erickson. The son does not have a middle initial. Also, I asked Mr. Samsel for a certified copy of the Judgment. Could you check on that, and can I get a copy of it?"

"I'll let you know. You should definitely have a copy for your files."

Tina wanted to say, "Yes, so I can show it to my new attorney," but she knew Mr. Baley wasn't the one who had failed to stand up for her. Tina was excited about her new attorney. She had met William Chambers when she was involved with a homeowner's dispute a few years before. He had been brilliant in his advice and handling of the situation, and Tina was very grateful. He was a partner in a large and influential law firm and their record was excellent. However, until William Chambers was up to speed on the case, she still needed someone who knew what was going on. She couldn't afford to have Mr. Baley "bail" on her now, she thought, somewhat amused at the play on words.

JULY 1992

Not much had happened on the case since April, and Tina tried to busy herself by playing golf and tennis. She realized how much she had missed seeing friends, too, so she tried to focus on her life other than the court case and, hopefully, the impending trial.

Finally, Tina had asked Samsel and Baley to forward all documents on file to the Law Offices of Melman, Stern, Jones, Sanders, and Chambers. Tina was optimistic that copies of court records that she had never received from Samsel and Baley would be forwarded to William Chambers, and he would have a chance to review her complete file. However, Samsel and Baley never sent the complete file; they left out crucial paperwork that was needed to appeal.

Joan was Mr. Chambers's secretary, and Tina knew that if she couldn't reach her new attorney, at least Joan would respond. Joan was pleasant and very efficient, and she followed through on everything that Tina had inquired about so far. Tina had asked Joan to forward any correspondence to her at her mother's address in New York for the month of July. Going to New York had kept Tina's mind off the case and was a nice diversion, since she was able to spend time visiting friends and relatives, many for the first time since the accident.

In mid-July, Tina received a phone call from Joan, excitedly telling her that she had just heard that Cisco Samsel was arrested for drug trafficking. Tina couldn't believe it! I paid Samsel to fly down to Mexico to check on the plane crash, and he actually was in the drug business? That must have been a free trip for him. Tina was ecstatic! She could hardly wait to call Roger.

A week later, Tina received a letter from Joan with the certified copy of the Judgment enclosed. She had been asking and waiting for her copy of the Judgment since March, and now she was actually holding it. Joan's letter was short, and when she glanced at the second paragraph, Cisco's name caught Tina's eye.

She laid the copy of the Judgment on the table and read Joan's words. *"For your information, we just heard that Cisco Samsel was indicted for money laundering in a twenty page Federal Court document. It has not hit the papers, but we will copy any articles and send them to you. We do not know if Mr. Baley is involved."*

Tina started screaming and jumping up and down, shouting to no one in particular. "I knew it, I knew it, I knew it! He didn't care about this case or what would happen to me. At least Judge Lockman will have to listen to our arguments in the courtroom, and, hopefully, he will believe me now! He wouldn't pick a felon's words over mine." As the ramifications of Joan's words started to sink in, Tina felt energized, like a mechanical bunny, and she couldn't stop moving. *Wow*, Tina thought, *this explains a lot. Did that money laundering have anything to do with Samsel's trips to Mexico?* she wondered.

Mr. Chambers was looking into the malpractice insurance that Samsel and Baley had, since Tina still hadn't resolved the fee issues with them at the time she suspended their services. She and Roger had been right—there was definitely something else going on, and Samsel had a hidden agenda the entire time he had been her attorney.

At the beginning of their relationship, Tina believed Samsel would represent her case well. As time went on, somewhere along the way, she felt that he turned against her, his own client. Tina recalled an incident with Samsel. On one of her interrogatory answers, Samsel insisted that she exaggerate and redirect the answer so that it had a completely different meaning. Tina didn't believe this was right, and argued with him.

He yelled, "I am your lawyer and you will do what I say!" He became argumentative and uncooperative.

I wonder whose side he is on? Tina asked herself.

NOVEMBER 1992

Judge Lockman was primarily an Estate Judge, but he seemed to get involved and handle any case Tina was involved in, including this new case with her ex-attorney,

Samsel, and the fee dispute. Tina felt the judge was almost like a dog that grabbed onto your clothing and wouldn't let go.

Mr. Chambers had done what Tina had asked. He had refused to back down from the wrath of Judge Lockman and stated that a trial would be the best way to resolve the fee dispute issue with Samsel and Baley. Judge Lockman, in Tina's eyes, still wasn't about to look at things fairly, and he ordered that $36,000 of the insurance money, the amount that Tina was disputing with Samsel and Baley, be held in an interest-bearing account. A trial for the attorney's fees issue was set for January 12, 1993. Judge Lockman stated in writing that there was no objection to this decision. Tina had asked the judge for additional time before the trial, so that Mr. Chambers could have time to review everything from the very beginning, but Judge Lockman denied her request without even considering it.

When Tina returned from New York, after spending the month of July with her mother, Mr. Chambers made it very clear that his firm could not continue to handle her case because of a conflict of interest. With Cisco's arrest, Mr. Chambers would have to be a witness, and he was also Tina's attorney, so he could not continue to represent her. He told Tina that she shouldn't take it personally, but his firm had decided they did not want to continue with this case after Cisco was arrested. *So what are they saying?* Tina wondered. *They don't want my case because of what Cisco did? They did not want a case that involved a shady attorney, or what? I didn't have my second attorney very long. Who will I get now?*

On December 1, Tina placed an ad in the *New Mexico Lawyer*, a trade publication, which was affiliated with the Bar Association in Albuquerque, New Mexico. Tina wasn't usually desperate, but after ten law firms in Las Cruces refused to take her case, she didn't have a choice. She needed help and she needed it a few months ago, before Cisco turned out to be such a snake.

The ad read, *"Plaintiff in plane crash seeks legal malpractice attorney: potential representation against former Las Cruces attorneys. (One was federally indicted in an unrelated matter.) Malpractice insurance carrier notified. Contact T.M. at ... "*

On December 2, Tina made her second desperate move in as many days. She wrote a letter directly to the judge.

Dear Judge Lockman:

On March 1 of this year, at a supposed settlement conference, as the victim I begged this court not to accept the Judgment presented by the opposing attorneys and the law firm of Samsel and Baley because I had not agreed with the offer presented to the Court and I had never seen the papers and the offer that my attorney presented

This Court accepted the Judgment against my protest.

On November 10, 1992, at a status conference for the interpleading of funds from the Judgment of March 1, you would not allow me to speak my mind and demand a jury trial.

On November 30, 1992, a request was made for objection and to request a jury trial.

On December 1, 1992, an offer of Judgment was filed with the court for the law firm of Samsel and Baley.

Why should Samsel be allowed to make an offer of Judgment in this case, when in this case I was denied that privilege? Remember, I did not make that offer of Judgment presented by Samsel and Baley.

Your Honor, what difference does it make if a man pulls a gun and takes your money or an attorney takes your

*money under a legal pretense? The result is the same: the
victim ends up with less money.*
I am begging you to please allow this jury trial.
Respectfully,
Tina Morgan

Tina reread what she had written and felt like she was
crawling on her hands and knees. This really wasn't her style,
not at all, but she was willing to do whatever was necessary.
Cisco Samsel had been of no help to her, and now she was
forced to go directly to the judge.

There were two issues at stake: the jury trial and the
money that she had agreed to pay Samsel in their first verbal
agreement. Tina knew it had been clear before, but it didn't
matter now—not to the Judge and, least of all, not to Samsel.
The 25% was supposed to come from any amount over and
above the $103,000 insurance settlement.

Tina knew there was plenty of money between the
two estates, or even just Russell's, since that's how the
attorneys for the Erickson estates were strategizing. But
Judge Lockman was trying to get her to take $64,000, with the
other $36,000 being held in an account that would ultimately
go to Samsel in 30 days, since the judge hadn't granted more
time. Then everyone could go their separate ways.

At this point, none of this mattered to her new attorney,
William Chambers because he already felt there was a conflict
of interest. Tina knew his firm didn't want to be involved in
the legal scandal of the decade. Las Cruces was a relatively
small town, at least in a who's who kind of way, and no
law firm in town wanted to deal with a lying, cheating, and
money-laundering peer. Even if it was the right thing to do,
a law firm that took on this goliath wouldn't win points with
other attorneys or judges.

But Tina couldn't and wouldn't back down now. She

recalled the day in the hospital and the first time Samsel had come to see her. There was another person with him—Mr. Bond. That was the next letter she would write. If the State Bar of New Mexico could question Mr. Bond, maybe he could vouch for Samsel's character, or lack thereof. Tina needed someone to find him. She needed Mr. Bond on her side.

"The only thing necessary for the triumph of evil is for good men to do nothing." Edmund Burke

CHAPTER TWENTY
December 1992

Tina had been feeling anxious, unsettled, nervous, and uncomfortable for a few weeks. She was in a catch-22 situation, trying to find a new attorney and, at the same time, trying to deal with a judge who would not extend the date of the trial. No one wanted to touch her case after the arrest of Cisco Samsel.

When she opened her mailbox the morning of December 9, Tina immediately spotted the envelope with the return address from the State Bar of New Mexico. Tina wondered if Pearl Samuel finally had the name of an attorney who would take her case. Pearl had given her leads on where to find more attorneys a few weeks earlier, but they had all refused to take over Tina's case. She was certainly glad Cisco Samsel was no longer representing her, as the final months before he was arrested were a screaming match of wits between them. One would think his arrest would make things easy for Tina and that the judge, or other attorneys, would want to take her side or have an open mind as to what occurred. What was hard to believe was that Samsel's arrest was complicating Tina's situation even more. Recently, there had been rumors, and one attorney had mentioned to Tina, that Samsel had strong Mafia ties. Most of the attorneys who had turned her down assured Tina that the short time frame before the trial was the reason they refused to consider taking her case. Tina really didn't believe this. She knew that Cisco Samsel was the reason no one wanted to touch her case.

The letterhead from the State Bar had the legal symbol of two equally balanced weights on a scale next to the words "STATE BAR of NEW MEXICO." "How ironic," Tina said to Roger, as she joined him on the patio and pointed to the letterhead so he could see the symbol. "The balanced weights imply that the State Bar represents fairness and equality. What I have experienced so far—from judges, to lawyers, to filing complaints with the state—has been a very unbalanced picture of the entire judicial system. In 1963, Dr. Martin Luther King Jr. stated: "Injustice anywhere is a threat to justice everywhere." Tina said, "I feel like I'm the kid on a seesaw and no one will play with me. I am sitting on the ground because no one will get on the other end to balance the scale. In other words, how do I go to court, when no attorney will take the case, and balance the scale?"

"That's quite a description," Roger said "and pretty accurate, too. Maybe you should devote your time to writing about the legal system," he laughed.

"Roger, this isn't funny!" Tina said.

"Hold on. I wasn't implying that it is funny at all. I was just trying to divert your attention. What does Ms. Samuel have to say?"

"I'm sorry I snapped at you. I know you are just trying to hold me together and add some levity to all of this, but I've about had it. Let's see here," Tina answered, looking at the letter. "It's interesting how fast I get a response when they just want to say 'No.' When I need information, it seems to take forever. I'll read it to you," Tina offered.

Dear Ms. Morgan:
Unless Mr. Bond has some information related to the allegations that you have made against Mr. Samsel, we will not attempt to locate him. We have limited resources, and

we do not attempt to locate people who can only "attest to the character" of any particular respondent lawyer.

In response to your request for a status update, I must summarize all of the information collected on Mr. Samsel and present it to the Probable Cause Panelist. It may take as long as 3 to 4 months before this matter is presented to the Panelist and a decision is made.

You will receive written notice of the decision once it has been made. We appreciate your continued patience and cooperation. "

"That's amazing," Roger said. "You give them a name, someone who had worked closely with Samsel, someone who really knows the true character of the man, and they will not get Bond's sworn testimony for you. Bond came to the hospital with Cisco Samsel when you first met, and they don't even want his input."

"They know I can't find him," Tina yelled. "They have the resources when they want to use them, but I am not important enough. They have nothing to gain, so they don't want to locate him. Roger, what if Bond is in the witness protection program?" "Or they simply don't care to devote those resources," Roger answered.

"I guess we can't argue with the State Bar, but it's not the last time Pearl Samuel will hear from me," Tina said. "Where is justice anyway? I am the victim. I should be the defendant. At least then I would have an attorney," Tina added glumly.

Tina spent countless hours speaking to and corresponding with more attorneys about representing her on the trial regarding attorney's fees against Samsel and Baley. William Chambers had also made it very clear that she should find substitute legal counsel for the malpractice suit against Samsel.

One of the attorneys Tina asked to represent her revealed

some interesting facts, which she outlined in a letter to William Chambers. Tina was getting so much conflicting advice, she knew the only way to cover all of the bases was to put what she knew in writing. If it was incorrect, William or someone else could clarify it in writing, and then she would have a hard-copy response for reference, which would be essential when another attorney came on board.

Dear William:
During my search for other attorneys, one attorney gave me his opinion at this point:
1. According to all papers filed in November, you are the attorney of record.
2. No attorney can take the case while you are the attorney of record.
3. If you withdraw at this time so close to the trial, no attorney would take the case and I would have no attorney, which leaves you vulnerable to malpractice by abandoning a client at such a late date.
4. If I allow you to withdraw, I have no attorney and no attorney will take the case. I cannot go to court without an attorney.

Tina went on to request that Chambers file a continuance, stating that the time constraints prevented her from finding suitable counsel. She said that a new attorney would need at least six months to prepare properly for the case. She ended the letter by stating:

There are two possible scenarios when we go to trial on January 12, 1993.
1. The judge says, "William, you know that you cannot be a witness and the attorney for the plaintiff. Therefore, you are disqualified as a witness." You then do the best

*you can. We will need an expert on fees. We also have
Graham Lennar and Marvin Vicobi as witnesses.*

*2. The other possibility is the judge says, "William,
you cannot be the attorney, so you are the witness and
Ms. Morgan must act as her own attorney since she was
unwilling to get other counsel." Again, we do our best.*

*At best, this is a big mess. At this point, you are still my
attorney and cannot abandon me now. I realize you do not
want it this way, but we have no choice. I've paid your firm
a lot of money and I need all of the resources of your firm
until other suitable counsel will accept my case.*

Sincerely,
Tina Morgan

Tina addressed the envelope, sealed, and stamped it. She
then started to the mailbox and thought, *Yes, this really is a
catch-22 for both of us. William is stuck with me, whether
he likes it or not. In some ways, the legal system has made
him a victim too. Where is justice?* Tina felt physically and
mentally exhausted and overwhelmed. She couldn't help but
wonder what had happened to the tranquil, fairytale life she
had before the crash?

Tina and Roger left for their planned vacation to
New York, which included, business, family, and pleasure.
Tina tried to be cheerful and not think about the various
scenarios that could play out while she was away, especially
in light of her less-than-favorable experiences and the
shortcomings of the legal system.

A day after they returned from New York, Tina received
a lengthy response from William Chambers. He had filed
and obtained a continuance. He also confirmed that his firm
was in fact the attorney of record, and no other attorney
could represent Tina while they were in that position. A
replacement attorney would have to be substituted.

In his letter, he stated: *Contrary to your Paragraph 3, I told you repeatedly that we would not withdraw and leave you without an attorney prior to the January 12 hearing date. I appreciate as much and probably more than you how devastating that would be to you. I told you on several occasions that several of my partners wondered what we were doing in the case and why we had not been replaced or withdrawn, and I explained to them (as I told you) that we could not and would not abandon you prior to the hearing and, if need be, represent you at the trial on January 12.*

William went on to explain that Mr. Frank, the attorney representing Cisco Samsel, had offered to reduce attorney's fees. He closed his letter by stating: *If you are unsuccessful in obtaining other counsel, as several lawyers have told you, there are advantages to putting this whole episode behind you. There is no direct correlation between Mr. Samsel participating in a drug operation and you being able to demonstrate direct financial loss as a result of his representation to you.*

You must be able to prove cause and effect (i.e. malpractice and financial loss flowing from the malpractice).

You now have a significant opportunity to retain other legal counsel. I must, therefore, advise you that our law firm will not represent you in the continued attorneys' fees hearing scheduled for June 28, 1993. We will not withdraw at this time, as I believe that would show Mr. Frank and Mr. Samsel some weakness. It would be best for you if we were merely substituted out by other counsel.

Very truly yours,
William Chambers

For a fleeting moment, Tina was ready to stop—stop looking for another attorney, stop fighting for malpractice and ridiculous fees, stop trying to stand up for herself and a legal system that was supposed to work for, not against, the victim. Maybe William was right. She should just put the whole episode behind her. The problem was, she knew it was wrong and, if she quit, Samsel would be getting away, and justice would not be served.

No, Tina would then be a quitter. "I can't give up now," Tina said out loud. "And I won't!"

Tina decided she could take a few matters into her own hands while she continued to look for a new attorney, such as tracking down Rico Bond. She finally found his mother's phone number. Mrs. Bond was vague and said Rico couldn't be reached. After more probing, although Bond's mother didn't come right out and say it, Tina figured out he was in the witness-protection program. Apparently he had agreed to divulge information about the drug trafficking operation in exchange for not going to prison.

Cisco Samsel is still throwing obstacles in my way, Tina thought.

In early February, Tina still had not heard from Pearl Samuel, so once again she wrote to the State Bar. William Chambers, however, had forwarded to Tina papers that neither she nor Chambers knew existed. Samsel and Baley had not given complete files to William's firm, so both Tina and her attorney had been in the dark about several issues.

Tina wrote:

Dear Ms. Samuel:

Attorney Chambers just sent the following papers that he received from Attorney Graham Lennar last week. These papers followed the motion to set filed by Mr. Samsel, but we did not have copies to present with the motion to set.

I'm sorry to bother you, but as we didn't have the file, I did not want to present an incorrect picture, and although Mr. Samsel filed a motion for a non-jury trial, Mr. Lennar

filed for a jury trial. Although a trial date was set, I had
never seen any of these papers.
   Sincerely,
   Tina Morgan
   Tina addressed the envelope, sealed, and stamped it. She
walked to the mailbox. *This mess just keeps getting bigger*,
she thought. "Quicksand, I'm walking in quicksand," Tina
said to no one in particular.

"There is no security on this earth; only opportunity."
Douglas MacArthur

CHAPTER TWENTY-ONE
Winter 1992

Tina had been pushed out of the Las Cruces legal system by every good, and even not so good, attorney. The Las Cruces judgment against the Erickson estate was filed by Tina's grandparents' attorney in the New York Courts. The firm had an outstanding reputation, but that clout came with a high price tag. Tina realized she couldn't keep up with the fees for long.

Getting an attorney in Richfield County, New York, seemed the logical thing to do. After all, she needed someone who knew the judges and the courts there. What Tina didn't know was that only the largest firms were influential when it came to the judges. A handful of smaller firms could hold their weight, but in large law firms, there was always a partner or two who knew someone influential in helping place or hear a case of their choice.

Tina thought back to her traditional Jewish upbringing and the special Seder dinner during the observance of Passover. A passage that explained the exodus of the Jews from Egypt described four types of people and how they would respond to the explanation of their exodus. In the passage, it talked about a wise person, a simple person, a wicked person, and a person who could not respond for himself at all. Tina thought of a conversation between a naïve man and a wise man. She played the scene in her mind. "Cases are not randomly given to judges," the wise man said. "Certain judges pick their cases."

"How could that be?" the naïve one said.

"It's who you know," the wise man said.

"Where is justice then?" the naïve one asked.

"Justice. You think the courts are just, naïve one? You think a judge who has a case before him will do the right thing? Or, will his ruling just happen to lean toward an attorney who just happens to be his friend or an attorney he socializes with when they are not working?"

"Well, he should do the right thing," said the naïve one.

"But will he do the right thing?"

The naive one stopped and thought. "I always thought I knew the answer, but now I'm not sure."

"Good," said the wise man. "It is better to be leery than to be naïve."

The experience with Cisco Samsel and Judge Lockman left Tina feeling drained, and she wanted to find a law firm that would represent her fairly and a judge who would listen to all the evidence without bias.

"I found an attorney by the name of Mr. Dorman. An attorney who was working on the case gave me his name. I certainly hope he can jump on this case and get something done. I just wish it was over," Tina told Roger, feeling uncertain.

"Just hang in there. Finding a firm in New York when trying to fight on the Ericksons's turf would be most effective. New York is where the majority of their assets are, including their businesses. Russell Jr. can't possibly think he can hide now. Surely things will speed up. I'm glad you found an attorney," Roger said.

"*Justice* is an elastic word," Tina said. "I can picture it, just like a rubber band. About the time you have it stretched to hold something just the way you want, it can snap. Tina snapped her fingers for effect. "And just like that everything falls apart. I want an attorney, a judge … all of them, to prove me wrong. I want to know that they can really see and decide right from wrong."

"Staten Island is an up and coming community and becoming the 'new' place to move to and start a family. We can hope it is less corrupt and that those in charge have a conscience and care about the people they serve." Roger commented.

"I hope you're right. His fee schedule is much more reasonable," Tina answered. "In fact, he said he might have some information today."

A few minutes later, the phone rang.

"Hello?" Tina answered.

"Hello, Ms. Morgan. This is Michael Dorman. I wanted you to know that I have sent a letter to Ericksons's attorney, Mr. Delgoto, notifying him that I have been retained to represent you. I also advised him that the judgment that has been outstanding since March of '92 has now been filed with the Clerk of the County of Richfield and, according to New York law, is now a valid New York judgment."

Tina wondered why Attorney Dorman had to file the judgment again when her grandparents' attorney had already filed it in New York. On the other hand, she was glad that Dorman was doing something and didn't want to question him.

Attorney Dorman went on, "I stated, also, that you demand full payment of the $425,000 settlement agreed upon by Russell, Jr. If he should claim that insufficient estate assets exist to pay the judgment in full, we will need copies of the estate tax returns, a listing of all estate assets and their current value, and whether or not any assets have been made to any other parties involved, including creditors."

"Well, Mr. Dorman, I have to say, I'm impressed with your prompt action. It's definitely a relief to know that the judgment is officially filed in New York," Tina said politely.

The truth of the matter was that Tina was terribly confused. Did she pick the wrong attorney for the fifth time? What was really going on?

Attorney Dorman cut into Tina's thoughts by saying, "I know this has been dragging on for a while, but hopefully we will get a quick reply and, even better, a quick settlement. It may be a short case for me, but that's okay. I certainly understand that you are ready to put this whole situation behind you, Ms. Morgan."

"You are right about that, Mr. Dorman; the sooner, the better. What time frame are we looking at for a response from the Ericksons?" Tina asked.

"I gave Attorney Delgoto a deadline of November 1. That should give them enough time to come up with the money or, in the worst case, the list of items I have asked for to substantiate their position if they say the funds aren't available."

"With all of the properties, businesses, and the shares that were in Russell's name, I can't imagine that the funds wouldn't be available," Tina said.

"After reviewing everything, I can't imagine it either," Attorney Dorman answered, "But until you have that payment in your hand, we can't rest completely."

"Thank you," Tina said. "I look forward to hearing from you soon." Tina hung up and relayed the conversation to Roger.

"It sounds like we're finally getting somewhere," said Roger, smiling and giving Tina a hug.

"I'm ready!" Tina said. "I'm ready to move on with our lives. I know I haven't been able to talk much about our future. I hope you understand. I just can't right now."

"As I've told you before, I'm willing to wait for you," Roger answered.

November 1 came and went. Before Tina knew it, 1993

had arrived and the judgment had still not been settled.

In early January, Tina received a call from Attorney Dorman.

"Ms. Morgan, I want you to know that Surrogate Judge Luccentti is on your side. From my experience, he is fair and even bordering on compassionate in the case of wronged victims. He has entered a Show Cause order, which means that Russell, Jr. will be served with a written notice and must appear in court by the end of the month or supply the information on his assets by January 15."

"It's good to know that there's a judge out there who cares, which would be one of the first in my experience." Tina tried not to sound sarcastic, but once again, nothing seemed to be happening.

"The good news is that multiple attempts, at different times of the day, have to be made to serve Russell Erickson Jr. with the order."

Tina asked, "So was it served or has this been dangling? In other words, Mr. Dorman, did we serve Russell Erickson Jr.?"

Attorney Dorman took his time and stammered as he said, "Well, ah, um, not yet, but we are working very diligently to take care of this matter."

"Keep me informed Mr. Dorman," Tina said in a disappointed tone.

"Worst case scenario is we will see Russell Erickson Jr. in court at the end of the month," Attorney Dorman replied in a positive tone.

Once again, Tina hung up the phone, feeling deflated and dejected. *How could this keep happening?* she wondered. *What is Russell Jr. up to? Why wouldn't he want to get this over with as well?* The only reason she could possibly come up with was that maybe he didn't have the money, or maybe he needed time to move it around. Tina was confident that the money should be there, unless… unless he was hiding it somewhere. He could have moved the money, paid it to someone else as a guise, paid expenses and loans as he had done in New Mexico, or somehow the assets had ended up in Pamela's estate, which wasn't part of the deal. Tina sadly contemplated all these possibilities.

Tina knew that Russell Sr. was too self-centered to worry about the safety of his own wife and the passengers in his airplane, so why would his son be any different? If his son could somehow get away without paying the $425,000, he would have just that much more to show for his father's negligence. The more Tina thought about it, the more agitated she became. Tina knew she'd wait until the money was available. What Russell didn't know was just how long Tina would wait.

The scenarios playing out in her mind were multiplying, but none of them were good. She put her face in her hands and wept. Her foot ached as a continual reminder of what had happened. When Tina played tennis or was on her feet too much, her slightly deformed ankle would swell, so there was a constant low level of pain that she endured. Even though she was in pain, Tina refused to give up tennis and dancing. Roger learned how to administer the Myotherapy treatment, and there was always relief after he worked his magic fingers on the affected area that ached.

Roger walked in and rushed to Tina's side. "Honey, what's wrong?" he asked, touching her shoulder.

"I'm just so overwhelmed. I thought once the judgment was filed and the case was handled by an attorney who was familiar with the Staten Island courts, things would start to move, but nothing is happening. Now, no matter how I dissect what is happening, I do not have a good feeling. Something is wrong, but I can't figure out exactly what it is."

"You need a break," Roger said. "Let's do something fun."

"I can't, Roger. Not right now. I'm sorry, but I can't concentrate on anything else."

Roger walked away, and for the first time, Tina felt like she was putting a strain on their relationship.

Not surprisingly, no one heard from Russell Jr., and Mr. Green, who made several attempts to serve him with the order, but they couldn't locate him. Finally, in late February, Mr. Green submitted a written statement to the court that he could not serve Russell Erickson, Jr. with the order to Show Cause because no one answered the door at his residence, or his wife would not state when he would be returning. As a consequence, Judge Luccentti's next entry to the court ordered that Russell Erickson, Jr. was restrained from distributing any estate assets. This time, Russell had until April 8 to comply. When Tina heard about this, she remembered all the times in the Las Cruces courts when money was set aside for her but was later used by the attorneys and Russell Erickson Jr. to pay other bills, even though the court said it was for her. Tina made a quick call to Dorman, who assured her that this would not be the case.

The days and months ticked away, and sometimes Tina felt like a bomb would explode at any moment. At other times, though, she felt at ease. Tina was doing volunteer work at the high school to occupy her time. It seemed that she always found someone she could help, but why couldn't she help herself?

Tina finally got an order allowing her to review the assets of the Erickson estate. Tina hired Gordon Bates, a precise, detailed accountant, to keep track of the financial information regarding the Erickson estate. Her decision to hire him was working out well. His fees were not as high as an attorney's, and he kept meticulous records, including Dorman's billable hours. Bates wasn't malicious, but he couldn't stand for the truth to be hidden, either, which worked to Tina's benefit.

Accountant Bates arrived at the law firm where Mr. Delgoto was a partner at precisely 10 a.m. on a Wednesday morning. "Good morning, Mr. Delgoto. I'm here to look at the accounting information for Russell Erickson, as we agreed."

"Morning, Mr. Bates." Delgoto was brief. He motioned to a small conference room.

"Help yourself. Those files contain all of the information we have at this moment. Of course, we are trying to get more records to help us both."

"Thank you, Mr. Delgoto." Bates thumbed through the files. At least they were in chronological order. He estimated he could get what he needed in about two hours. He had only been in the room for 15 minutes when he heard a familiar voice.

"Hey, Michael!" he heard Delgoto say cheerfully. "Come in, come in. What brings you here today?"

He heard Attorney Dorman mumble something and then both attorneys, laughed. Delgoto and Dorman chatted about a variety of topics—traveling, sports, women, restaurants—everything except the Morgan vs. Erickson case. Accountant Bates completed his work at 12:10 p.m. As he was leaving, he stopped to thank Delgoto. Attorney Dorman was obviously shocked to see Bates, and his deer-in-the-headlights expression was clear evidence.

"Good day, Mr. Delgoto, Mr. Dorman." The two men hadn't talked about business once.

Bates stopped for a sandwich in a deli next to the law firm. He took his lunch back to his desk and called Tina.

"Ms. Morgan? This is Gordon Bates."

"Hello, Mr. Bates."

"I was just in Mr. Delgoto's office and Attorney Dorman was there. The bad news is that they were shooting the breeze for two hours and didn't discuss your case once. You may be charged for hours that he wasn't working."

"Okay, Mr. Bates. Thank you for the information."

Tina was shaking when she hung up. She didn't have money to pay an attorney who only made excuses. She was tired and angry. She had tried to be patient, thinking maybe Dorman really couldn't find Russell Erickson Jr., but now she suspected that he wasn't even trying. She'd had it. It was time to find a new attorney.

In the past, Tina hadn't been able to get an attorney to take her case. Now, she didn't know how hard it would be to get rid of one. Dorman would be the fifth attorney on this case that she would have to replace.

"THE SEAT OF KNOWLEDGE IS IN THE HEAD; OF WISDOM IN THE HEART. WE ARE SURE TO JUDGE WRONG IF WE DO NOT FEEL RIGHT." WILLIAM HAZLITT

CHAPTER TWENTY-TWO
FALL 1993—SPRING 1995:
TINA'S LIFE IN LAS CRUCES

At this point, Tina's case wasn't even moving at a snail's pace; it wasn't moving at all. The Judgment was now filed with the New York Courts. The case seemed to have all but disappeared as the new attorney, number 6, familiarized himself with the case. Tina had attorney number 3 in Las Cruces working on other details of the Samsel case. The files that had been sent from Las Cruces as "background" material contained, in reality, information that was more than sufficient for a case by itself. There would be no immediate justice for Tina. When Samsel was aggressively trying to convince Tina to settle without a jury trial, he told her that a jury would not see the extent of her injuries since she had healed so well. He also stated with conviction that since she had a savings account and property, these factors would work against her, and the jury wouldn't give her a fair settlement. Tina couldn't forget those words, because in her mind, a jury would be fair. When the jury knew that the accident was caused by pilot error, and that her left foot was so severely injured that it could have been amputated, Tina felt that the jury would make a fair and just decision.

Fall had always been Tina's favorite time of year. Although the leaves didn't change with the breathtaking crimson, scarlet, and gold of the Northeast, fall in New Mexico was a welcome respite from the sweltering summer heat. She loved the warm days and cooler nights and mornings. It was in the month of October that she met Hunter, at Jane's Halloween party, and that fact reminded her how short and fragile life can be.

"I've been thinking," Tina said to Roger one morning. "I have choices to make. I could keep obsessing about the pending court case in New York, even though we know nothing about what is happening right now, and this scenario probably won't change anytime soon. I could continue to put this case paramount in my life, or I could go on. I need to do something constructive. I just saw that volunteers are needed for the Junior Achievement program that is added to the curriculum of the marketing classes in many of the area high schools. With my background, I think I could give the kids some real life experiences."

"I think that would be great, Tina," Roger said sincerely.

"You're just saying that to get me out of your hair for a while and so you won't have to hear me complain about the lack of justice in our legal system," Tina teased.

"I think you could teach those kids a thing or two about the judicial system. No, seriously…" Roger said.

Tina interrupted before he could finish. "Don't worry, I won't teach law to them. I'm trying to get away from that for a while, remember? It will truly be a good diversion."

"Okay. Go sign up and find out what your schedule will be."

Tina knew she didn't need Roger's permission, but she felt even better that he was supportive of this decision. Tina had a bachelor's degree in business administration; she had majored in marketing and minored in management. After Tina married and had children, working in retail just didn't work out for her so she went back for her master's and professional diploma in education and school counseling. The Junior Achievement volunteers needed to be able to help students start a company, select officers, issue stock shares, and select a product. The product would then be manufactured and sold. The profits were used to pay salaries and the students learned how to pay dividends on the stocks. At the end of the project, the company was liquidated. Tina was eager to work with the students and was excited about the hands-on opportunity they would have.

The next day, after school was out, Tina went to Las Cruces High and met Mrs. Gold, a veteran teacher who taught the marketing classes. It was love at first sight. Tina and Mrs. Gold talked and talked.

"Just call me Cece," Mrs. Gold said.

"Okay, but I'll call you Mrs. Gold in front of the students," Tina said. "How many classes do you have each day?"

"I teach four marketing classes a day. We also have a cookie business. As long as we buy Otis Spunkmeyer's frozen cookie dough, the company lets us use their ovens at no charge. Students look forward to freshly made, home-baked cookies. The smell travels up and down the halls and the students have a choice of three types of cookies. It's a win, win situation for all."

Plus, we have a captive audience, Tina thought. *We have the students and staff and none of them can get enough.*

"It sounds like you're very busy all of the time," Tina said.

"I am busy, but I enjoy what I do, and the students are very special. I'm the lucky one. This program gives students real-life experiences right here in the classroom. It is textbook learning coming alive. Without someone to assist me, however, some of the quieter kids can be pushed into a corner. I know with a little more attention and direction, this is the perfect venue for them to come out of their shell."

"I would be honored and privileged to work in your classroom with you," Tina said.

"We had a volunteer for a while, but when there was a

student protest and other student problems, the volunteer didn't feel comfortable staying," Cece told Tina. "I feel we will be able to reach all of the students in this classroom. I love the hands-on concept but want to make sure that each student has the chance to really experience it. Once they have the excitement of sales in their blood, they will love what they learn and be able to apply it. Tina left, feeling elated.

Over the next few weeks, Tina felt that Cece respected and appreciated her as much as Tina enjoyed helping her. It was a match made in marketing heaven. Cece gave Tina the chance to add her own experience to the mix, and the students were amazing. They enjoyed the program, and most of them excelled.

Tina told her friend, Helen, about the wonderful Junior Achievement program she was involved in and how much she enjoyed what she was doing. Helen replied, "I graduated from Las Cruces High, and my fondest memories are of the school store. We set it up, sold items, and had great success. Since you ran a jewelry business, you could certainly teach the kids how to run a store," Helen said. Tina wondered why a school store didn't exist now.

"What a great outlet for teaching marketing," Tina said enthusiastically.

"Oh, that would be perfect if I could get this current administration to add a school store. If we had the school store, I think we would have something for every student to do and really get involved."

Tina thanked Helen for her advice and kept thinking about the real possibilities of a school store for Las Cruces High next year.

At the end of the semester, Tina approached the principal with her idea. "It sounds feasible, Tina. Let me think about it and I will get back to you on Monday. I think you have to speak with Mrs. Gold, since she would be responsible for operating the store through her marketing classes. We will talk to her and see what she thinks. She's the only staff member who could supervise a school store, since it would have to be under the direction of a LCUSD (Las Cruces Unified School District) teacher."

Tina hoped Cece would agree to the idea. As it was, Mrs. Gold worked more than any other teacher. Her plate was already overflowing. However, Tina also knew that Cece was the kind of person who would take on one more thing if she believed her work would benefit the students. The marketing teacher thought it was a wonderful idea, and the students were informed that there would be a school store the next school year. The students voted on a name and the school store, dubbed the Badger Den, was born. It was located in a large office space that housed the attendance office, as well as other offices. Tina spent the next two years working with the teacher and the students in the marketing classes on Tuesday and Friday mornings. The store was opened before school and after school and during lunch. Mrs. Gold seemed to work 110 hours a week, and Tina knew that with her help, Mrs. Gold was able to teach her classes and run the store. They all worked together to set up display cases, purchase notebooks, calculators, and other school supplies, as well as cookies, candy, drinks, and food that didn't compete with the school cafeteria. This project was very successful and beneficial to all the marketing students.

One day, Mrs. Gold stopped Tina as she was leaving for the day. "I am thrilled with the store, Tina. We have all learned so much and the students are so happy, and they are also working harder than ever. The school store is a great experience and teaching tool for the hands-on part of the class curriculum. It's probably the best teaching and learning experience they can get at this point in their lives. Thank you, Tina," Mrs. Gold said.

"I am just as thrilled to be a part of it," Tina said. "Using the profits to help the less fortunate is such a good experience for the students. I know many of our students and their families struggle financially, but through this experience, they learn that there are people in much more dire circumstances.

"I have noticed students that were loners are now mixing better in the classroom. Also, students who speak English as a second language are participating and expressing their opinions. I see so many positive things going on."

"You are right, Tina. Some of the students are making more friends," Mrs. Gold commented. "They have become more outgoing, and the more popular students are respecting their opinions, too. Everyone is working so well together."

"They really are," Tina replied. "Have you noticed how much Daisy's English has improved in such a short period of time? She would start a sentence in English and then ask for a word or the name of something so she could finish her sentence. Now, her English is great. She is outgoing and the students in the class truly respect her."

"I think our class could be called marketing, English, communications, finance, accounting, and retail 101, all rolled into one," Mrs. Gold said with a chuckle.

"You're right!" Tina said. "This is an experience of a lifetime for our students and it will help them with whatever they decide to do after they graduate."

The Badger Den thrived for the rest of the school year and through the next year. In the spring of the second year, Daisy was getting ready to leave class. "Could I talk to you, Ms. Morgan, please?"

"Certainly, Daisy, what can I do for you?"

"I was wondering if I could... I mean if you could

mention to Mrs. Gold that I would like to give the speech at our end-of-school-year banquet," Daisy said, tentatively. "I have learned so much, and I never could have done it at the beginning of the year. I love speaking to the students and teachers. I love selling to them and telling them how they are helping others."

"Daisy, I think that is a fantastic idea," Tina said. "I'm very proud of you for everything you've achieved in this class and for all your hard work with the Badger Den."

"Thank you for your help," Daisy said, and waved as she ran to her next class.

As Tina was leaving the school, she was reflecting on what a great year this had been and how much had been accomplished. CeCe Gold is such a remarkable women! She spends all her extra time and energy on her students and this school store. She works so hard and gives so much. Does the school district know what a gem they have?

At the beginning of Tina's fourth year working for Mrs. Gold's marketing class, a new principal for Las Cruces High School was hired. The Badger Den was in its third year of operation. One morning in September of the new school year, the principal peaked his head out of his office and asked Mrs. Gold to attend a meeting in his office that afternoon. Mrs. Gold had heard rumors, but she had hoped they were just that. Mrs. Gold walked calmly into the principal's office, but there was uneasiness in her gut. The Food Services supervisor was there, too, and she wasn't smiling.

"Please sit down, ladies," the principal said. "I'm afraid we have a problem."

"What kind of a problem?" Mrs. Gold asked. "If it's more storage space for the cafeteria..."

"No, that is not the issue," the Food Services supervisor broke in. "Your store is cutting into our profits, and the cafeteria is operating for the benefit of the district. We just hired two new staff members this fall, and we hardly have enough for them to do."

"I'm afraid the Badger Den is in conflict with the Food Services operation at the school," the principal explained.

"Could we give you some facts of the success of this program?" Cece asked.

"I am aware of what the store has done for the marketing class, and it is impressive," the principal admitted. "The Food Services supervisor brought some federal and state mandates to the school board's attention that mention you cannot sell some of the foods you are selling. I've talked to the district, and the points brought up by the Food Services supervisor are being supported by our school board. I'm afraid we're going to have to shut the Badger Den down on October 1."

"What?" Mrs. Gold exclaimed, feeling like she had just been handed a death sentence. Mrs. Gold looked from the smug, stoic face of the supervisor to the kind, understanding expression of the principal. "Is there any room for negotiation?" she asked, trying not to sound desperate.

"I'm afraid not," the principal said. The Food Services supervisor crossed her arms and nodded smugly.

Mrs. Gold wanted to tell the principal about the lives that had been changed, about the kids that had confidence, about Daisy who spoke fluently in front of a roomful of students, parents, and teachers. What were they thinking? After she left the office, Mrs. Gold wondered what she would tell her students tomorrow and, especially, what would Tina say when she told her the news.

The next day, Tina arrived early, and Mrs. Gold pulled her aside to tell her the devastating news. "No, no," Tina said. "This is not right! Why us? This is just not fair!" Tina stamped her foot down hard on the floor.

"You're experiencing the worst part of a large school district, Tina. Unfortunately, someone has agreed this is the thing to do and, as you know, it's the principal's first year and he doesn't feel he can make waves, so the Food Services supervisor found the perfect time to get rid of us," Mrs. Gold explained. "Since I'm going to be retiring soon, they know I can't afford to cause much of a rift."

"I'm an unpaid volunteer, and I don't have anything to lose," Tina said.

"You don't have to do that," Mrs. Gold said, but sounded somewhat hopeful.

"I know I don't have to, but I want to. What are we going to tell the students?" Tina asked. "One of the reasons some of the students took this course is because there was a school store and they were going to have hands-on experience, working in and running the store. How do you think they are going to feel, and how do you think their parents are going to feel if their children are no longer able to have this experience? I think we should have a meeting with the students, the Food Services supervisor, and the principal to see if we can blend some services, instead of totally separating them. Maybe that would be more effective."

"Oh, Tina, that's a great idea. If the students are there, too, and we have a plan, maybe we will get results."

"This may turn out to be a good learning experience for the students," Tina said. "There may be a good lesson to learn if the students see that we can make change by using reasoning and education, not by demonstrations and violence." *Maybe even Ms. Sour Face will come around*, Tina thought.

Tina arranged the meeting with the principal and the Food Services supervisor after class. Eight students were in the room with Tina and Mrs. Gold, and everyone had agreed to be on their best behavior.

When the principal and the Food Services supervisor walked into the room, the students politely stood and greeted them. After they all sat down in a semicircle, the students asked a few questions to get a better understanding of why plans were made for the Badger Den to close. When the fourth question was asked, the supervisor rose from her chair, banged her hand flat on the table, and said, "I don't have to take this!" and marched out of the room.

Tina was stunned and the students looked scared and helpless. The principal was speechless. *What a bad example for our young people*, Tina thought. *Our School Store is closed and the Food Supervisor will not talk to us.*

Every ounce of Tina's energy went into saving the school store. Her master's in Education and Professional Diploma in School Counseling aided her. She called the State Board of Education in Albuquerque to get a copy of the mandate stating why Las Cruces High couldn't operate a school store. Interestingly enough, the secretary told her there wasn't one. The information that was available would be mailed to her immediately. After the material arrived from Albuquerque, Tina read it and realized there was no mandate but a few memos from the principal to a teacher years ago. Tina showed the alleged mandates to the principal, vice-principal, and other administrators. Tina called her friend on the school board and wanted an explanation about the mandate that wasn't.

"Why is our school store being closed when other schools in the district with even larger school stores and more merchandise are staying open?" Tina asked. "What is really going on? We have the right to know."

Tina's friend, Mrs. Jenkins said, "The district has to have the same rules for everyone." "If the school store at Las Cruces High is shut down, the other high school stores in the district will be shut down, too. We are working on it,

Tina. We have a problem and we will take care of it, just be patient."

"Patience is not my virtue. I never have patience!" Tina said excitedly. "We are losing this whole school year. It just doesn't seem right. The students worked so hard to establish this wonderful store and the results can't be measured by a food supervisor's whim to single out our school store and shut it down. "What are her school credentials," Tina asked?

Mrs. Jenkins said, "The only difference between the Badger Den and other stores in the district is that the Badger Den is located next to the cafeteria. The other school stores have a separate space. They don't share the space with other school offices and are not next to the cafeteria."

When other schools got wind of the closing, they didn't offer to go to the school board with Tina or band their forces together so no school would lose a store. Instead, rumors circulated among the teachers about Tina and Mrs. Gold, accusing them of ruining the other schools' opportunity to have stores, which might be forced to close also.

The students at Las Cruces High asked if they could organize a strike to get attention for the cause, but both Mrs. Gold and Tina said they should use positive persuasion and the press to help the word get out about the benefits of the store. The students rose to the occasion and brought their parents to the school board meeting, where Tina had asked to be on the agenda to speak. Their hard work and planning fell on deaf ears. The newspaper reporter was there, but the publicity just made the other schools with stores shun Las Cruces High even more.

In February, the students attended the largest DECA conference of the year at a wealthier school in the district. DECA is an international association of high school and college students studying marketing, management and entrepreneurship in business, finance, hospitality and marketing sales and services. The students, at Las Cruces High, took pictures of their school's store, with the vast array of merchandise and fancy equipment.

The next month, before the school board meeting, Tina called the local newspaper and asked them to attend this month's meeting. Tina, the students and their parents, marched back to the school board with their arsenal in hand. The press also was there.

The pictures and the students' speeches were very impressive. Finally, the decision was made to reopen the Badger Den. The school gave the Badger Den a new space that was better than the space they had before. The fight had been more than worth all they had gone through. Tina's court case may have been stalled, but this case had ended in victory.

Tina made sure that, from then on, the principal, the school board, and other high-ranking administrators were periodically notified of the positive effect the marketing classes had on their classmates and the community. Tina called it marketing and advertising. She felt it was necessary to brag about the good that was taking place in these classes. Tina made sure to stay away from the Food Services supervisor, and she had nothing more to do with that department.

One day, one of the students said to Tina, "When I graduate and go to college, I want to get married, have a family, and then go back to a school and help the students learn from my experiences, just like you." This experience was something the student could never have learned from a textbook, and the feeling Tina experienced was indescribable. Volunteers make a difference! Tina was ecstatic about her volunteer work and the joint student and parent effort over this past six months. It was a fight fairly won. The students were already getting the benefits of their hard work. What greater reward could there be?

"A GOOD LAWYER KNOWS THE LAW AND A GREAT LAWYER KNOWS THE JUDGE." ANONYMOUS

CHAPTER TWENTY-THREE
FALL 1993—BACK TO THE LEGAL SYSTEM

Tina wasn't sure who Attorney Dorman was working for or if he was making any effort to work on her case. Dorman continued making excuses and telling Tina that he was "trying." Even after Accountant Gordon Bates had informed her about Dorman being in Attorney Delgoto's office, Tina continued to give the attorney the benefit of the doubt, thinking that perhaps he was on other business with Delgoto and that he wouldn't bill her for those hours. Tina had written down the day and time of Bates's call, and when Dorman's statement arrived, she quickly glanced at the date. Dorman had indeed billed her for four hours of his time, from 10 a.m. until 2 p.m., on that day.

Tina was upset and angry that she had not discharged Dorman earlier. When she finally tried to discharge him, Dorman refused to sign the paperwork that would remove him from representing her case. This was extremely strange. Why wouldn't he let go, when on the surface it appeared that he wasn't even interested? By this time, Tina was extremely frustrated and disgusted. It seemed that throughout this case there was one constant: Tina was constantly battling with attorneys, as well as with the Ericksons for information they refused to properly provide. It just seemed that all her efforts were going nowhere; it didn't seem to matter what state or city Tina was in. The type of attorney she continually picked was working against, and not for, Tina. What was going on, and why couldn't she make the right decision when it came to choosing an attorney?

Tina sat down one afternoon and made a list of each attorney and the characteristics they had in common. It seemed that all the attorneys were from small firms. Maybe they didn't have the resources. It was obvious that the attorneys to date hadn't listened to her. It was obvious that they did not follow through and do what they discussed when she was in their office. It was also obvious that Tina was being taken for a ride. Tina kept thinking that maybe a private investigator could get the information she was asking for. She knew that PIs were trained in methods to obtain information, and maybe in this case, which seemed to be one setback after another, the PI would take charge. It was so tiring starting over with a new attorney every year or two, and that is exactly what Tina had been doing. Another Attorney, Another Promise, Another Two Years, Wasted.

In the meantime, Bates's accounting firm had requested that Attorney Dorman contact Attorney Delgoto to get copies of Russell Erickson Sr.'s birth certificate, driver's license, or high school diploma. The accounting firm agreed with Tina that these documents would help clear up the confusion about Russell Erickson Jr.'s name being written with the middle initial "A." on some documents and not on others. Lately, Russell Jr.'s name included the middle initial "A." but not "Jr." On current documents handed out by the New York attorneys for Russell Erickson Jr., his late father's name no longer included the middle initial. However, in early court papers in Las Cruces and in paperwork prior to Erickson Sr.'s death, his name on a variety of legal documents, including companies and properties he owned, included the middle initial "A."

Russell Erickson Sr.'s will included the middle initial. Tina didn't have a signed copy of the will, but Christina's will had her husband's name with the middle initial. Tina had always been detail oriented, and she had spotted the discrepancy when Samsel and Judge Lockman were on the case. No one seemed to think it was a big deal. The "A." actually looked as if it had been written in and added to some of the documents at a later date, not when they were originally signed—possibly, or probably, after Erickson Sr.'s death. Tina's suspicion that Russell Erickson Jr. was becoming his father, at least on paper, was becoming eerily true. Roger was the only person who even acknowledged that this might be the case, and anyone else involved with the case from a legal standpoint refused to discuss it.

Now that a request had been made in writing by Bates's firm, Delgoto had to respond. Somehow, Dorman was still hanging around, much to Tina's regret.

"Maybe since Attorney Delgoto and Attorney Dorman seem to have a relationship, Dorman will get a response from him," Roger said to Tina. "I truly believe there's a reason for everything, and maybe that's why Dorman hasn't signed the release, because in an odd way, we still need him." Ever the optimist, Roger continued to be the rock Tina could lean on for support when she thought she was ready to crumble.

"Oh, Roger, you do have a way of looking at things. If you weren't so positive, I probably would have run to the top of a mountain and stayed there," Tina said, actually smiling.

In mid-September, Roger's prediction proved correct, and Attorney Delgoto did respond to Attorney Dorman in a letter. Of course, Delgoto and Dorman were on a first-name basis. In fact as it turned out, they had been friends for 20 years.

Starting with her first attorney, Cisco Samsel, Tina had asked repeatedly if it would be beneficial in this case to hire a private investigator. She was certain that a PI could track down copies of some of the documents or find archived information from Russell Erickson's high school, revealing how his name had been spelled when he was younger.

Tina had been convinced that Erickson Jr. was trying to become his father, and it had to be because he was hiding something. It could explain why he had physically been hiding, so that he couldn't be served with any orders from the court.

Attorney Dorman had forwarded the letter to Accountant Bates, who forwarded it to Tina. If this was true, it still didn't answer why some of the documents had an "A." in the deceased Erickson's name. The letter read:

> **Dear Richard:**
> **Russell A. Erickson advises me that he does not have any access to his father's birth certificate or driver's license, which he assumes he had with him when he passed away. To clarify the names, however, he offers the following information: He states that his father was born Russell Erickson, without any middle initial. Our client, who is referred to as Russell Erickson, Jr., is in fact Russell A. Erickson, and does not use the "junior." It has been used in the estate only for the purpose of clarification. I have enclosed a copy of the last corporate Federal Income Tax Return filed for Erickson Aircraft Corporation. No other returns have been filed on behalf of the said corporation since Russell Erickson passed away.**
> **Sincerely yours,**
> **James P. Delgoto, Jr.**

Tina felt this letter said nothing, but, in a way it said everything. At this time, if Tina had the information that was buried in files in Samsel's office, she would have been able to prove her theories. This was paperwork submitted by the law firm defending Russell A. Erickson's estate back in Las Cruces, New Mexico. It was answered by Russell Erickson Jr. to "Personal Injury Uniform Interrogatories," and it was dated December 2, 1991.

It was filed in the Superior Court of the State of New Mexico. Question 1 asked, "State your name and address."

The answer was simple.

RUSSELL ERICKSON JR.

As of December 2, 1991, this was his name, without a middle initial "A." Today, his name is Russell A. Erickson. Of course, there is no "junior"; now that his father is deceased, he can drop that suffix. He was able to succeed with this scheme because Tina had used different attorneys and she never had access to all the paperwork. Therefore, it was relatively easy for Russell Erickson Jr. to switch names with his father. His attorneys were more than happy to protect him on the legal end. This man lied continually, and he got away with it because no one representing Tina Morgan had followed through until the truth was uncovered. Russell Erickson Jr.'s word was taken as truth, when in fact it wasn't. Years later, Tina found a copy of his driver's license in an old file of attorney and court papers. The copy looked as if an "A" had been inserted between his first and last names. Tina had never seen these papers and she wasn't sure if anyone of her attorneys had seen original documentation of his driver's license, and none of Tina's attorneys had acknowledged her suspicions or asked to see the original. Living over 2000 miles away, Tina was never present in court when Russell Erickson Jr. appeared. Tina offered to come, but was told by the attorneys that it wasn't necessary. This advice proved to be lethal, as it was necessary to be present in court when Erickson Jr. was questioned under oath. This way she could have objected and had her attorney question him in depth on statements that may not have been accurate.

Russell Erickson Jr. was then asked "whether plaintiff or anyone acting on their behalf had been interviewed or spoken with defendant." Russell Erickson, Jr. answered as follows

Defendant spoke with plaintiff shortly after the accident. She expressed how grateful she was to Russell Sr., who she felt had saved her life. She related how calm and controlled he was during the few minutes prior to the crash. She explained how he went about trying to land the plane on a paved road in front of them but apparently unable to reach it, how brave and comforting Mrs. Erickson had been during the last few minutes and how she had consoled her by holding her head in her lap as the plane went down. Ms. Morgan also indicated that she smelled something unusual in the cockpit. She thought perhaps something was burning but could not identify it. She was aware that they had lost power in one engine and that they had turned back toward the airport. She also knew, shortly after, that they lost power in the second engine, but she seemed to have no additional knowledge of details of what was happening. All she remembered after the crash was struggling to climb out of the plane and crawling away from it prior to it exploding. The tone of Ms. Morgan's comments was one of gratitude and obvious deep feeling towards both Mr. and Mrs. Erickson. She explained she had been sitting next to Mrs. Erickson and that they were behind Mr. Erickson, who was in the pilot's seat, and Mr. Smith was to the right of Mr. Erickson. She was very impressed by the calm that was maintained by both Mr. and Mrs. Erickson in the cabin when they knew the plane was coming down.

Tina never saw these papers until recently. Unfortunately, if she had the paperwork, she could have proved her point. *I couldn't defend myself and my feelings 15 years earlier, but I can now. I want to set the record straight,* thought Tina.

The only reason, I called Russell Erickson Jr. was to say I was sorry that his parents died and to pay my condolences.

Had I been able to answer the statements Russell made under oath, this is what I would have answered, under oath.

1. I never said I was grateful and never felt Russell saved my life.

2. When dining with the Ericksons in Baja Del Sol, they both lied to me when I asked them what happened on the flight down to Baja Del Sol? Christina had stopped reading her book, stiffened and looked around before going back to her book?

3. I stated that Russell was calm before crashing the plane because there was no talking in the cabin. I mistook panic for calmness.

4. Russell did not answer the tower when they asked our location. There is enough paperwork to verify this.

5. At the time of the accident, there was no way that I knew we were near a large wash or a paved road, as I wasn't paying attention. Cisco Samsel gave that information to us after he returned from Mexico. I could not have known this on the seventh day following the plane crash.

6. I was only aware that the plane's engines stopped. I was not aware of 'loss of power.'

7. I know the engines were physically turned off. I was in an Areostar plane months later, and had the horns turned on. This horn did not start blasting until after both engines were shut down.

8. Russell never attempted to restart the engines or go through a check list.

9. I was grateful to Christina for suggesting that I put my head on her lap, as I did not want to witness the crash.

I was never grateful to the Ericksons for turning my world upside down and killing my Hunter because they refused to take care of the problem with the engines when they landed in Baja Del Sol for the long weekend.

I guess the apple doesn't fall far from the tree and Russell Erickson Jr. could lie just as well as his father, Russell A. Erickson. All the paperwork submitted by the Ericksons's attorneys in both states used different names for father and son. Following the crash, everything was Russell Erickson Jr., and at the end everything was Russell A. Erickson—different names for the same man

Tina returned to the present and looked over the last corporate income tax return that was filed. The statement showed a loss, which Tina knew was typical for many businesses, so this company wasn't where her settlement would be coming from. She hadn't expected to recover money from this business, but actually seeing the big minus sign in front of the $24,000 figure made Tina even more apprehensive than before. The first thing that Tina wondered was what happened to the $99,000 airplane salvage check from the insurance company? It wasn't even on this statement. Did it also get added to Christina's estate? Tina had noticed that all income went into Christina's estate and all expenses when into Russell's estate. Gordon Bates, the accountant, had also requested proof of ownership on the other three businesses the Ericksons owned, but as of yet, this information hadn't been provided. "I wonder how many years we will have to wait for that," Tina said aloud to an empty room. She was getting used to talking aloud to herself. She did that when she tried to understand a letter or when she was going through court documents or when she was thinking of the pros and cons of an argument she wanted to develop.

FEBRUARY 1994

Tina's former attorney, Mr. Dorman, had not been paid since he sent his final bill. In response to Tina's request, he refused to sign the release necessary so the new attorney could get all the paperwork. Months went by—almost 10 to be exact—and finally in mid-December, Mr. Dorman sent the following brief, but pointed correspondence:

So long as my bill is paid in full, I will be pleased to cooperate with your new attorney and to permit him to make copies of any papers in my file. If my bill is not paid, I shall make claim in the court for the amount due at my standard billing rate.

He also reminded Tina that his rate had been reduced from $225 per hour to $125 per hour, since he had also been counting on profiting from a portion of the settlement once it was awarded by the New York courts. Tina was beginning to think all attorneys were alike. They pushed you into a corner until you couldn't breathe, and the only way to come up for air was to give into their demands. Fortunately, Tina had an exact accounting of what Dorman had charged her and what she had gotten in return, which wasn't much.

"I guess it's easy to charge a reduced fee when you plan on double billing and billing for time when you are not even working," Tina commented to Roger after she read the letter out loud. I am glad I hired Mr. Kantor, attorney number six, and he has filed papers in court requesting Dorman to return some of the funds.

Just when Tina thought she was taking a step forward, the next minute she felt like she was taking two steps back. Not only did she need a new attorney to pursue the judgment against the Erickson estate, but she needed this new attorney to make a case against Attorney Dorman and his ongoing fees with nothing to show for it.

Judge Luccentti ruled in Tina's favor and required Dorman to return some of the fees Tina had been required to pay. Tina was happy that the judge would be working on the case with her sixth attorney, Mr. Kantor, an older gentleman with graying hair. Tina felt comfortable around him; he reminded her of a patient father who would support and guide her through the still unchartered territory of the tumultuous legal system. It was Kantor who presented the facts of Dorman's fees and his lack of action and lack of results to Judge Luccentti, so that the judge could make a quick ruling.

Kantor proceeded to file the necessary paperwork, and he appeared in court in mid-January, 1994, but as usual, the next step took several months and Tina wondered if a different judge would be assigned to the case. In early June, Tina received a letter from Joseph Kantor:

Dear Tina:
I appeared in court today and Judge Delgoto ...."
Tina had to catch herself from falling. Could it be? Attorney Delgoto was now *Judge* Delgoto? This couldn't possibly be the U.S. court system at its best, could it? How could the attorney who was representing the Ericksons, the defendant, possibly be an unbiased voice for her in court? The answer was, HE COULDN'T. Judges must have their own fraternal society, so that if some of the law partners in the firm representing the Ericksons are also judges, then it explains why this case was going nowhere. When Tina relaxed, she realized that Delgoto wasn't sitting in as the judge. Tina took a long drink of water, sat down, and kept reading:

...and I argued the application to compel Erickson to give information on the Estate. Judge Delgoto directed that this matter be conferenced with a law assistant of the Court. The Court has set a date of August 23, 1994, as the control date to report back.

As I mentioned to you, I want to question Erickson about the transfers of stock to him as a gift and his statement

under oath in the Estate tax return that his father had
made no gifts.
   Very truly yours,
   Joseph Bennett Kantor

Finally, Tina had someone who wouldn't dance to the Ericksons's music, but would confront these discrepancies head on. As refreshing as that was, it didn't change the fact that Mr. Delgoto was a part-time judge. This probably meant that he had lots of friends in high places, Mr. Kantor was finally the attorney who was able to obtain the asset appraisal of the Ericksons's properties. He even convinced Delgoto to obtain an affidavit from Mr. Hanson, Russell Erickson's longtime CPA.

According to Hanson, Erickson Sr. transferred his interest in Erickson Realty Company and the property to his son prior to his death.

The appraisal on the building the Ericksons owned that housed another business, S & S Fire Suppression Systems, Inc., came in at $447,000. Tina had driven by the building and was sure it had to have a value of over $1 million. It was sitting on a main road and there was a small stone house in the front and a huge factory-type building in the back. Another mistake made by Tina's attorneys was that they did not order a separate appraisal on the property conducted by an independent appraiser. These mistakes did not help her case. Tina realized that if one is dealing with a case where there are possible lies, it is most important to get independent information from private investigators and appraisers.

In total, the gifts given to Erickson Jr. totaled just under $600,000, which was why, Hanson went to explain, no tax return had been filed. Russell Erickson had used his lifetime exclusion of $600,000 when gifting his stock.

"How convenient," Tina mused. "The numbers for the

property, equipment, and stock all add up to a perfect, or perfectly planned, amount."

By the end of August, Mr. Kantor wrote to Tina, telling her that he had appeared in court with Mr. Delgoto, and he said the following:

I insisted in the discussion that there be an examination of Mr. Erickson under oath. Mr. Delgoto had questioned whether he could satisfy my demand by the use of written questions. I stated that I did not want written questions, because in my experience the responses to written questions are legally crafted by the lawyer rather than the extemporaneous response of the person being questioned without counsel's input.

To that end, I will be serving a notice to take Mr. Erickson's deposition on September 21, 1994.

Best regards,
Joseph Bennett Kantor

"Yes!" Tina shouted. "Yes! Mr. Kantor may be the only one who can hold his own. He also implies that lawyers may tell their clients exactly what to say, whether it's the truth or not."

Maybe, just maybe, they were finally getting somewhere.

"FEW THINGS ARE IMPOSSIBLE TO DILIGENCE AND SKILL. GREAT WORKS ARE PERFORMED NOT BY STRENGTH, BUT PERSEVERANCE." SAMUEL JOHNSON

CHAPTER TWENTY-FOUR
DECEMBER 2004

Tina appreciated that Mr. Kantor was a straight-shooting attorney, who always followed through on what he told her he would do. Over the next few months, Erickson's attorneys, Mr. Delgoto and Mr. Goldman, tried to belittle Tina's requests for more information on the properties and the gifts that were given to his children. Mr. Kantor continued to pursue obtaining any documents or records that would substantiate the fact that Erickson Jr. was hiding something.

Mr. Goldman even wrote to Mr. Kantor:

Your client may think there is a gold mine at the end, but it is not there. All of Mr. Erickson's assets were heavily mortgaged.

Ms. Morgan is either going to have to accept the facts we present or she can expend her own resources, as well as deplete whatever she might ultimately recover from the Estate, if she is not satisfied. At this point, I have advised the executor that it would appear that nothing we furnish on a voluntary basis to Tina Morgan is going to satisfy her and it might be better to just let a Court throw her claims out and dispense with all this 'free' discovery of privileged material.

"Wait a minute," Tina said to Mr. Kantor, when he shared this information with her. "First of all they have never furnished anything on a voluntary basis, and secondly, aren't they being a little hypocritical? I have never been looking for a "gold mine"! I have been looking for the truth and for someone to tell me there is money somewhere to pay for my medical bills in this quagmire of insufficient insurance. I understand that Mr. Erickson wasn't planning to die when he was in perfectly good health, but he should have been adequately insured, especially if his properties and other assets were heavily mortgaged."

"You're absolutely right, Tina. And that's why I'm not ready to give up on this.

Maybe the plane wasn't insured properly, but Russell Erickson had definitely made arrangements so his children would be provided for in the event of his death.

What we have to prove is that your injuries and medical expenses were also an unforeseen circumstance, just like his death. As a result, his children have to share those assets with you."

"I know this is tough, Mr. Kantor. You were thrown into the middle of this mess, and I really appreciate you sorting out the facts and moving forward to try and secure the judgment. I had not agreed freely to the $425,000 without collateral, but Erickson Jr. did. I guess the difference was I just assumed it was there to be collected, and Erickson Jr., on the other hand, knew he wasn't going to pay. He must have realized that he could hide the assets by switching his name with his father's name.

"Well, Tina, the good news is that Judge Luccentti seems to be on our side once again. We were successful in getting an examination of Erickson Jr.. Attorney Delgoto had the nerve to request that the examination be conducted at his office, but I gave him two dates, both in January 1996, at the Courthouse, not in at his offices."

"That is good news," Tina replied.

Mr. Kantor forwarded Tina a copy of the deposition. It did pin Erickson Jr. down on a few details, but for the most part, it covered the businesses that were owned by his father when Erickson Jr. took over the primary operations of the Erickson conglomerate.

Months turned into years and not much happened in the New York Courts. In May 1997, Tina and Roger returned from visiting relatives and Tina was relieved to see a fax from Mr. Kantor stating that the Final Adjournment and deposition date had been scheduled for July 15. She could actually be in New York on that date, if she was needed, and sent Kantor a fax stating this. Tina also included several unanswered questions.

She felt like a parrot asking the same question over and over, but once again she asked Mr. Kantor if a private investigator would help delve into some of the missing pieces of information and clear up some of the discrepancies that seemed to be the theme of the Erickson camp. The topics ran the gamut from accounting issues to once again, who Russell A. Erickson, alias, Russell Erickson Jr., truly was.

Tina also questioned the November 1991 New York State Estate Tax return, which revealed $4,498,241.19 in deductions. How could this possibly be when the value of the estate, even in the Erickson's deposition two years earlier, was claimed to be just $30,000? Tina had gone back and checked the commas and the period in that figure, but there it was in black and white. Over $4 million! This was more than a red flag, since this sum of money—deduction or not—had never been mentioned by anyone in the past.

Who was hiding what, and why? Tina wondered. *In his final deposition, Russell Jr. also said funeral expenses were 'around $8,000,' when an earlier deposition showed that he indicated those same expenses were closer to $30,000, but that was when they were stealing the available money from the Las Cruces Estate, back in 1992. That was during Erickson Jr.'s first deposition. At that time, Erickson Jr. said under oath that his name was Russell Erickson Jr. without* *the initial "A."* As Tina was writing this, she remembered her old friend who had always said, "A liar has to have a good memory."

Tina also asked Mr. Kantor, in writing, if Erickson Sr.'s accountant, Mr. Hanson, had ever been questioned regarding the ownership of land and gifts, since he had also given a deposition.

Tina never did get all of her questions answered. In July 1997, Mr. Kantor, who had been having health issues, was ready to retire. Mr. Kantor suggested Jerome Melman as his replacement. Melman would become attorney number seven. He was a much younger man, very tall and very fit. He had blue eyes and medium-brown hair, along with a square jaw and silver-colored glasses. Once again, it meant that Mr. Melman, the new attorney, would need a few months to gather information and get up to speed on the case. In October, Tina wrote to him to let him know that she would send more records by the end of the month. Going through the documents raised more questions.

Tina wrote to her new attorney. "I ceased using Samsel's law firm after the March 1992 judgment. Ten days later, I went to William Chambers. Why did Delgoto, Erickson's attorney, send documents to Samsel in 1995? That was plainly to prevent me from having the chance to object to the accounting. Do I have recourse here? With what monies were the bank notes paid off? What collateral was this note based on?" Tina wanted to point out that the accounting records were not consistent and there were no canceled checks or other evidence to back up the money spent. Tina was frustrated since the accounting records that were sporadically given to her had changed from time to time and also from attorney to attorney. No one, including Tina, had a complete set of records to verify the inconsistencies.

As Tina continued with her life in Las Cruces and her

volunteer work at the high school, progress with the case continued slowly over the next year. In September 1998, Tina wrote a suggestion to Mr. Melman in an e-mail:

My son used a bounty hunter to collect on a $6,000 bad check that the County Attorney's office was handling. The thief told the court he could not pay my son, but a week later, he called him and said he would pay if this bounty hunter left him alone. It was very effective, and very legal. My other son, who lives in New York, also told me that in the jewelry business, Hassidic Jews are called upon to collect debts for the other jewelers and manufacturers, because they are very effective.

My point is that a good detective could go back through the files and find people who can attest to what the Ericksons have done to hide their father's money.

Once again, no action was taken, and Mr. Melman did not follow up on using a private investigator.

"A LIAR HAS TO HAVE A GOOD MEMORY." ANONYMOUS

CHAPTER TWENTY-FIVE
AUGUST 1999

No paperwork of significance had been filed in the courts for a few years, but now, finally, Russell Jr. was scheduled to give another deposition. The purpose of the deposition was to clear up some issues regarding the Ericksons's estate assets and their accounting methods, but instead it opened a Pandora's box of improper accounting and discrepancies.

Attorney Melman called Tina in September to go over the results of the deposition.

"Russell's deposition was interesting, to say the least," Mr. Melman told Tina over the phone. "One of the glaring inconsistencies was his statement that all funeral expenses were less than $10,000."

Before Melman could explain, Tina couldn't contain her outburst, "What? Russell Erickson Jr. is lying!" she screamed. "In an early interrogatory, dated December 2, 1991, Russell Erickson Jr. was explaining the accounting and expenses for the estate. He mentioned that there was no real profit from the sale of the two condominiums because $30,000 plus of that paid for the funeral expenses for both of his parents. At that time, all the expenses for the couple were charged to Russell A. Erickson's estate. They were raping Russell's estate of any available monies. Money that they received from the insurance company went into Christina's estate, which the judge had declared separate, even though New Mexico is a community property state. In other words, I was told the net proceeds from both properties were primarily used for funeral expenses far exceeding $10,000!

That's why there was nothing left from those properties to help me pay my medical bills."

"That's what I was going to explain, Tina," Mr. Melman said patiently. "You're right. I have paperwork here listing $28,000 to $38,000 for combined funeral expenses for Russell Sr. and Christina.

"Maybe if Russell Jr. hadn't dragged his feet for years, his memory would be a little better," Tina said sarcastically. She continued, "He doesn't even know his name. The earlier paperwork clearly states that when the court asked Russell, 'Please state your name,' he said for the record it was Russell Erickson Jr. In his deposition, dated June 13, 1999, when he was asked to state his name, he said it was Russell A. Erickson. Now he has a middle initial! What do we do? It sounds like it's our word against his, and that hasn't gotten us too far in the past.

"I wish I had better news, Tina, but the bottom line is that if the money's not there, it's not there. Despite the fact that Russell Jr. downright lied, and one of the depositions is a lie, it doesn't change the fact that the money is gone."

"Is that where it really went, though?" Tina asked. "Could he have pocketed it somehow?"

"Unfortunately, that is certainly possible," Jerome Melman said.

Looking back all these years later, Tina thought, *This could have been avoided if I had all the paperwork pertaining to this case from the six previous attorneys*. One thing Tina came to understand was that, with each court procedure, there is paperwork and it is up to you, the client, to get all of it from your attorney. Of course, this is easier said than done. What if the attorney sends out paperwork or makes a motion and doesn't tell his client about it?

Attorney Melman broke into Tina's thoughts by saying, "You're right about one thing. After all this time, the next judge is going to want to close this case. This probably isn't the best time to tell you this, either, but we've had some very crooked issues uncovered in the Richfield County Court system lately, and no one is sure which judges and attorneys are involved, and we won't know until all the facts are uncovered."

"Just a minute," Tina said, not concerned about the scandal, "You said the NEXT judge?"

"Oh, I'm so sorry. Maybe you didn't get the letter explaining that Judge Luccentti is retiring."

"No, I haven't seen that one," Tina sighed. "He's been the first judge that I thought actually had some compassion and could look at this case fairly. I can't believe it! So, do I dare ask who the judge is now?"

"The judge's name is Kantino. Maybe you should sit down, Tina."

"I'm pacing the floor, Mr. Melman. I am not calm and I can't sit," Tina said. "I feel so helpless… not that I could do much even if I was right there, but being so far away makes me feel not only out of touch, but out of control."

"I can understand that, Tina. Here's the thing. Judge Kantino is the first cousin of Attorney Bradesco, one of the partners in the firm Donnelli, Ambeck, Delgoto, Bradesco, & Copeano, who just happens to be handling the Erickson estate."

"Erickson's attorney!" Tina blurted out. "I can't believe this! Isn't there some law against this?"

"Not a law, but most judges wouldn't want a case like this, even if it's just for their family's sanity. It's not easy, and no matter what the outcome is, there can be finger pointing. It's hard to maintain a good reputation, not to mention good family relations."

"Can we request another judge?" Tina asked. "Is there anything that says a relative cannot be a judge?"

"I'm afraid not, especially with all of the issues the county is investigating right now. There's too much red tape and the case would take even longer," Mr. Melman explained.

Months passed, and the case seemed to be frozen in time. Tina couldn't stand it any longer and she picked up the phone and called her attorney, Jerome Melman. "Hello, this is Tina Morgan."

"Hello Tin…"

Tina broke in immediately and said, "I have been patient, Mr. Melman, for nine years and where has it gotten me?"

"It's the system," Mr. Melman explained to Tina. "With all of the issues going on up here in Richfield County, it's better to be patient right now."

"How long can I afford to pay attorney's fees and get nowhere? It has been almost 10 years. I'm sorry," Tina said, "I am starting to panic."

Ten months later, in June 2000, Judge Kantino recused himself from the case. *Why did the judge take so long to step down? Did he actually have a conscience, or was this case so bizarre that he didn't want any part of it?* Tina wondered. Whatever the reason, it was totally out of Tina's control, and the never-ending saga was about to take a downward spiral.

When the new judge was assigned, Tina didn't think too much about not getting an update for a few months. The judge would have to go through the files, possibly contact both attorneys, and bring himself up to speed before even considering a date to award the judgment.

To Tina's chagrin, the months literally turned into years. Attorney Melman couldn't get any answers either. Finally one day he called and told Tina the files in her case were lost. The new judge was in a building across the street from Judge Kantino's chambers, and during the transfer, the files disappeared.

Tina had been having lunch when he called; she expected

bad news regarding this case, since good news usually never came her way. "The files just disappeared?" Tina said. "It took, Judge Kantino over ten months to recuse himself after deciding that since he was the first cousin to the attorney for the defendant, he should not be involved in the case. The records and files just go missing? Any coincidences here? Don't you find this odd and highly irregular, Mr. Melman?"

"What can I say Tina? We have to just wait and see."

Once she was off the phone, Tina started to ask herself, *How could files, legal files for a case that had already been pending for years, get lost? Someone had to carry them across the street, and now they were nowhere to be found? What is going on?* Tina was certain this was all planned, but how could she ever prove it?

Tina continued to talk to herself, having an internal conversation with her naïve and wise alter egos. *Did Russell Erickson know all the judges who had handled and were handling this case? Did he have the kind of connections and clout in this courthouse to be capable of judicial steering? Could he delay this case many more years?*

Possibly, said the wise one.

Would an attorney having a cousin who is a judge really give him clout? asked the naïve one. *Possibly*, said the wise one.

This is America, where there has to be justice.

Why? asked the wise one.

This is America, the greatest country in the world. This business of falsifying or losing records and interfering with justice in our courts just doesn't make sense.

You really think so? asked the wise one.

I did, but I don't now. I don't know what to think or what to believe.

Tina went on with her life as best she could. She and

Roger were happy and enjoyed a good life together. Still, the case hung over her like a bad cough that she couldn't shake, or clouds that wouldn't let the sunshine through.

A couple of years later, Tina woke up one late spring morning to sunlight streaming in through the windows. She opened her eyes to the sharp contrast of the mountains against the clear blue sky. *What a perfect day*, she thought. Sunday was a free day, and she didn't want to waste it by staying inside. She almost bounced into the kitchen and kissed Roger on the cheek. "I have a surprise for you."

"If you're thinking of spending the entire day outside in this beautiful weather,..." he started to say.

As Tina often did when she was excited or upset, she broke in. "I know you don't love hiking, but it is such a beautiful day, isn't it? I thought I would make a picnic and we could go to Dripping Springs. The falls there are quite a sight and we could eat by the water. Both trails are relatively short, and we could go to the mountain cave, too!"

"You really want me to go on two hikes in one day?" Roger teased.

"Please?" Tina asked, playfully batting her eyelashes.

"Okay. It's worth it to see you happy, Tina. Just remember, if I get blisters, you'll have to rub my feet and kiss my toes!" Roger said.

"I'll get the food ready, if you want to get the sunscreen, camera, and, oh yes, some band-aids in case you do get blisters. If you could grab the water bottles, too, that would be great. Do you want to leave in 30 minutes?" Tina was talking fast and Roger smiled.

It really was good to see Tina acting like her old self. "Whatever you say, dear," he said.

They drove to the Organ Mountains east of Las Cruces and parked at the visitor's center. From there it was a short walk to the trailhead.

"Let's go up to the ruins first," Tina said.

"What did it used to be?" Roger asked.

"It was actually built as a resort, but was used as a sanitarium for people suffering from tuberculosis," Tina explained.

"That's cheerful," Roger said.

"Well, at least they had a lovely setting," Tina commented.

"Yes, they did," Roger answered.

As they hiked, birds sang and a cardinal swooped across the path in front of them. He landed in a tree and his brilliant red feathers glistened in the sun. "He's stunning," Tina whispered.

A light brown bird, with just a touch of light red around the edges of its feathers, landed in the tree next to him. "She's not as pretty," Roger said.

"Why is it the males are the spectacular-looking birds of the species?" Tina asked.

Roger laughed, "So the females can find us," he answered.

As they made their way past the old Boyd Sanitarium, they found the rock stairway to the left of the former dining hall. As they climbed the steps, a deer and her fawn stopped in a clearing on the right to watch them. Tina stopped walking so she wouldn't scare them. The mother deer flared her nostrils and they both turned and ran, tails straight in the air.

They could hear the falls before they saw them. The stream was full from an unusually heavy snowfall late in the season, and the falls pounded on the rocks below. As they came over the last crest in the hill, Tina stopped in her tracks, "Oh, look, Roger!"

The sunlight on the spraying water cast hundreds of little rainbows. Cottonwood trees hugged the banks of the pool where sunlight and shade played tag with each other, as if chasing after the colors of the rainbow. It was a breathtaking site, and no one else was around. Suddenly, Roger slipped his arms around Tina's waist. She turned her face up to his and felt the cool spray of the water. They held each other tightly and slowly and hungrily kissed.

It was a magical moment, and Tina realized how much she had missed being a normal person. They had been married for almost eight years now, but Tina had been so wrapped up with the court case that she hadn't really been there for Roger. As usual, he hadn't complained.

"I love you, Roger. We really need to do this more often," she whispered.

"I love you, too, but you don't need to whisper. There doesn't seem to be another soul around for miles. This was a wonderful idea, by the way," he told her.

They sat in the shade and watched a coyote drink out of the pool while they ate their sandwiches, cheese, and fruit. They talked about everything except the pending case, which was fine with Tina. She felt more relaxed than she had in months. After they had rested and soaked their feet in the cool water, Tina asked, "Are you ready for another hike?"

"Thought I'd just stay here and take a nap," Roger said, closing his eyes.

"Come on, we need the exercise," Tina said, tickling him.

"Okay, okay," he said, trying to hold her at arm's length. Only if I get another long, leisurely kiss," said Roger as he grabbed her waist.

"Yummy," Tina said as they parted.

"Where are we off to now, my princess?"

"We'll hike back to the fork in the trail and take the other path. That will lead to La Cueva. It's a mountain cave that was thought to have been a shelter for the prehistoric Mongolian Indians."

"It sounds fascinating, but can I ask how far it is?"

"Just a mile or so," Tina answered.

"I think I can make it," Roger said, leaning against the cottonwood as he stood up.

"Are you okay?" Tina asked, concerned.

Roger straightened up and started to chase her. "Of course I'm okay. You'd better run, or I'll get there first."

As they approached the cave, Tina stopped suddenly. "I saw something move."

"Maybe a prehistoric creature," Roger teased.

"No, really," Tina said, quietly.

They were very still for a moment and Tina strained to hear what sounded like a kitten crying.

"Oh, look!" Tina pointed to the hill to the right of the cave. A female bobcat was carrying her baby in her mouth.

"She must be moving her den," Roger said. The bobcat turned to look at them and then scampered off.

They finally made it back to the parking lot late in the afternoon. There were fewer cars now, as most of the hikers had left. "Funny," Tina said. "As long as we were in the canyon, I felt energized. I could have stayed even longer, but now that we are back and I'm sitting down, I have to admit, I'm tired." Tina rolled down the car window to let in some fresh air. "I also want a nice long shower."

"No, I can't believe it!" Roger laughed. "You have more energy than anyone I know."

"I guess the fresh air, sunshine, and being in love wear a person out," Tina replied.

Tina and Roger lived on the eastside of town, so they didn't have far to travel once they were back on the main road. As they passed their local shopping center, a car sat on the side of the road with a dented fender. A police car was still parked with its lights blinking. "At least, no one died in that accident," Tina commented, knowingly and with resolve.

The end of the afternoon and evening were quiet. Tina

soaked in the whirlpool tub and let the jets swirl and massage her aching muscles. She had added bubbles to the water and the scent helped her relax even more. She had soaked for almost an hour, when Roger poked his head in. "Ready for something to eat" he asked?

"I am hungry. I'll be right out." Tina said as she slipped into her revealing nightclothes, knowing Roger would like it even better if she wasn't "dressed" while they ate.

Shortly after 8:30 p.m., the phone rang. It was Tina's friend, Jack, from the Singles Club.

"Hi, Tina, I just wondered if you had heard about Jane?" he said, coming right to the point.

"No, Jack, what about Jane? We have plans to get together for lunch next week," Tina replied sounding just a little anxious.

"Jane died," Jack said in a strong, calm voice."

Tina couldn't quite comprehend what he was saying. "What did you say, Jack? Could you repeat that?" Tina asked, with alarm and concern in her voice and tears coming to her eyes.

"Jane died this afternoon, Tina. She was in an accident coming out of the shopping center. She misjudged the distance and pulled out into oncoming traffic. A car couldn't stop and hit her fender."

"Wait, do you mean the Safeway shopping center near us?"

"Yes, Tina. That's where it was."

"No! OH, no," Tina said crying. "We saw the car, but I didn't realize it was hers. There was hardly any damage. It just looked like a small fender bender. What happened? She couldn't have died from that!"

"She had internal injuries," Jack explained. "You know she had chemo all winter, so her bones were really brittle. The impact from the seat belt caused her rib to crack and it punctured her lung. She bled internally. She waited a long time in the ER. They were short staffed on a Sunday afternoon and were really busy. The hospital staff thought the same thing—just a small fender bender, nothing serious. While Jane was waiting in a room, she silently bled to death. Her body was weak, and I guess in the end, it was in God's hands."

Tina was in shock. She thanked Jack for calling, and she told Roger the news as she crumpled in his arms. They talked for a while and Roger held her tightly as they fell asleep. At 1 or 2 a.m, Tina woke up and tiptoed into the kitchen. She was so sad. Tina took out a pen and paper. She had loved Jane and had so much to tell her. Now she would never get the chance, so Tina wrote her dear friend a letter:

Dear Jane,
Did I ever tell you how much I admired your talents, your creativity, and your artistic ability to blend, sculpt, sew, paint, weave, and design the fabrics of your life into useful gifts for others to enjoy?

Did I ever tell you, you were like a fairy godmother, mother earth, and a naive child, all wrapped into one? Jane, you were the eternal optimist, the compassionate soul who always had a kind word for all of us.

You were generous, sweet, kind, warm, gentle, and loving in oh so many ways and in so many circumstances. You never seemed to judge; you always seemed to understand.

Your house was open to everyone. You were always so trusting, so understanding, and always so willing to help.

Did I ever tell you what a gutsy lady you were? You were never afraid to take a chance, never afraid to be alone and to travel alone, never afraid to meet people.

You were always there for someone, or anyone, who would need to talk or need the comfort of your shoulder or the wisdom of your words; no matter what happened, you would always say ," It will always work out; it will be okay."

Did I ever tell you, you always made the sun shine when you were in a room, and that you always wore such vibrant colors to match or blend with your dancing, blue eyes?

Did I ever tell you how much I looked forward to and how much I enjoyed your hand-painted Christmas cards of Love and Peace and Joy?

Halloween will never be the same! Your parties were the grandest and you--the fairest of them all, with your long flowing dresses and a garland of flowers in your hair.

GOOD-BYE, DEAR GRACIOUS LADY, YOU WILL BE MISSED, But NOT FORGOTTEN!

"I HAVE ALWAYS FOUND THAT MERCY BEARS RICHER FRUITS THAN STRICT JUSTICE." ABRAHAM LINCOLN

CHAPTER TWENTY-SIX
APRIL 2004

Tina was planting summer flowers by the pool when the phone rang. She shook the dirt from her gloves and wiped the sweat from her brow as she answered.

"Hello?"

"Tina! It's your attorney, Jerome Melman. I just received a letter stating that Judge Santelli has transferred the case to Judge Mancuso and a pretrial conference is scheduled for May 3 at 2:15 p.m. It's a Tuesday and less than two weeks from today, and we have to be there."

"Excuse me?" Tina was incredulous.

"I thought you'd be thrilled to be moving forward, Tina." Mr. Melman sounded a little bewildered.

"Well, Mr. Melman, my concern is that you filed all of the necessary paperwork in 1998. Let's see, if my calculations are right that was SIX years ago. Then the files disappeared for four years. How did the files turn up? Did they just walk in the room last week and seat themselves on Judge Mancuso's desk? This is just so bizarre! For over four years, the files are missing and no one can explain to us how everything was lost, missing—MIA. And now they want us—me—to jump on a plane in less than two weeks? How can we be prepared?"

"Not much has changed, Tina. The judgment is the same and we just need to see what the judge has to say."

"Then why is it a pretrial conference? Why aren't we just going to trial?"

"After all this time, I'm sure the judge has a few questions," Melman reasoned. "It's actually in our best interest."

"I'm sorry if I don't seem as confident as you do, Mr. Melman, but so far, nothing has been in our best interest.

"I'm looking at my calendar right now, and unfortunately my husband and I have a major commitment. We have a wedding party that we are hosting, and as I'm sure the judge can understand, this commitment was planned well in advance and certainly longer than the two-week notice given to me to appear in New York."

"I will check for you, Tina. Courts are funny—I'm just letting you know beforehand that they may require you to submit some kind of documentation regarding your prior commitment."

"That is funny, Mr. Melman. I will be more than happy to do that. I will write a letter now, stating why I cannot be there on May 3, and I'll fax a copy of the invitation. I will be available in June. Maybe that will give you more time, too, if you need it."

"I'm sorry this is so sudden, Tina. But I have a feeling that we may be able to finally wrap this case up for you."

"I'm sorry if I don't seem more appreciative, Mr. Melman. I do thank you for your time, and I know you took this case as a favor for a friend. I know you have worked hard and tried to get some answers when we have been stuck in limbo for the last four years. Now you want me to be excited, but in all honesty, I don't know how to feel."

Tina clicked off the phone and sank to the ground next to the flowers that she needed to plant and water. *My flowers need soil and water to live*, Tina thought. *It's up to me to respond to their needs. Isn't it up to our American courts, the judicial system that our country was founded on, to respond to the needs of plaintiffs who have been wronged? Doesn't America provide justice for all?*

Tina could agree with Mr. Melman on one point: the end was drawing near. It was the final outcome that she wasn't so sure about.

Tina included a copy of the wedding invitation with her faxed statement: "At this time, the May date is impossible to keep because I cannot appear in court on that date." Maybe the extra time was on her side. At any rate, she felt more in control of the situation, knowing the ordeal would finally be over. Or would it? Nothing was as it seemed, so why should this be any different?

When Tina arrived at the Newark Airport, Dennis, her cousin was there to pick her up and take her to his home. He was going to make the trip with her to the Richfield County Surrogate Courthouse. He, too, was Tina's angel. They had grown up together as children, and even though they didn't live near each other anymore, there was a tie that went down to the very core of their existence.

The next morning, bright and early, they left Jersey for the early-morning date with Tina's attorney before they all headed out to the Richfield County Surrogate Courthouse. The day was fresh and the sky was blue, not overcast and threatening. *Maybe this is a good omen*, Tina thought. Soon, they were focused on the drive, waiting on toll roads and crossing over bridges in stop-and-go-traffic. They found a parking spot next to Jerome Melman's office and managed to climb the steps and reach the door as the clock from a nearby church struck 9 a.m.

Tina and Dennis were greeted cheerfully by Mr. Melman as he led them to his office. Tina couldn't wait and just blurted out in a slightly loud and anxious voice, "What is going to happen? How long is this going to take? Why are we even here?"

"Wait a minute and calm down, Tina. I will explain what is going to happen. The judge wants to see us in his chambers to try to settle this without using the taxpayers' money on a trial. He…"

Tina interrupted, remembering her unanswered wishes for a trial in the New Mexico Court System years before. "I want a jury trial. I was denied a trial before. I want one now. I don't want to make any more concessions."

"Okay, Tina, I understand," Jerome said, "but we don't have a choice. We have to see the judge."

"I don't want that judge," Tina screamed. "Didn't you say he was the law clerk of the judge who was Bradesco's cousin? Doesn't Bradesco's firm represent Erickson?"

"Tina," Melman said, "we went over all this before. It isn't going to help to get excited. Let's just see what the judge has to say." Tina shook her head, resigned to another bad day.

They arrived at the courthouse in a fair amount of time. It was a beautiful courthouse—very statuesque, stately, and large but had character. It was more than 15 years old, which, by New York standards, was on the new side. The courthouse was named after Michael Santonio, who was a judge. His life had been tragically cut short when he ruled against the plaintiff in a sexual harassment and employment discrimination case. The plaintiff's father, a retired police officer who was saddened by what he saw as injustice in the verdict, killed the judge before taking his own life.

Tina, her cousin, and her attorney walked through the long halls and took the elevator up to the courtroom, where they saw Erickson Jr. and his attorney. Tina didn't know Erickson Jr., but that had to be him. There was also a guard. They sat on the oak benches and waited for the judge. Finally Judge Mancuso appeared. He was dressed in a suit, not the black robes usually associated with judges. He introduced himself and said he would like to meet with each party separately in his chambers. Erickson Jr. and his attorney went in first, and then it was Tina and Mr. Melman's turn. *It looked like a play with the front of the courtroom as a stage. We are going to go behind the scenes,* Tina thought. Tina and her attorney walked up to the stage area and then went through a hall backstage. They continued to walk until they came to the judge's office and his chambers. There were two rooms attached. First, there was an outer office that was quite small and then a larger judge's chamber that had chairs and a big desk in the back. Four summer-school law students were already seated, with their backs to the windows. Judge Mancuso explained that these students were his interns and they would be listening in on the conference. At this point, Tina had no idea what to expect.

Judge Mancuso explained that he was trying to assess the situation and see if there was any way this could be settled without a trial. He explained that the Erickson estate was very anxious to settle. He pointed out further that this had taken over ten years, and it should be off the books by now. He stated that the Erickson estate wanted to make a monetary offer, and then he asked Tina what she thought.

Tina just said, "NO! I want a trial." After another half hour, they were led out of the chambers, and Erickson Jr. and his attorney followed the judge back to his chambers. This back-and-forth procedure went on all morning, with a one-hour break for lunch at 12:30. The afternoon session was exactly the same. At about four o'clock, the judge said to Tina, "We will meet here tomorrow at 10 a.m." Tina just looked at her attorney and said nothing. When Tina got outside, she asked Mr. Melman if this procedure was normal. Could a judge keep you in his chambers all day and then demand that you return the next day? Jerome said that this was unusual, and he had never experienced anything like this before.

The next day started the same way, except this time when Judge Mancuso came to get Tina and her attorney, she asked the judge if her cousin Dennis could also attend the session in his chambers. He said it would be fine, so Dennis had a chance to experience firsthand this very unusual and very unorthodox procedure. Tuesday was a continuation of Monday, with alternating visits to the judge's chambers. The students were not invited to these. Tina was told in no uncertain terms that if a decision could not be made before trial, then Judge Mancuso would be the judge, and he could choose to give her less than the amount suggested today at this settlement conference. The amount offered was not enough money to pay for the medical bills and attorneys' fees that Tina had to come up with out of her own pocket. Would this never end? Tina didn't know what to do. She only knew that she didn't want to settle for the extremely small amount of money the Ericksons were offering to give her.

A break for lunch was finally called, and Tina, Dennis, and Jerome Melman left the courthouse. Dennis commented that he couldn't believe what he was witnessing. Tina asked her attorney again if he had ever experienced this type of arm twisting. And, again, Jerome said no.

As the afternoon progressed, the dollar amount offered, which would not even cover Tina's doctors' or attorneys' fees, was raised slightly. To Tina, it was another long, tiring, and wasted day. Tina started getting angry and felt like she was being held hostage, with limited choices. She knew that in the New Mexico Courts, the judge who handled the settlement conference did not handle the trial. Tina asked Jerome Melman why Judge Mancuso would be handling the trial. Jerome said simply, "He is the trial judge." No other explanation was given. Tina went on to explain that in New Mexico, this was not possible.

At 4 p.m., the judge adjourned their meeting until the next day. "I will see you tomorrow, Tina," the judge said. So, once again, they would be heading back to the courthouse tomorrow. As before, they awoke early and traveled through the early-morning, rush-hour traffic over the bridges and back to a "Hall of Justice," that in Tina's estimation, wasn't "Just" at all.

Another day and more of the same. Tina was the victim and Tina was the hostage. She didn't see a way out. Was that the idea, to wear her down and make her agree against her free will? Tina asked the judge when it was her team's turn in his chambers.

"I don't want to go to trial with you as the judge, and I don't want to settle! I still don't feel, I can get a fair trial. What choices do I have?"

"Well, you can fire your attorney and then ask for more time and a new trial," said the judge. Tina observed a smirk on the judge's face and a satisfied tone in his voice.

"I don't want to do that," said Tina. *I want this over with*, she thought. *Which judge would I get next? Another attorney's relative of this very large law firm or another law clerk?* There didn't seem to be an end and really no advantage to getting another judicial member in a system that already stacked the deck against her.

Next Tina asked, "What about the other lawsuit that Erickson won? What happened to all that property? Why don't we have an up-to-date accounting on the assets of the Erickson estate? His estate cannot be dissolved as long as this lawsuit isn't resolved."

"Well," said Judge Mancuso, with an authoritative voice. "It's like this, Tina, your attorney should have applied for an update on the assets of the Erickson estate, and he did not. Now you are not entitled to this information. He told the court he was ready for trial."

"He was ready!" Tina blurted out, "but that was over five years ago."

"Well, he did not get an update," the judge said.

"You didn't give us any time. You wanted us here immediately," Tina said.

"He should have made a motion to extend. He did not," the Judge said.

Tina sat there quietly and thought, *Screwed again!*

The judge broke into Tina's thoughts and said, "You know, Tina, in a case like this, you get the most expensive attorney you can afford."

Just what Tina needed to hear, another word from the wise. It was probably very good advice but it didn't help Tina or her case. A few minutes later, Tina said, "Your honor, I need lunch. It is almost 1:30, and I need to eat."

"Okay, let's adjourn till 2:30. See you back in court then," the Judge said.

Lunch was a good break. This had been a long, grueling session that was full of subtle threats. *Oh, I was given lots of choices*, Tina thought. *I can fire my attorney and start over, or I can fire my attorney and start over, and over, and over.*

During lunch, Tina asked Jerome Melman if the attorney with Erickson Jr. was Delgoto, who had given them so much trouble over the years. "Yes," Melman said. "Delgoto is here, and his law partner is Bradesco, whose cousin intimately knows Judge Mancuso. It seems like one big happy family. Where is justice? This is a joke and it is on me."

After lunch, the judge called the Ericksons's camp into the chamber first, and then it was Tina's turn. By then it was almost 3:30—and another long day. If nothing was settled today, tomorrow would be the trial. Tomorrow, the judge could decide to give Tina less than the meager offer presented. The judge started by saying the Erickson's offer would go up by $5,000. At this point, Tina said, "I want to go back to Mexico, when this is over, and give $5,000 to each of my two Angels. I need another $10,000. This money is NOT for me but for them." Wearily, the judge said he would take the offer to them, and we left. We were called back in shortly, and the judge said that had been their final offer.

"They will not budge."

"Then I won't budge," said Tina.

At this point, Mr. Melman who was sitting very quietly after the dressing down by the judge about his mistake of not getting an extension for a current accounting on the estate, said, "Tina, I will give you the $7,000 that you owe me. You don't have to pay me any more money. I have the retainer, and you have already paid me for my time."

"Thank you, Mr. Melman," Tina said. "That will help, but I still want the extra $3,000 to give to my angels."

"You won't get any more money from the estate," Judge Mancuso said. Then the room was quiet. Dead Quiet. It was after 4 p.m. and there was still a standoff. "Okay," said the judge, "we will all be in court tomorrow at 10 a.m. for the trial." With that, they all rose. As they walked out of the chambers into the small outer office, Tina started to think. *This is all I can get. I can ask for a new trial and dismiss my attorney and get rid of this judge, or I can take the money and end this nightmare.*

As they reached the hall, Tina took longer steps so she could reach the judge, and then she said, "Judge, I will take the offer."

With that the judge said, "Let's go back into the chambers." He gave them directions for the next day and then called in the Erickson team.

We have to return on Thursday morning for the final insult, Tina thought.

*"IF IT WERE NOT FOR INJUSTICE, MEN WOULD NOT KNOW
JUSTICE." HERACLITUS*

CHAPTER TWENTY-SEVEN
JUNE 9, 2004

It was the final day of a four-day, drawn-out "discussion," as Judge Mancuso so kindly referred to the contested accounting proceeding in the Surrogate's Court. Judge Mancuso started the session by summing up the events of the thirty days prior to the "settlement discussions" and stating that the discussions were very productive. Tina, on the other hand, viewed these settlement discussions as confinement in the court for the three days prior to the trial, with little choice but to fire her attorney and start anew.

During the morning, before the court convened, both sides agreed to sign general releases against any past claims either party might have against the other. Tina wanted to be sure that there would be no repercussions following release of the book she planned to write. So she had Mr. Melman add the following statement to the recorded document they both signed: "releases any claims for the past, present, or future."

Today, the attorney for Erickson Jr. was Mr. Bradesco. The name sounded familiar, but at the moment Tina couldn't recall the connection. Today, there was no attorney named Delgoto, whose name had been associated with the Erickson case in the past. *Very interesting*, Tina thought. Why did they change attorneys? Tina had forgotten the connection, and this was not to her benefit. The connection was that Judge Mancuso had been Judge Kantino's law clerk for 15 years. Judge Kantino was the first cousin of Mr. Bradesco, who happened to be in court today as one of Erickson's attorneys. After 15 years of working together on a daily basis, Mancuso and Kantino would certainly be more like brothers than even first cousins. Did the files disappear on purpose until Judge Santelli could transfer the case to Judge Mancuso?

Judge Mancuso swore in both Russell, the petitioner, and Tina, the objecting.

Judge Mancuso: *How are you doing today?*

Tina: *Good.*

Judge Mancuso: *Do you swear that the answers you're about to provide to me in this matter will be the truth, the whole truth, and nothing but the truth?*

Tina: *Yes, but will you like them?* Tina thought, *What else is there, if not the truth?*

Tina had an agenda and she knew the answers she provided in court today might be used in a book she was planning to write after this whole debacle was over.

Judge Mancuso: *I like whatever answers you give me, ma'am. Okay, have a seat, please. Be comfortable. You have heard Mr. Bradesco's settlement offer and you want to settle it along those terms?*

Tina: *That is the choice that I have. I have no other choice, so that is the best decision to make.* Tina thought back at this point. All the attorneys. All the mistakes. Getting stuck with a judgement not backed by collateral. Not being able to find another attorney in Las Cruces to take the case and reverse the judgement. Choice, what choice? Moving the case to New York because she thought she felt she would be treated fairly by the courts. Dismissing her grandmothers law firm because she thought an attorney in the locale where the courthouse was located was better. One mistake after another and in the end, here I am.

Judge Mancuso: *Okay. You have some options, and it's*

certainly, you know, your call to decide on an option. I want to make sure we're on the same page. You have options. You can choose among them, and they have different consequences, certainly. But is this the option that you feel is the right option, and is it what you want to do today?

Tina: *Because of the situation of my choice of counsel throughout this case, from way back in Las Cruces, and the choices that I have made, I am going along with this one now, which is to end this and get on with our lives.*

Judge Mancuso: *Okay. Do you feel that you understand the terms of this settlement agreement?*

Tina: *I understand the terms to be that he doesn't sue me and I don't sue him, as far as I understand, and this part of it will be closed.*

Judge Mancuso: *Any claims that you have against this estate would be waived in exchange for their payment to you of the specified amount and the exchange of those general releases.*

Tina: *Right.*

Judge Mancuso: *Is that what you understand the terms to be?*

Tina: *Correct.*

Judge Mancuso: *And you feel you can comply with this portion of the agreement?*

Tina: *Yes.*

Judge Mancuso: *Okay. You've been represented by Mr. Melman in this matter. Have you had an adequate amount of time to speak to him about it?*

Tina: *Yes, sir.*

Judge Mancuso: *Do you need any more time to speak to him about it?*

Tina: *No, sir.*

Judge Mancuso: *Do you have any questions for either*

him or me in regards to the terms and conditions of the stipulation?

Tina: *No, sir.*

Judge Mancuso: *Okay. Are you satisfied with the legal representation you've had in this matter? I'm not talking about the New Mexico case from which your judgment arises; I'm talking about this matter.*

Tina: *I don't think it matters what I think. I didn't have a choice, sir. I didn't have a choice.*

Judge Mancuso: *It matters to me that you're satisfied with the advice that you're receiving. Are you satisfied with the advice, or do you want time to get a different attorney or something else?* Tina thought of the past week and the judges words, that Mr. Melman didn't ask for a new accounting of the estates assets prior to this week so we can't ask for them.

Tina: *Well, you said we had no time to do anything and couldn't change anything, and the trial was going to proceed today regardless, and so...*

Judge Mancuso: *You didn't ask me if you could get a new lawyer. If you want to get a new lawyer, that's a different question. If you simply don't want to go to trial and don't want to settle, then, you know, we do have to go to trial. Trial is scheduled for today, and your attorney is ready, willing, and able to proceed. I have to be assured that you're satisfied with the legal advice and representation that you're receiving from Mr. Melman at this time.*

Tina: *I have agreed upon the information given to me.*

Judge Mancuso: *Okay. You've agreed with him that this settlement is the proper way for you to go; is that what you're indicating?*

Tina: *That's because of my lack of choices. This is the only way to go. Lack of choices meaning staying in this Court and not going to a different Court, and all the other*

*things. So, therefore, as long as we have to stay here, then
let's just finish it.*

Judge Mancuso: *When you say "here," what do you
mean, New York?*

Tina: *The New York Courts, sir.*

Judge Mancuso: *Okay. Well, then. Let me ask you this.
This settlement today; is this something you're doing freely
and voluntarily? Is this your decision to do this?*

Tina: *I have agreed to do it because...*

Judge Mancuso: *You know, Ms. Morgan, I don't want
equivocation in this record. I'm prepared to try your case
right now. We can start.*

Tina: *But we aren't prepared, and you know that
because we don't have up-to-date information, which we
were never given and which we didn't ask for. I understand.
So therefore, from what we have, and what I'm allowed
to do under these circumstances, we are going along with
this, and I'm going along with whatever needs to be done
to close the case.*

Judge Mancuso: *This matter has been outstanding for
many, many years.*

Tina: *But it hasn't been worked on for many years
either.* Tina thought back over the past four years when
the case records had mysteriously disappeared off the desk
of one of the judges and no one could find them. *Was this
my choice or was someone in the drivers seat? Was their
someone steering this train to the judge of their choice? Was
there someone who wanted Judge Mancuso? After all, he
was the law clerk for over a decade to the judge who is a
first cousin to the defendants attorney. Oh yes, Justice,* Tina
thought; *where have you gone?*

Judge Mancuso: *I understand that's your position
with regard to it, but I'm not taking a settlement that's
not freely, voluntarily, and intelligently entered into by*

the parties. I'm just not going to accept it. So, I'll tell you what I'll do. I'll break for fifteen minutes; you can speak to Mr. Melman. If this is a settlement that you want because you want it and you're doing it voluntarily, fine. If you feel that you're being threatened or coerced or forced, then you don't take it, and we go to trial.

Tina: *Well, we're not ready for trial and we can't go to trial today, so there's no other choice.*

Tina knew that Judge Mancuso did not like her answers, but she was not ready to back down yet. She wanted it recorded that what had happened was not fair and not just.

Judge Mancuso: *I'm going to give you the options. There are choices to make, and you need to make them. Then you need to be able to answer the questions I have to ask you with regard to it, because I will not accept anything or any settlement where I feel that there's some equivocation as to whether it's been freely, voluntarily, knowingly, and intelligently entered into. I'm going to take a fifteen-minute recess, and then you will let me know what you want me to do. We'll meet again at five after noon.*

Well, there's a new word, Tina thought, as the recess was taken. *Knowingly! I'll bet all of you know something after all this time.* This time, Tina knew what she was doing, and she was ready to move ahead. Drawing this out and making the judge listen to her was her right.

Tina turned to Jerome Melman and innocently asked, "Didn't Judge Mancuso say he would like any answer I gave him? So why are we having a recess?" Tina knew she had pushed the envelope as far as she could. She had made her statements so they would be part of the court records forever.

Judge Mancuso: *Come to order. We're back on the record. We've had an opportunity, maybe forty-five minutes, to have the attorneys speak with their respective clients. At this time, we are going to try to put the settlement* on record. Ms. Morgan, I was speaking to you, and I think where we were was I was asking you if you felt that you could comply with the terms of the stipulation that Mr. Bradesco spread on the record.

Tina: *Yes, sir.*

Judge Mancuso: *All right, and this is what you want to do?*

Tina: *Yes, sir.*

The Court: *All right, I have indicated to you that you have options. Trial could be an option, or other applications could be an option, and settling could be an option. At this time, is this the option you have chosen?*

Tina remembered that in the judge's chambers, there were no other options. She remembered that he told her if they went to trial, he could award her less money than was offered in this settlement. So why would she want that? The judge said to get the case moved or a new trial date, Tina would have to fire her attorney and get a new attorney. So what was the positive choice in all this? What was supposed to work in Tina's favor? Tina couldn't see any positive solution. So in answer to Judge Mancuso's question, Tina answered, *"Yes, sir."*

Judge Mancuso: *Have you done so voluntarily, knowingly?*

Again, Tina thought, *Freely and voluntarily? I was sequestered in the judge's chambers for three days? Knowingly and intelligently...."*

Judge Mancuso (continuing): *and intelligently to make this decision?*

Tina: *Yes, sir.*

Judge Mancuso: *Has anyone forced you, threatened you, or coerced you into making this agreement?*

Tina thought again, *The judge told me that my choice was to get a new attorney if I wanted more time. The judge told me my attorney made a mistake. The judge told me to get the best law firm if I wanted to win. This case had cost a fortune and I didn't have more money.* Tina felt she was being forced into this decision, but she had no reasonable recourse. Therefore, she answered, *No, sir.*

Judge Mancuso: *You're doing this of your own free will?*

Tina: *My free choice, yes.* Tina had taken a minute and thought of the time and money it would cost if she continued this case. *What guarantee would there be that I could win the amount of the judgement so that I could pay all my bills? How many more years and how much more money would this take?*

Judge Mancuso: *Okay. And you're satisfied with the legal representation from Mr. Melman?*

Tina: *Yes.* Tina knew that Mr. Melman made a crucial mistake but to Tina it was not worth any more time. He had tried.

Judge Mancuso: *Are you under the influence of any medications or alcohol or drug that could prevent you from understanding the terms and conditions of this agreement?*

Tina: *No, sir.*

Judge Mancuso: *Do you have any questions for me?*

Tina: *No, sir.*

Judge Mancuso: *Okay, Mr. Erickson. Please stand up and raise your right hand.*

The judge proceeded to ask Erickson the same round of questions, all of which he answered with "Yes" or "No."

Judge Mancuso: *Okay. And you both understand that this will be the final resolution to the proceedings of this particular estate?*

Tina: *I understand, yes.*

Mr. Erickson: *Yes.*

Judge Mancuso: *All right. Very well! Mr. Bradesco,*

do you know when the funds in consideration of this will be paid?

Mr. Bradesco: *Immediately, your honor. I'll tender the check.*

And with that, he handed the check to Mr. Melman.

Mr. Melman: *Thank you, Mr. Bradesco. All releases have been signed.*

Judge Mancuso: *Very well. The matter will be marked settled.*

As they left the courthouse, Tina turned to Mr. Melman. "Thank you, Mr. Melman. I will be in touch. I need to get copies of files from you. Now that I have some money, I'm going back to find my angels. I'm going to Baja Del Sol to find the man who saved me and the doctor who gave me the critical care needed to save my foot."

"That's wonderful, Tina. Let me know how it goes. I'm interested. I'm sorry this couldn't have ended differently."

"It's okay. It's over! I can work on my book and go on with my life. We really weren't given choices, and I wasn't interested in finding attorney number eight. Judge Mancuso wouldn't have changed his mind. It was his court and it seemed that he was handpicked by the Erickson law firm and the previous judges. He was definitely in charge. He may have seemed interested, but he didn't really care about me. He's probably someone's cousin, too!" Tina laughed. "It really is one big happy family up here at the Richfield Surrogate Courthouse," Tina replied. *What a scam*, she thought. *So this is justice? What would we do without justice?* Tina knew she was being sarcastic, but at that moment, she just couldn't help it. Once again, Tina had stood alone. Tina thought of the quote: "A good attorney knows the law. A great attorney knows the Judge." That is how this case had always been, ever since she crawled away from the broken wreckage on that hot November day.

No more thinking about what was. Now Tina could get on to what would be. There was relief in just knowing this chapter was finished and a new chapter could be written. Tina had other things to think about. She had to plan a trip to Baja Del Sol, Mexico.

"WE HAVE A CHOICE; TO PLOW NEW GROUND OR LET THE WEEDS GROW." JONATHAN WESTOVER

CHAPTER TWENTY-EIGHT
AUGUST 2004

Tina was back in New Mexico. Now it was time to make the plans to find her angels. Tina wanted to wait until after the rainy season in Mexico, when the weather would be less humid and the temperature somewhat cooler.

After the trial, Tina felt like a heavy burden had been lifted. For almost fourteen long years, Tina felt as if she had been on a roller coaster. It was a long ride with bumps and turns and never-ending hills, a ride in which she had no control. Even though the outcome wasn't what she expected or wanted, Tina knew she was now in control. Maybe now she could find some answers. Answers that could help reduce the guilt she felt as the sole survivor. Tina also was hoping, beyond hope, that the trip to Baja Del Sol, Mexico, in October, would clear up some questions that remained unanswered after all these years. The biggest piece of the puzzle would be to actually find the men who saved her. Tina felt that was like finding a needle in a haystack. She had already made inquiries and found the location and phone number of the doctor who had given her so much critical care when it was needed.

In May of this year, Tina retired from her eight years of volunteer work at Las Cruces High because the marketing teacher, Cece, was retiring and Tina knew it would not be the same working with another teacher. Tina felt comfortable knowing that there would always be a school store and she had helped make that possible.

Now, she would use her time and energy to find her

"angels." Tina really was excited to take a new path that was positive. On a stifling August morning, Tina was reading the Sunday paper and, as always, she glanced at the "States" section, which highlighted two or three newsworthy features about different states around the country. The Pennsylvania headline jumped off the page, and for a moment, Tina couldn't breathe.

"Small-plane crash kills 3 and injures 1," she read.

Erie—A small plane attempting to land Saturday night crashed about a half-mile short of the runway at Erie International Airport, killing three people and injuring a fourth, airport police said. The pilot had apparently wanted to stop to refuel in Jamestown, N.Y., but couldn't, the airport police chief said. Two men and a woman were dead at the scene, he said. Another woman was airlifted to Mamot Medical Center, where a spokesperson said her condition was still being evaluated.

Almost without thinking, Tina ran to her computer and looked up the address of the Mamot Medical Center in Prarie. Then she wrote a letter:

When the time is right, please give this letter to the lady who survived the plane crash, as it may be of some comfort and provide some strength to her.

On, October 14, 1990, I was the sole survivor of a plane crash in which 3 others died. For years, I asked, Why Me? For years, I felt guilty. For years, I felt I should have done something more. For years, I felt I should have helped the others. The truth is, I was just lucky. I couldn't have done anything. I was hurt myself.

The one thing that people said to me was that "your work is not done here on earth." I don't know that, but

I do know that every day is a gift. I know that no matter what your injuries are, you must get well. You have to live for the others. The doctors did not believe how fast I recovered from my injuries and the progress I made in a very short time. No matter what your injuries, you must do the therapy. Go to therapy every day instead of a few times a week. Work at getting well as you would at your job. For the time being, this is your only job. Don't give up. Homeopathic as well as conventional methods of therapy should be used.

I wish I could tell you that you will forget and that time will fade this nightmare, but you will not forget. Every time there is a plane accident or a news article about a crash, you will relive it again as if it were yesterday. But that is okay. You can live with that. You will be strong. You are a survivor. If you ever need to talk, you can always call me.

Tina listed her phone number and ended the letter by telling the woman that she was going to go back to Mexico to find the men who saved her and to the area where the accident had happened.

Writing about going back to Baja Del Sol made it real. Yes, she and Roger were actually going to do this! She mailed the letter to the editor of the *Prarie Times. Hopefully, the editor can get this letter to the hospital and to the right person*, Tina thought.

Tina remembered when she was recovering following the plane crash, she had hired her attorney Samsel Cisco who was fluent in Spanish, to fly to Mexico and bring back all of the articles, pictures, and information from any documents and newspapers he could find concerning the plane crash. He had also given Tina names of the people he had spoken to about the crash, and Tina had kept all the information.

After the settlement, Tina took out the files and circled the names in the articles of the people she wanted to meet.

Finding the doctor was the easiest. Tina and Roger knew a doctor who had a practice in Baja Del Sol and in Juarez, Mexico. They sent him the newspaper articles about the plane crash in July, and his assistant, Sunny, was able to find the attending doctor, Dr. Miguel Mendosa F. who still practiced medicine in Baja Réal, but not in the same remote clinic where Tina had met him. Dr. Miguel Mendosa was getting ready for his morning patients when the phone rang. It was Sunny, from his friend, Doctor G's office. Do you remember a plane crash, fourteen years ago?" Sunny asked. "The woman you treated would like to talk to you."

The doctor's mind flashed back to that November day when a petite American woman had been rushed into his clinic. He used CPR to try to revive her fiancé, but to no avail; he lay dead on the floor next to her. Dr. Mendosa worked quickly to clean the woman's foot and set her ankle. When she left that night to be transported back to the States, Dr. Mendosa wasn't sure if she would ever walk again, and if so, if she would always walk with a limp. He always wondered how she recovered.

"Dr. Mendosa?" Sunny questioned, breaking his thoughts.

"Yes, I'm here. And, yes, I would like to talk to the woman."

Sunny said she would give Tina the information so she could arrange a meeting. Tina had two angels she wanted to find. At least they had located the doctor. With that information, Tina and Roger booked their flights to Baja Del Sol to meet the Doctor and find the man that found her among the smoldering pieces of the wreckage and the tall, lush desert landscape.

OCTOBER 14, 2004

Tina couldn't sleep the night before they left for Baja Del Sol. Her mind raced with what might happen—and what might not.

We can't do anything about the past, so if we are healthy, we just go on. Hunter is always with me, she thought as the moon cast shadows in the dark room. *His picture is in the house and his memories are in my heart, but the physical man is no more. I am happy to have known him and to have had the love we shared. But life goes on like pages in a book, and we go on. One chapter ends and another begins.*

"DON'T BE AFRAID TO TAKE A BIG STEP. YOU CAN'T CROSS A CHASM IN TWO SMALL JUMPS." DAVID LLOYD GEORGE

CHAPTER TWENTY-NINE

On the plane the next day, Tina could barely contain her nervous energy as she fidgeted and moved in her seat every few minutes. She would pick up her book and try to read, and then put it down.

Roger turned to her and put his hand on her knee. "Calm down, honey. Everything is going to be all right." They had been on many planes since the plane crash almost fourteen years earlier, but Roger wondered if Tina was fearful of flying back to the same area?

"I'm so excited, I just can't sit still. We will find them Roger. I know we will," Tina said with determination and resolve. It was the same resolve that helped her recover after the crash.

"You have waited a long time for this," Roger said, "and we will be successful! I'm sure there is someone who will at least remember the newspaper articles and the crash."

Tina sat quietly through the rest of the ride, remembering the trip she made almost fourteen years ago. It had been a beautiful day and the trip was easy and without turbulence, except for the body language that Christina had displayed for only a minute. Now, Tina was making the same trip with Roger, who had stood by her and supported her through the merry-go-round of the courts, attorneys, and judges.

Tina started to think that today she was returning to an area where she had lost so much. By finding the angels that kept her alive, she would close one chapter in her life and open another. *This could be the beginning of new friendships*, Tina thought. *These men made a difference and without those* quick-thinking medical procedures and good hearts, I might not have had a second chance. *These men are my heroes.* What makes a hero? Tina contemplated:

A HERO is someone who chooses to do the right thing, the human thing, regardless of the possible consequences.

A HERO is someone who could loose his job or, worse yet, his life, but chooses to help another human being.

A HERO doesn't have a specific age or skin color.

A HERO is not from one particular race or religion.

A HERO has a Heart!

A Hero has a Soul.

A Hero has a conscience and with his heart and soul, he makes a decision to save a life.

These men, who I will find, are heroes, she smiled. Tina then turned her thoughts back to October 14, 1990, and the events of that day.

Why didn't I tell Hunter I was ready to spend my life with him? Why didn't I ask the stranger to place me next to Hunter when we were lying in the desert? Why didn't I call Christina back and question her when she told Hunter that Russell went to the airport earlier to check something out? Why didn't I just say, 'We are going to stay a few days longer in Baja Del Sol because we like it so much. Please go on without us.'

I guess the biggest "why" is why did the Ericksons want to fly in a plane that had a problem? Why didn't they have the plane checked out a few days earlier?

Why didn't they talk to each other in the plane when they knew it was going down?

Did they plan a suicide? That's enough, Tina told herself. *You have to put this out of your mind. You have to be positive. How many people get the chance to thank those who have come to their aid?*

Turning to Roger, Tina said, "You are my lucky charm.

I love you. You have supported me throughout this ordeal. Now you are taking me back to a past that did not involve you. Thank you, my dear, sweet man."

Roger put his arm around her and Tina laid her head on his shoulder. Roger closed his eyes and dozed for a while, but when Tina closed her eyes, all she continued to see was the past and the cabin of the Areostar. She remembered the radio asking for their location. She remembered how Hunter, concerned for her well being, had turned and asked if her seat belt was secure. As she stared into his eyes filled with concern, she said nothing, but only nodded, yes. Why didn't she tell him that she loved him? Why, why, why? This trip is bittersweet.

Tina said, "By coming back to Mexico, I am burying the past, but at the same time uncovering the past. Hunter has always been in my heart and in my mind, and today, I feel his presence beside me. I am so lucky to have had Hunter in my life. And I am blessed to have you, such a wonderful man, in my life to love."

Maybe Tina dozed off, too, because she suddenly was aware of the sound of the plane's landing gear lowering. She opened her eyes and looked out the window. *The mountains and vastness of the undeveloped land are still here*, she thought, as the plane quietly made its descent toward the airport. Tina felt calm, knowing that the shimmering Sea of Cortez would be waiting for her. She loved the sight of the sea, and it always took her breath away.

"We're here!" she said, squeezing Roger's hand as she kissed his cheek. "We're here!"

After they gathered their luggage and found a van, they drove to a cozy hotel across from the sea, where they would be staying.

Their room had Internet service, which Roger and Tina needed because they had an online business and they needed to be able to access their accounts and customers. As soon as they unpacked, Tina couldn't wait to leave the room. "Let's go down to the marina and see which hotels have Internet service so that we can be close to downtown." Tina wanted to be as close to where she had been with Hunter all those years ago. Tina felt that the heart and soul of Baja Del Sol was in the downtown area, with the spacious marina filled with large, interesting boats, grand yachts and small, surrounding shops that were filled with beautiful native ceramic figures, trinkets and paintings. The hotel they were in now was halfway between Baja Del Sol and Baja Réal. It was just in the middle, neither here nor there. When you were staying in the downtown area, Tina felt like she was part of the town and its people. Once they unpacked, they headed for the street and took a taxi. They asked to be let off near the marina.

When they got out of the taxi, Tina was astounded. "Roger," Tina said, "this is so different than it was fourteen years ago. There was only one hotel—at the most two—and now the marina is filled with buildings, hotels, stores, many restaurants, and, look, even a mall. What have they done with this sleepy little fishing village?" Tina looked around, with her mouth open and her eyes wide.

Roger broke into Tina's thoughts as he said, "Let's walk. It's really hot just standing here." They started walking away from the marina and toward the beach, where Tina remembered there had been many hotels. Walking along the beach was one of Tina's favorite things to do; it reminded her of her youth and where she spent her summers until she was twelve years old.

The older hotels did not have Internet service, but some time-shares and condos had Internet hookups. Tina knew that crucial to their business was the ability to communicate quickly with their customers, especially first-time buyers who didn't know what to expect.

Tina and Roger walked into the lobby of the Baja Villas Beach Resort, which was built by a Mexican family in Baja Del Sol. The family started with four large villas on a dirt road that had a view of the ocean. As the family's business grew, they added rooms and the hotel became a time-share resort, offering beautiful views and accommodations. The resort had been built in stages until it reached the beach. There were swimming pools and restaurants and a beautiful restaurant on the roof.

The young man at the reservation desk informed them that the hotel did in fact have an Internet office that was available to guests. In the next breath, however, he commented, "We do not have any rooms available tonight,"

"Oh," Tina said. "Do you know of another hotel in the area with Internet service?"

"Not in this immediate area. You might try the new resort, which is about ten miles south of town. I'm sure they do," the clerk said. Tina and Roger walked out of the hotel. The marina was just down the block and the bustling downtown was a stone's throw away.

"Well, this would have been perfect," Tina sighed, as they walked down the steps and headed back out to the street.

"Excuse me, do you need help?" asked a handsome man with a tanned, honey brown complexion and a dazzling, white smile. His hair was jet black and he had black, bushy eyebrows. His brown eyes, which sparked with warmth and interest, were what Tina noticed most.

"We wanted to stay at your hotel, but there isn't any room. We need to have Internet service so that we can access our website. This is the only hotel around here that has it and we wanted to be close to the marina and downtown," Tina said quickly.

"I can help you," the man answered. "My name is Carlos. I know someone who can get you a room." Tina and Roger followed him back into the hotel, while he spoke with the reservations clerk, who continued to search for any openings.

"I'm sorry," he finally said, glancing up at them. "I have nothing! A new group of time-share owners came in this morning, so there will be nothing available tomorrow either."

Tina and Roger followed the kind man back outside. When they were in the parking lot, he turned to them and said, "The morning clerk is my friend, so let me see what I can do. Give me your name and phone number and I will call you tomorrow at 8 a.m. and tell you what I have found." They thanked him and decided to stay another night at the hotel they were in because they needed Internet access.

The next morning, at precisely 8 a.m., the man, who introduced himself as Carlos, called.

"My friend said there would be a room available in a couple of days and you will have Internet access. Carlos said that the hotel across the street has a room for tonight. It's clean and has a very fine view of the sea but no Internet service."

Later that morning, Tina dug out the newspaper articles from October 14, 1990. "Roger, do you think we should take these articles to Carlos? Maybe he could help us," Tina said.

"It's a great place to start, and he speaks English." Roger agreed.

They ate breakfast and Tina and Roger gathered their luggage, caught a taxi, and headed to the La Vista Hotel. Their room had a breathtaking view and they were close to everything. Then they walked across the street. Carlos was in a covered booth, eager to sell time-shares.

"We thought maybe you could help us," Tina said, as she handed him the articles.

As he read, Carlos raised his bushy eyebrows and his brown eyes became as large as saucers as he stared at Tina. "This was you?" he asked softly.

"Yes, and I need to find this man," she said pointing to the article. "His nickname is Chi Chi."

After thinking a few minutes, Carlos said, "I have a friend and his family is from Floridas. He might be able to help. I will call you at nine o'clock tomorrow morning and tell you what I have found out," Carlos said. "Could I keep this article?"

"Yes," Tina said. "Just protect it for me."

Tina and Roger spent the day at the beach and shopped in town. They ate fabulous Mexican seafood at a restaurant overlooking the marina where small boats and large yachts were docked. Roger would be able to stay in Baja Del Sol only another three days because he couldn't leave the business for too long. Tina was glad she could spend some time alone with him; this had been their first vacation not visiting Roger's family or hers. Those trips were always fun, but not quite the same as having Roger all to herself.

All through dinner, Tina could not help but wonder what, if any, information Carlos would have for them.

At exactly nine the next morning, Carlos called, just as he had promised. "I think I have located this man who goes by the nickname Chi Chi, in Floridas. I have to go to the airport this morning, but I will be back by noon. Why don't you come by and talk to me?" he asked.

"We'll be there!" Tina answered.

At noon, Carlos was waiting for them and he was extremely excited. "The article mentioned Floridas. I have been told that there is a man there who goes by the nickname Chi Chi, just like the article said. We should go there and meet with him in person. I think I have the right location in Floridas. It is to the left on the far side of town and after you get to the statue of a women, you make a right turn as soon as possible. Tina and Roger made plans for their trip with Carlos to Floridas on Sunday. They didn't know if this was a wild goose chase or whether to believe that this was actually the man they were searching for.

Carlos was not only kind, but he was extremely generous. At no point did Carlos ask for money. He had the car, he was the driver, and he made the plans. Tina, Roger, and Carlos were excitedly looking forward to Sunday.

"By the way," Carlos said, "I have a room at Baja Villas for you. Someone had to leave early, so you can stay tonight if you like."

Roger agreed and he and Tina then went with Carlos to the reservations desk at the Beach Resort. "The room is $225 per night," the clerk said.

Tina felt her cheeks turning red. Never once had they asked about the price of the room; she had assumed it would be comparable to the price they were paying across the street. "I'm so sorry," she said, as she turned to Carlos and then back to the reservation lady. "I will be here another week after Monday, and this is just too much money to pay for one person."

"We offer a discount, so the room will only be $171.00."

"I am so sorry," Tina said again, as she shook her head and turned back to Carlos and gestured for them to leave. In a low voice, Tina said, "We just can't afford the extra cost."

As they left, Carlos said, "Don't worry," he said in a gentle soft voice, "I will see if I can make arrangements for you to use the Internet office.."

Tina couldn't believe their good fortune. Carlos spoke English, he was always on time, and he kept his promises. Never once did Carlos pressure them to go to a high-powered time-share breakfast or ask them to buy a time-share. Carlos was a very special man, and they were so lucky to have met him. Tina was finally going to meet her angels, and now Carlos was her third angel.

"HE IS NO FOOL WHO GIVES WHAT HE CANNOT KEEP TO GAIN WHAT HE CANNOT LOSE." JIM ELLIOT

CHAPTER THIRTY

Roger and Tina were so lucky to have met Carlos, who knew someone in the small town of Floridas who knew Jose Santos Spiros Flores, the man who had rescued Tina following the plane crash in the desert . This week was full of anticipation and Tina was extremely excited. *Will we actually find this man or not? How will I know for sure if this is the man? What questions should I ask him right away and what should I say?* Tina's mind raced with the possibilities. Although they had a free day, Tina had too much on her mind to really relax. She couldn't stop wondering about what tomorrow would bring.

The next day was cloudy and you could see rain clouds in the distance. Tina almost wondered where she was and what happened to that beautiful, blue sky? They met Carlos and after getting in the car, Roger suggested they fill up with gas. They drove with Carlos for more than an hour-and-a-half around curves, up and down hills, and through the countryside to the small town of Floridas, north of Baja Réal, where they were going to meet with Jose Santos Spiros Flores. They didn't have an exact address and after they had passed the statue of the women, they stopped and asked a stranger who pointed to a house just a little farther down and across the street. As they pulled into the family's driveway, Tina, Roger, and Carlos could see the family seated outside at a table having their noon meal. Carlos got out of his car as two men approached, and they started to speak. Carlos asked if one of the men was Jose Santos, explaining why they were there. "I am not the man you are looking for," the shorter of the two men told Carlos in Spanish. "He is my uncle. He still lives on the ranch, not too far from the gravel pit where he used to work. With the rain showers today, the washes will be flooded, but I will get a message to him tomorrow. I remember my uncle telling the story. He always wondered what happened to the little lady with the very badly damaged foot."

Carlos asked Roger to give Jose Santos's nephew $10 for gas money so he could send someone out to his uncle's ranch, which was across two washes and difficult to reach. Tina was beside herself having to wait even longer to meet one of her angels, but she knew in her heart it would be worth the wait.

The next day, Jose Santos called Carlos, and they set up an appointment for a few days later. After all this time, Jose Santos wondered what the American Lady wanted?

Roger had to leave for the airport the next day and, once again, Carlos wanted to help. He offered to take Roger. "Are you sure?" Roger asked. "It's at least an hour away. It is Monday and you have work. I don't want to be any trouble."

"It will not be a problem. On the way to the airport, I would like to show you something very special," Carlos said. Carlos drove Roger by the site where Dr. Miguel Mendosa's clinic once stood. He wanted to show him how that remote, tiny clinic had grown. Roger had never seen the small clinic, but, Tina had described it to him so he had a visual image based on her description. Now, Roger saw a beautiful, large, sprawling hospital.

They arrived at the airport in plenty of time. The men got out of the car and Roger turned to Carlos and gave him a hug. "This is for you, Carlos. Thank you for all you have done for us." Roger gave Carlos expense money for all he had done. Roger knew, however, that it would never be enough to repay the kindness Carlos had shown.

After Carlos returned to Baja Del Sol, the meeting with Jose Santos was planned for the next evening in the parking lot of the City Club, a warehouse super store, much like a Costco or Sam's Club. Tina was ecstatic. "Today my dream will come true," Tina said to herself on the morning of the meeting. "Will I actually find this man or not? How will I know for sure if he is my real hero? What questions should I ask him?" Tina's mind raced with the possibilities.

It started out like any other beautiful, warm, sunny day in Baja Del Sol. But today was special. "Today, I am going to meet one of my angels," Tina said aloud. "Today, I am going to meet Jose Santos Spiros Flores. Today, I am going to find out more about the plane crash that happened almost fourteen years ago to the day."

That evening, Carlos and Tina arrived first. As they sat in the parking lot waiting, Tina tried to stay calm, and she closed her eyes. *After all, I really don't know who I am meeting or if this man is really my angel*, she thought. A few minutes later, a dark green Ford Explorer pulled into the parking lot, and Carlos and Tina got out of the car and waved. The minute he opened the door and got out of the car, Tina knew he was "The Man," her angel. She didn't know whether to laugh or to cry. For that one moment, Tina was speechless.

He is even wearing the same type of cap with the stiff brim that he took off and put on my head that very hot day in the middle of the desert, Tina thought. He had brought his family with him. Carlos gave instructions to Jose Santos to follow Tina and Carlos to the restaurant where a table was waiting for them. It was the kind of restaurant that Tina called "inside outside" because it had a courtyard with a large, high wall, and the table was in the courtyard, but the setting was much like being in someone's patio home. Jose Santos had a grey mustache but his eyebrows and eyes were still dark. His eyes still had the kindness that Tina remembered, and he had the same ruddy complexion. Jose Santos brought his wife, his niece who spoke fluent English, and his daughter. Tina sat in the wonderment of the moment. Here was her angel.

Sitting around the table, eating dinner, Jose Santos recounted the part of the story of how he found Tina, and the pieces of the puzzle began to fall into place. "It was lunchtime, around 1 p.m., and I was eating, when I heard an explosion. I stepped away from the gazebo to take a look, but the other men and the machinery were working and everything seemed fine. The other workers couldn't hear the noise because they were working the noisy equipment in the gravel pit. I started eating again and then heard another explosion. This time I stepped out farther and did a 360-degree sweep with my eyes. Then I saw the billowing smoke and orange flames. The area on fire was in the direction of my home, Jose said, so I started to run to the site, which was in the far distance. As I got real close, I saw that there was a plane accident. I heard you calling to me in Spanish," Jose told Tina. "Then I saw you, and after you spoke and asked for water, I moved you under a tree and placed my cap on your head."

Jose took a sip of his water and then told us about how he found Hunter so close to the plane and when he tried to get him on his feet, Hunter took one step and he staggered and had to be helped back down. "I ran back to the gravel pit to get help," Jose said. You didn't speak to Hunter first? Tina interrupted. All these years, I thought you had found Hunter first and spoke to him. Funny how your mind can play tricks on you? Hunter called out to you when you left. I heard him. He said, Wait, don't go. Stay! Please stay. Jose Santos didn't go into too much more detail, and Tina asked him more about his family.

The dinner was lovely and getting to know this angel, Jose Santos, was a dream come true. After dinner,

Francesca, Jose Santos's wife, said in Spanish, "My husband would like to know if you want to go to the crash site."

"Yes, I would like to go. There are questions I would like answers to," Tina said. *Maybe I can find them there*, she thought.

"I will take you," Jose Santos said. Carlos and Jose Santos made plans for that weekend. Jose Santos and his family would stay at his sister in law's house. They would stay overnight in Baja Del Sol, and Sunday morning they would all meet once again at City Club, and they would all go to the crash site together. Tina couldn't believe her fortune. She was overwhelmed. This was a miracle.

On Sunday morning, Jose Santos brought his wife Francesca, their niece Lulu with her son Nexar and their daughter Irena who had been four years old when Jose Santos rescued Tina from the crash site. Now, at the age of 18, Irena was studying to be an architect and her older sister, who wasn't there, had graduated and was now an attorney. Tina could understand how such a lovely family came from such a compassionate man. Carlos and Tina followed everyone in the Jeep. On their way, Jose stopped near Baja Réal for breakfast, since he knew it would be hours before any of them would eat again. He also insisted on paying for breakfast. They continued driving for what seemed like another hour.

It was almost noon when they turned off of the paved road onto the dirt road belonging to the Common Property of the People of Mexico. The road had been graded so it was not bumpy, as it had been when Tina was riding in the ambulance all those years ago. This time during the ride, Tina could look out the window. Of course, they still were not near the area where the crash occurred, but they were not far from Jose Santos's home. The terrain was lush and sandy, much like it had been fourteen years earlier, and there were cows and steers grazing on the foliage. They continued driving and Tina was both excited and apprehensive. They were traveling on the same path that the ambulance took all those years ago. *Of course we're not traveling nearly as fast as the ambulance was traveling when it was taking Hunter and me to the clinic*, Tina thought.

The road ended, but they were able to keep driving over the dirt and then through a very wide, shallow wash that was wider than a football field and longer than the eye could see. It was filled with loosely packed sand, small rocks and stones and broken pieces of wood and trees. It was the end of the rainy season and the terrain was lush with green bushes, tall trees, and cacti. The desert broom was over three-feet high and the Jeep had to drive right over them. They finally stopped where the Brava Sura, the gravel pit business, had been. They would have to park there and walk the rest of the way, Jose Santos said.

Carlos rushed out of the car and was already taking pictures. Francisca, who had stayed in the city the night before, was not dressed for the hike so she opted to wait in the car,

Abandoned machinery sat rusted and broken. Small structures without windows or doors and some without roofs stood like skeletons that had been long dead and abandoned. The buildings were arranged in a cluster and Tina could visualize how it must have looked so many years ago: an office for the boss, a room for the men, and a gazebo for shelter, where Jose Santos had been eating his lunch on that fateful day.

From the Brava Sura, they walked on foot. They walked in the heat of the bright sun through washes and up and down steep, narrow areas. Parts of the path were clear but only fifteen-inches wide, and in other places the brush was thick and menacing. The terrain was hillier and rougher than Tina had remembered. *How did four men possibly carry me in a coat down the narrow gullies and up the steep, rocky hills?* she wondered. *And how did Jose Santos even find us with all of the trees and overgrown bushes?* Now she understood why her legs had been scraped and bumped by the brambles and shrubs. The men had been gentle and careful, but there was no way to avoid the thorny bushes on the rocky slopes.

As our little group continued to walk in the hot noon sun, Jose suddenly stopped and said to Carlos that we should all wait and they would be back shortly. It was a nice break sitting under the Palo Verde tree with its canopy of green leaves and shade. Irena said she was 4 and that her father had brought her out here about a month after the accident. Lulu, her cousin was our interpreter. It seemed like we waited almost a half hour and then the men appeared grinning and they said, "we found the site of the crash". We all started walking again and as we crested another hill, Tina stared at the site.

"This is where the plane came down," Jose Santos said. As they walked to the spot, Jose said, "Look, here is a piece from the plane. Now look way down there," he pointed. "That is where I found you, Tina. See that tree? That is where I carried you to get you out of the sun." He walked over and touched a tree. "See where this limb was torn off? It was broken when the plane hit." Jose Santos walked a little further. "Here are more pieces of the plane." Then everyone started looking for pieces of the plane, and in a short time, Carlos had made a pile of all the parts they had found. He took as many pictures as he could. Some pieces were broken but other parts were clean and almost like new.

Pieces of burned plastic were scattered about. *Maybe the windows,* Tina thought. They found fiberglass with blue and silver paint on it—the steel blue and silver of the beautiful plane. Tina remembered that day when they had arrived at the airport and all the planes were lined up. This plane had been the prettiest plane, but Tina now knew, it also had been the deadliest. *Here I am, holding a piece of that plane fourteen years later*, she thought, *holding a piece of my history, a piece of the day that I could not change and that changed the course of my life. And here I am, at the same time, 1:10 p.m., in the same place the plane went down, twice in a lifetime in the same place at the same time. How incredible! How surreal!* Tina thought.

Carlos's voice broke through Tina's thoughts. "Look what I found!" he said. He was holding the circuit board for the glidescope. The board was damaged, but the label on the side was as bright and shiny as the day the factory had installed it. It wasn't something that had been brought out here on a picnic, and it definitely wasn't the sort of thing that one would expect to find in the home of an average Mexican family. No, it was part of the twin engine Aerostar with the call letters #N7777Q. This is where the plane landed. This was truly where the plane fell apart. This is where the wings caught in the large trees and one was torn off the body of the plane during that fateful landing.

It was quiet in the desert, and this time there was no smell of fire or the urgency to get medical help. The desert had slowly grown over the swath of land that the plane had ripped clean of vegetation during its landing on the desert floor. "What a day," Tina whispered as they left the area and walked back to the car. The small group talked awhile, and then it was time to go.

After walking back to the cars, Francesca, Jose Santos's wife, invited them to have a drink with the family.

As they left, Tina stared at the dirt road that was flat enough and clear enough to land a plane, and then at the wide wash, with soft sand that would have been a safer place to land. The desert itself was full of cacti, trees and bushes—obstacles that could cause the plane to flip and catch fire. Tina knew the pilot had choices and still didn't know why he hadn't made it back to the airport, or at least chosen a better place to land. Tina recounted his choices in her mind: *Russell could have landed in a wash that was almost 100 feet wide. He could have landed on the dirt road that wasn't as wide, but was flat and devoid of foliage. He could have continued back to the airport, as we were very close Or he could shut down the engines and land in the thick, lush desert of the Southwest.*

The decision and choice he had made led to the death of his wife; himself; and Hunter, Tina's intended husband. Maybe he panicked when he realized this accident was his fault because he had time to have the plane checked out properly, but didn't. Russell and Christina knew something was wrong, but didn't take any action to correct it.

"Here I was, standing with the parts of the plane, the memories of the past, the angel who found me and the angel Carlos, who found Jose Santos so that I could fulfill my dream and close a chapter in my book," Tina said to herself.

Tina was quiet as she thought about the adventure. It seemed like a short time and then they were at the home of Jose Santos and Francisca. Their ranch-style home was isolated and not more than half an hour from the Brava Sura. Sitting in the peace of their backyard, they enjoyed cool iced tea and cake. Francesca once again said, "Jose wants to see you again, and his birthday is on Wednesday."

Tina looked at Carlos and said, "Let's have a party! Cake and dessert in Baja Del Sol, and bring your daughters!"

On their way back to La Vista Hotel, Carlos drove by the sprawling, modern hospital that Dr. Miguel Mendosa had helped build from the ground up and where he was now Director of Medicine. Tina was looking forward to meeting this special man, who had come so far in the medical profession and had done great things for his people. The next evening, she would meet with the good doctor and his wife. "It's too bad that we weren't able to meet with Dr. Mendosa while Roger was still in town. I really wish Roger could meet him, too," Tina said to Carlos.

The next evening, Tina eagerly awaited the couple's arrival outside the La Vista Hotel. She couldn't help but remember how kind and gentle he had been as he tried to soothe her broken body that day so many years ago. When the doctor and his wife drove up to the hotel, there was a parking space in front. Tina watched as they exited the car. The doctor was about 5' 9" tall, small boned, and lean. His hair was dark and sprinkled with gray. His brown inquisitive eyes had a twinkle in them. After all these years, Tina could not say that she remembered him. He was the doctor in the articles who, with his quick thinking, protected Tina, and she knew her life would have been much different were it not for his care. If he hadn't attended to her foot immediately, she most probably would have needed a prosthesis and may not have been able to fully enjoy golf, tennis, and country dancing again.

When Tina saw the doctor, he put his arms around her and gave her a big hug. He introduced her to his wife, Inez. They went across the street and down the block to the Baja Villa Beach Resort, where they climbed the stairs to the rooftop restaurant. The setting was more beautiful than a postcard, as the Sea of Cortez glowed from the setting sun, holding the cruise ships safe like precious jewels. From their perch in the restaurant, they could also view the beach and the town weaving its way along the coastline. The water was calm, and as the full moon came up, rays of light glistened and sparkled on the water.

It was magical, yet so real. Tina and her angel were

sitting face to face after all this time. They talked about the past and what the doctor did that day. He spoke English, he was skilled in critical care, and he had 23 years of experience. He helped give Tina back to her mother and sons, and there simply was not enough thanks to give to this incredible man.

As they talked about their lives and their families, there was yet another good side to this tragedy. Dr. Miguel Mendosa and Inez's five children all were smart and successful. One was an architect, one a doctor, one a housewife, one still in school, and Jose Rafael who was still making a name for himself. Both Dr. Miguel Mendosa and his wife beamed with pride when they talked about their children. The night ended almost before it began, and Tina knew she wanted to see them again.

"We're having a birthday party later in the week here in town for Jose Santos, the man who found me in the desert. I would be honored if you could both come," Tina said.

The doctor thought about his schedule for a moment and then shook his head. "I'm sorry, Tina, but I have to attend a medical conference this week. I wish we could be there, but please visit us again."

Tina bid this special couple farewell, but knew she would return to Baja Del Sol and see them again. Today was the day Tina had a chance to walk in the footsteps of the past. How many people get that chance?

That night, in Tina's journal, she wrote, *"Everyone of us has a good story to tell, but how many of us know the ending? And how many endings are new beginnings? How many times do we end one chapter in our lives, only to open another? Returning to an area, where in minutes, everything around me was taken away and then, miraculously finding all the angels that helped keep me alive, only brought another new beginning. A beginning of friendship with the kind strangers that would not let me die."*

"LIFE IS A BOOK AND YOU ARE THE AUTHOR.
YOU DETERMINE ITS PLOT AND PACE AND YOU—ONLY YOU—
TURN ITS PAGES." BETH MENDE CONNY

CHAPTER THIRTY-ONE

Jose Santos's birthday party was another highlight of the trip. He brought his wife, two daughters, and future son-in-law. The pool area at the La Vista Hotel, with the Mexican décor and mariachis, provided a festive atmosphere. There were only a few other people there, so it was as if they had the space to themselves. Carlos had helped Tina buy the goodies and cake earlier in the evening, and they had decided on a Winnie the Pooh theme with hats and tablecloths. Everyone got into the party mood quickly, and Carlos took pictures. It was like being with family.

Everyone put on their party hats and ate an amazing Mexican meal. For dessert, they had a big, chocolate birthday cake and Mexican favorites, such as flan and caramel cake with milk. There is no birthday party without a piñata. They had bought a cowboy piñata. A piñata can wear an assortment of faces and characters, like Superman, Mickey Mouse, a Princess, assorted animals, such as horses, pigs, dogs or lions. Some piñatas are three or four feet high. They are hollow inside and that is where candy and goodies are stored. After everyone is lined up, the first person gets a big stick or bat and tries to hit the piñata. However, they are blindfolded and someone else has a string tied to the piñata and pulls it up and down so it is not easy to hit. We let Jose Santos bang away, until he finally broke the piñata, and everyone scrambled to pick up the candy on the floor.

Everyone had such a good time, and Tina felt truly blessed. She knew she had to leave soon, and she could hardly believe how close she felt to these people after just knowing them for a few days. She would be sad to go, but Tina knew she would be back, because Jose Santos had promised to invite her and Roger to the wedding of his daughter Rhonda to Ramon the following year.

When Tina arrived back in Las Cruces, she couldn't stop talking. She had to tell Roger about every detail and about the exceptional people he hadn't been able to meet. Finally he said "Tina, you have had an amazing journey, but you have to be exhausted. Get some sleep and we can talk more tomorrow."

Tina slept for a while, but she awoke at 1 a.m., her mind racing with everything that had happened. She couldn't sleep, so she wrote in her journal:

OCTOBER 22, 2004
AFTER THE JOURNEY HOME

I'm home now. In some ways it is like two different worlds, and in some ways it is like awakening in one's dream. You can still visualize all that you saw. You know it is real because you can touch the people and visit the places you had visited 14 years before. Even though I am back home now, I can feel all the emotions around me.

Looking back, this was really an unbelievable journey. To be able to find just the right person who was living in a really remote area beyond Floridas is just incredible.

Everything that happened was so amazing and special. Best of all, I met the most exceptional human beings. They are all wonderful, kind, and genuine people. It is such a pleasure to know them.

Tina shut her journal and then made a list. She would send a digital camera and printer to Carlos with a note of thanks. She would send each of Dr. Mendosa's daughters jewelry specially made for each of them and send a Palm Pilot to their son. Then Tina had another idea: she would set up a scholarship fund for students in the field of medicine, in Dr. Mendosa's name. "Yes," Tina said aloud, "this will be better." On Monday, she would also contact Ramon Garcia Harachi Casta, Rhonda Mandez's fiancé who was an attorney, so she could continue to send the money she promised Jose Santos. The to-do list was long, but Tina couldn't wait to get started. Finding her angels had been like finding a needle in a haystack, and luck and fate had stepped in along the way.

Tina felt it was almost like someone above was guiding them and making good things happen. It was certainly a welcome change from the past fourteen years. There was peace, joy, respect, and love in Tina's heart when she thought about her angels.

*"When someone shares something of value with you,
and you benefit by it, you have a moral obligation to
share it with others."* Chinese Proverb

CHAPTER THIRTY-TWO
Baja Del Sol Revisited:
December 7—December 12, 2005
December 7

Tina and Roger were once again flying to Baja Del Sol, Mexico. It was just over a year since she had found her angels. Her adrenaline was racing and Tina realized that she felt almost more excited this time, not because she was anxious, but because she was looking forward to seeing the families she had treasured in her heart for the last year. Tina knew she and Roger would learn more about the men and their families and be able to talk and spend more time together. This time, all that had been unknown and mysterious a year ago was now clear. They had their friend and ever-ready traveler, Carlos, to thank for that. He had almost single-handedly helped Tina find all the pieces of the puzzle that, for fourteen years, had been scattered over many miles in this part of Mexico. He had helped Tina pick up the pieces and put them in their rightful place. The resulting picture—the completed puzzle—was a sight to behold: Tina, Roger, her angels, and their families. Lives that had been entwined by a tragic day were now being reunited, and that, to Tina, was a miracle. These men and their families were a gift that Tina could not place a price tag on, and all the trials and tribulations in the American court system weren't nearly as important as these people who had helped her regain her life. In just two days, they would be going to a wedding, and the joy and celebration of this trip was overwhelming.

After they settled in, Tina and Roger called their friends to set up the schedule for the next four days. The biggest disappointment was that their hotel, with the beautiful view of the sea just a year ago, was now blocked by a larger hotel that had been built in front of it. The tourist ships, with their huge hulls and multi-storied decks, stood like sentinels in the Sea of Cortez. The *Holland American Line* loomed largest of all, but Tina and Roger could no longer see the ships from their balcony.

DECEMBER 8

Friday was their day to relax and enjoy. That evening, they met with Dr. Miguel Mendosa and his charming wife Inez. They went up to their perch high in the sky of the Baja Villas Beach Resort. The outdoor restaurant still overlooked a spectacular view of the coastline, the outline of the large hotels, and the lights of the growing city. They spoke about many things. Tina wanted to hear from Dr. Mendosa about his experience in the small clinic in Baja Réal. The doctor explained that he had been a general surgeon from 1970-1990 prior to October 14. He had trained in the emergency room of the old General Hospital in La Rosa. His specialties were varied and many, in addition to his training in critical care medicine. At the time, he had twenty-three years experience and was the perfect doctor for Tina.

He could remain calm while assessing difficult and complicated situations. With all of his talent and excellent training, he was the attending physician in this remote clinic on that day. He had been offered the post of interim medical director because of problems in Baja Réal. They needed a surgeon trained in anesthesiology, obstetrical and caesarean surgery and epidural anesthesia.

Dr. Miguel Mendosa possessed the necessary skills and experience.

"I was really lucky to have you there," Tina said. "And on top of your excellent care, you spoke English!"

Tina then talked about the wedding that would take place the following day, and Dr. Miguel said he planned to attend the ceremony and that he knew the bride's parents. Roger and Tina said good-bye as they made plans to meet the next day.

DECEMBER 9—THE WEDDING DAY

Lulu, Jose Santos's niece, and her husband, along with their two children, picked Tina and Roger up at their hotel, and they all arrived at the church at 5:30 p.m. The church was spectacular. Tina was surprised that such a beautiful and state-of-the art, modern Catholic Church had been built in this small town of ancient architecture and tradition. Impressively, the citizens had saved for the construction of this church, and it had taken six years to build, with the priest working closely with the architect. The contemporary glass and stone provided contrast to the light-colored wood used in the church's construction, and a sculpture high above the priest provided imagery of birds of peace circling overhead.

The design of the white cross complemented the architectural style of this breathtakingly, beautiful church, and behind the cross was a metal sculpture that formed an arc, which accented the contemporary beauty of the church. The warm, welcoming church was light and airy with very high ceilings. Tina and Roger felt as if they were in God's house. This house of worship was named Casa De Cristo. Tina thanked God for being alive and in this paradise.

When the beautiful wedding ceremony was over, Tina turned toward the back of the church and, true to his word, there was Dr. Miguel and his wife Inez. Roger and Tina went to greet the doctor and his wife, and Dr. Miguel explained that he did indeed know the family. They all went to congratulate the newly married couple and their parents, and Dr. Miguel Mendosa spoke directly to the bride, saying, "I delivered you and your sister."

Immediately Rhonda's mother, Francesca smiled and said, "Yes, I remember you!" Everyone smiled and hugged each other.

This is truly amazing, Tina thought. *Wonders never cease. My angels are connected to each other, and they were brought together by this hand of fate from the fatal crash so long ago.*

The wedding reception was held in a large hall that had been decorated for the occasion. The atmosphere was festive, and a band of lively musicians played continuous music, adding to the celebration. The bride was very beautiful. Her hair was worn up with soft wisps of curled hair dropping down the sides of her face. Her elegant dress was white satin adorned with tiny pearls woven into the fabric. The groom was dressed in formal attire. The bride and groom were a handsome couple.

Jose Santos had told his friends about Tina and Roger, and everyone treated them warmly and as friends. They sat at the main table along with the beautiful bride, groom, parents, and grandparents. It was really very special. The table with the wonderfully prepared Mexican dishes and the large assortment of food was truly a banquet. Following the wedding feast, the dancing resumed. The ceiling of the building opened up revealing the heavens. Tina and Roger, the wedding party, parents, grandparents, guests, and children danced and visited all night under a magical, starry sky. The celebration continued until 2 a.m. the next morning.

Tina wanted to contribute to the wedding and add to its uniqueness, so she brought a box of 100 lighted braids for the children. The younger children got in line to pick up the braids.

The little girls put them in their hair, and the boys clipped them around their wrists and made bracelets, while others attached them to their shirts and ties. The children were enjoying the sparkling braids, and the older children and young adults also stuck the sparkling lights in their hair or wore them as jewelry. Even some of the older women put the braids in their hair. Tina was happy that she could in some way bring joy to everyone there.

DECEMBER 10—THE FIESTA

The next day, Tina rushed to get ready, because Dr. Miguel's daughter was coming to pick them up. At 11:30 a.m., Marisol, her husband, and their two children arrived, and they drove to Baja Réal to spend the afternoon with Dr. Miguel Mendosa, his wife, and family members. Their home sat high on the hillside and overlooked the blue shoreline and Sea of Cortez. The multiple patios were filled with flowers in an array of reds, pinks, and oranges. Green houseplants overflowed their colorful Mexican pots. Everyone ate the delicious homemade meal and enjoyed this cozy environment, with children running and playing as they talked. The time passed very quickly, with Dr. Miguel proudly speaking about his family. Two of the doctor's daughters, Marisol and Inez, joined the luncheon, and Tina and Karen, the two other daughters, were spending time together in La Rosa. The "children," now successful adults, were creating their own bright futures. It was a wonderful afternoon, and Tina and Roger felt like part of the family. It was a day to remember.

DECEMBER 11, 12, AND 13

Tina and Roger had to find Carlos. They didn't know if he was in Baja Del Sol again, because they had lost track of him when he moved his family back to Puerto Vallarta. Carlos had moved two or three times in the past few years. Luckily for them, Carlos's uncle had a small shop near the La Vista Hotel and his uncle was able to help them. He told Tina and Roger that Carlos was living full time in Baja Del Sol and was working for the Hacienda Del Sol Resort in the Sales Department. Tina was so excited that she forgot to ask for Carlos's cell phone number as she took Roger's hand and steered him out of the shop and into the street. Tina and Roger tried for the next two days to call his office, but they were unable to reach him,

Tina had to find Carlos today since they were leaving in a few days, so she decided to go to the resort. "I have to find Carlos," Tina said to Roger. "Let's go look for him because this day is ours."

Tina did not know if he would be at the resort, but at that point in time, it seemed to be her only hope, and she had to try. She wanted to know if he was doing well and that he was happy. Tina knew his job should be going well, since Carlos was hardworking, bilingual, intelligent, and charismatic.

Tina and Roger walked to the bus stop at the shopping center because Tina enjoyed mingling among the people wherever she traveled. In addition, being from New York, she knew that public transportation was the best way to get around in a city. As Tina and Roger stood on line with the twenty or more people waiting to get on the bus for Baja Réal that hot, sunny day, Tina's mind was racing with happy thoughts. To Tina, it wasn't if she would find Carlos but when. Once again, fate stepped in to help. Tina approached a petite young lady with shiny, long hair and asked her if this was where to catch the bus that would take them to the

Hacienda Del Sol Resort. As luck would have it, Tina had picked the one person out of the crowd who was going to the hotel. They introduced themselves and when the already full bus arrived, twenty or more people began to step on to the bus. Tina couldn't imagine how they all would fit, but they did. Some people went to the back of the bus and others stuffed themselves into the front section. Sylvia, Tina's new friend, stood by the open door and signaled for Roger and Tina to get on before her. *The kindness and generosity the Mexican people expressed to foreigners in this little town was amazing,* Tina thought.

The bus ride was just over twenty-five minutes. As the bus stopped to pick up more and more people, Tina would not have thought that the bus could hold that many people. And just as she thought that, four more people piled in. Tina sat in utter amazement. In New York, a bus driver wouldn't stop at the next stop if the bus was full and no one was getting off. Here in Mexico, the drivers tried to accommodate everyone.

The front door of the bus was left open as the driver maneuvered down the street, and the last man who boarded the bus looked as if he might fall out at any minute. He seemed unperturbed by this and had wedged himself in the doorway, holding on, as if he was accustomed to traveling this way.

Sylvia told us that they would be getting off at the next stop. We walked from the highway on to a private road, which joined three separate hotels and condos and led to the sea. The day was bright and sunny, with a clear blue sky and a slight breeze, making the day picture perfect. They walked at a quick pace, single file, down the narrow path a half mile to the security guard house. Once again luck was with Tina because Sylvia, who spoke both Spanish and English, was with them and helped translate for the security guard, who did not speak English.

It took about twenty minutes, but they finally confirmed that Carlos Fernandez Ramirez was an employee of the hotel and was working in the Sales Department of the Time Share Villas. Sylvia smiled at Roger and Tina, as she could understand Tina's excitement about finding her friend who, they had been told, worked there. Before they said good-bye, Tina wanted to show her appreciation to Sylvia for all of her help; she slipped off her multicolored pearl bracelet and gave it to Sylvia as a token of her gratitude.

They proceeded walking toward the hotel, and Sylvia eventually bid her good-byes and went her separate way. Tina and Roger continued to the sales office, which they wouldn't have found without the help of one of the hotel employees who personally escorted them to the office. The receptionist, who sat at a table outside and in front of the sales office, listened to their request. She explained that Carlos was not working that day. Tina asked for a phone number for Carlos. The receptionist offered to call him, since she was not permitted to give out phone numbers of employees. Carlos's cell phone was busy and she said she would try again.

While she waited, Tina took her journal out of her bag and wrote the following entry:

Window of Opportunity - Seize the Moment
  In life you cannot wait for the moment. You must make it. In life you cannot give up before you even try. You can't say what is the use or think negative thoughts. There is no way, so why try, or, it won't work, so why bother? I always believed that if I try, I can succeed. If I want to find Carlos, I will! Think Positive!

It was as if writing in her journal strengthened Tina's resolve, and now she could taste success. She could feel the future. When the receptionist called again, Carlos answered and she explained that there was an American lady and man looking for him by the names of Tina and Roger. After she handed the phone to Tina, Carlos immediately said, "Stay there and I will come and get you."

"Carlos is like a cowboy on a horse, except instead of a horse, he rides in a red Jeep Cherokee. And at a moment's notice, he will get in that car and drive anywhere," Tina said to Roger.

About half an hour later, Carlos appeared. The hours of calling and mailing and trying to locate him were over. Carlos, with his dark shiny hair, bushy eyebrows, suntanned skin, and sparkling brown eyes, was standing in front of them. He had not changed a bit since the last time they had seen him. He smiled warmly at Tina and Roger; he was kind, generous, always happy, always ready to help, and always ready to travel.

The first thing Carlos did after hugging Tina and Roger was to excuse himself and return with T-shirts from the fancy new resort where he worked. After he gave them the T-shirts, Carlos excitedly said, "I want you to meet my family."

Off they went. "Just a minute," Tina said, "I have to stop and get some gifts for your children and wife. We didn't fill our suitcases with gifts from home because I did not know if I would find you here in Baja Del Sol." As they drove into town, they went back to the large City Club, which Tina had visited the year before. Tina and Roger picked out gifts for the family. For the girls, ages 14 and 11, Tina bought clothing. And for little Martin, they bought small cars that rocketed through the air, a perfect gift for this shy, quiet five-year-old.

When Tina asked Carlos what his wife wanted for their new home, Roger asked if she liked pots and pans?

Carlos said, "Yes." Roger chose a large box containing an assortment of pots, pans, and kitchen gadgets.

Tina later told Adelina, Carlos's wife, "I would not like a gift like that. I do not like to cook, and kitchen trinkets would not be a gift. That would mean work." They laughed, talked, and played dominoes. Tina and Roger thoroughly enjoyed themselves with Carlos and his family. After sharing a delicious meal and wonderful conversation, it was time to return to the hotel.

The next evening, Tina and Roger were planning to host a mini-fiesta for Tina's angels. They were going to use the pool area of the same small hotel they had used the year before. This time they would have dinner and, of course, a dessert selected by Carlos. Tina picked out flan, the rich Mexican custard, but Carlos picked out a big gooey chocolate cake that would turn out to be a great hit at the party.

*"I SHALL GROW OLD BUT NEVER LOSE LIFE'S ZEST, BECAUSE
THE ROAD'S LAST TURN WILL BE THE BEST." HENRY VAN DYKE*

CHAPTER THIRTY-THREE

Tonight was Tina's time to have all her angels together. This was to be a reunion of a past experience that was stricken and saddened by death on a day that had been picture perfect and a vacation that, until the crash, had been equally perfect. *Never forget the dead for they are our strength. They give us the examples and backbone to carry on and succeed,* Tina said silently.

Tina thanked her angels for coming to the party, and they all toasted, laughed, and reminisced. "Today, I once again have my Jose Santos, my first angel. He found us and then walked through that terrain of cactus, large trees, and desert brush overgrown from the summer rains to get us the help we needed. He picked me up and placed me under a tree and gave me his hat to shield my face and head from the hot, sunny day. He ran back to his place of work, drove his truck back to town, alerted the police, and then led a team of men, including the medic and others, back to the field of devastation left by the plane as it laid engulfed in flames across the desert floor.

Tina continued, "And with us at this party is Carlos, who kept his promise and met the challenge. He and he alone found Jose Santos. Somehow, I made the right choice and found the right man to help fit the pieces of the puzzle together.

At this table is Dr. Miguel Mendosa, who is one of the reasons I have my foot today. He took this broken, mangled, and bloody foot and scrubbed it to remove the dirt and germs because he knew that infection would lesson the chances of saving my foot. He then protected my leg and foot by putting it into a cast so it would be kept clean on the journey back to the States. He knew a team of doctors could perform surgery and save the foot. Under the circumstances, my foot works pretty well.

Tina smiled and raised her glass and said, "My heartfelt thanks to my three angels and their wonderful families! Cheers!" Since the night was cool, the party took place inside the hotel, in the bar area. It was comfortable and they conversed freely. Dinner was served and a good evening was had by all.

The next evening, Tina and her angels had a chance to talk. Tina asked Jose Santos more questions about the rescue party. Tina mentioned the stretcher that the rescue party had used to carry Hunter to the ambulance. Jose Santos immediately said "no" and explained to her, with Carlos interpreting, that they didn't have a stretcher.

Tina said, "I saw Hunter on a stretcher."

"No," said Jose Santos. "That was the broken wing of the airplane."

"What?" asked Tina in amazement?

"Yes, we ran back near the burnt-out plane and retrieved the broken wing," said Jose Santos. Tina knew there hadn't been a stretcher for her, but she had always thought Hunter was carried on a stretcher

"Necessity is the mother of invention" certainly were words that held true in this case. How creative those men had been!

When Jose Santos returned to the Gravel Pit and told his boss at the Brava Sura that he needed employees and equipment to get the wounded people he had found in the desert, his boss yelled, "Stay put, do not go! Nobody is leaving here. They could be a bunch of drug dealers."

Jose had done what he knew in his heart he had to do for

the human beings in need. He left his job site and jeopardized his job and his family's security to rescue complete strangers. If Jose Santos had heeded his boss's words, Tina and Hunter would have been in the desert much longer and things could have turned out much differently. Tina remembered a quote by Romain Rolland, "A hero is one that does what he can. The others don't." Yes, Jose Santos is a true hero.

Jose Santos was Tina's eyes and ears the day of the crash because he continued to explain things that had nagged at her and she had never been able to understand. *How could everything go so deadly wrong when life had been so wonderful and right? Can I finally put the guilt behind me?* Tina wondered.

Tina finally realized why the small planes she heard in the sky that day couldn't find them. When Russell had not answered the tower, the tower used his last coordinates to look for the plane. That was sixty miles farther north. Jose Santos told Tina that the attendant gave Hunter a shot for pain. This medicine may have made him more comfortable, but also may have slowed his heart rate. In Tina's mind, he seemed to be so alert before the ambulance team came to the area. Hunter answered all their questions but, according to Jose Santos, Hunter was in a dazed state. Maybe that was the wrong medication for the situation? Tina didn't blame anyone. The situation had been an emergency, and the men at the scene had to make split-second decisions.

Jose continued his story: about a week after the crash, the FAA came to the crash site. Jose Santos wasn't at work that day because his wife was sick and he had taken her to the hospital in La Rosa. The foreman of the Brava Sura told the investigators that they would grade a road to the crash site for a price. As long as the foreman was paid well, he was at their service. They graded a section of the desert from the Gravel Pit to the crash site for all the investigators in their vehicles to get to the site. When Jose Santos returned in the afternoon, he was speechless. He couldn't confront the foreman because he didn't want to jeopardize his job, but his boss was accommodating now, when on that day fatal day he had told Jose Santos not to go back to the crash site.

Tina learned that in emergencies and difficult times, there are two kinds of individuals: those who seize the moment and do the right thing and those who seize the moment to take advantage of those in need. Heroes are ordinary people, but when they are needed, they find inner strength and do the right thing. Heroes seem to be goal oriented, to stay focused on the problem at hand, and to come out ahead.

During the evening, Tina and Roger learned about Jose Santos's background. He and his wife had sacrificed a lot when their children were growing up, but they knew that education was paramount and their children would have opportunities they themselves never had. From middle school through high school, the children lived away from home. They went to a boarding school in Floridas for middle school and then lived with their aunt and uncle to attend high school in Baja Del Sol. Jose Santos and Francesca visited them on weekends. Even though it was hard, they knew their children would get a better education, and they could still make sure their values would be handed down to them. With a good education, Jose Santos and Francesca felt their children could grow up to be successful, responsible adults.

Jose Santos smiled and chuckled when he spoke about his wife. "My wife got married to me, I didn't marry her," he said of their wedding day on October 29, 1983. He told Tina that he loved her more now than ever. "Francesca is the love of my life. She is my helpmate and sometimes my voice. She understands me and always knows what I am thinking. We are soul mates."

Carlos told Tina about his life. His parents had divorced

when he was five-years old. He lived with his father in Mexico and visited his mother, who had become an American citizen, on holidays in California. Both of his parents remarried and he eventually had twelve siblings. On holidays, they would all get together at his mother's home. They all loved each other and got along very well. Carlos was right in the middle of all of the children. He learned to speak English in California and went to a teacher's college in Mexico. For his internship, he was sent to an area of southern Mexico that was a two-and-a-half-day drive from where he grew up. In his class, he taught fifty children, who spoke in a Mexican-Indian dialect, to speak English and Spanish. He believed that if he taught the children that they, in turn, would teach their parents, and that is exactly what happened. He worked there for eight months and then got another job on the coast of the Pacific Ocean. The classrooms were smaller and he was closer to an area he loved, as well as closer to his family. He worked there for nine years. After ten years of teaching, Carlos moved to the United States and then worked for Empire Beach, which was between Empire City, California, and Tijuana, Mexico, where he worked in the landscaping business for six years.

When Carlos got homesick, he moved to Puerto Vallarta, where one of his brothers lived. Carlos got a job in time-share marketing at one of the new resorts right away, since he was bilingual. He loved meeting people and changing lifestyles, so this job was a perfect fit. More importantly, people loved him, because he was honest, helpful, trustworthy, and sincere.

For lunch one day, Carlos stopped at a local taco stand, run by Adelina. One look and he could not take his eyes off this beautiful, gentle, intelligent woman. Carlos was 40 years old at the time, and Adelina was 32. She had three very young children and was going through a long, drawn-out divorce. Carlos, who never ate tacos, began eating at

Adelina's taco stand as often as he could. When they fell in love, they knew they would have to be patient and wait to be together.

Tina had learned that emergencies bring out two kinds of men: good and evil. Her angels were very, very good. Carlos had said, "When you find something good for your life, you can change everything because you have a good reason to live and enjoy your life. You see everything more clearly and vividly when you have good feelings and a reason to live." Carlos continued, "If I do good things for others, someone will do something for my children. Good deeds are like a boomerang and if you do good things, you will get good things, but if you do bad things, then bad things happen. You need the feelings behind the facts. The eyes are the window to the soul. If you look into a person's eyes and see no emotions—anger or joy—that is not a good thing."

Tina couldn't agree more and she knew that her angels were definitely some of the finest men anywhere. "My angel, Dr. Miguel Mendosa, was the right doctor for my circumstances on that fateful day. I have always believed that luck and fate play an important role in whether one lives or dies," Tina said.

Tina said she asked Dr. Mendosa what made him want to become a doctor, and he explained it this way:

"I was a quiet, friendly boy who had always shown leadership and organizational traits. As a young boy, I was shy but highly regarded by my peers." With his teacher, Miguel organized a club for children called the "Club Cadets." It was similar to the Boy Scouts, and they went hiking and did community service. Dr. Mendosa said, "I was just an average boy who liked singing, guitar, soccer, football, music, and painting. However, I was a dreamer. I wanted to become 'somebody.'

"In high school, I read a book called *Casadores Microbe.*

It was about important men, and I was so inspired by these men that my dream developed to become a doctor. This is where I was different from most boys my age, and I took a different path. I took correspondence courses and started studying to become a doctor. My grandmother was the official military photographer in Baja California South and later opened the first photography studio in the same area. She was well known and lived in La Rosa near me and my family. My great grandfather was a pioneer in commercial shipping, sailing and diving. My father was in the military and later a small trader. He did not have the notoriety or wealth of his parents, but his father made a living and they were comfortable."

On October 14, 1990, Dr. Miguel had been married twenty-three years to the same good woman, and they had five children: four girls and a boy. He was fifty-one years old and made sure his children went to schools in Guadalajara; Washington Tri Cities; La Rosa; Tijuana; and Long Beach and San Diego, California. His career in the medical field had spanned forty years. Dr. Miguel, as Tina affectionately called him, commented that he loves his work and wants to continue as long as possible. This brought to mind a quote by Baltasar Gracian, "Great ability develops and reveals itself increasingly with every new assignment". It was easy for Tina to see that Dr. Miguel loved new assignments and new challenges.

Tina's angel held many medical posts and continued to serve the public. He went from serving in a small, remote clinic to serving as the head of a large, beautiful hospital. He was also Surgeon General of the region where he practiced for thirty years.

This evening, Tina learned so much more about her angels, and then it was time to say good-bye. There would be next year, and Tina knew they would all be together again.

Time was up and Tina and Roger would be leaving Baja Del Sol in two days, but before they left, Roger suggested they buy a time-share. Tina was reluctant to buy a time-share, especially in a foreign country. The two stood close, holding hands, and looking out over the beautiful Sea of Cortez, with the shimmering light of the moon lighting the water. Tina felt like reaching out and never letting go of this magical, beautiful city with the blue water and endless beaches. It was the end of a special, but bittersweet trip. As if reading her thoughts, Roger held Tina in his arms and kissed her. "Look at it this way. If we buy a time-share, we will always have a home here, so we can come back and visit your angels and their families every year." That's all it took; Tina agreed.

Tina still couldn't believe how odd and coincidental it was that these three men were tied together with the configuration of their names. Jose Santos, who found her in the desert, had two children that were both delivered by Dr. Miguel Mendosa. Since Jose Santos did not come to the clinic with the ambulance, he did not know that fact at the time. Mexico is a country of double last names, and, to say the least, Tina found it very confusing. Every person has two last names and their children have both the mother's and father's last names, and the husband and wife have last names that include their families' names. They are similar, but different.

Even Carlos's name was interesting. Tina's hero, Carlos Fernandez Ramirez, who found Jose Santos, had the two last names that just happened to be the names of both the doctor; Miguel; and his wife, Ines. Her mother's name was Ramirez, which was an interesting Mexican name. And Carlos and Rafael both had Fernandez as part of their last names. Of all the people she could have asked for help in Baja Del Sol, she found Carlos, and he was tied to her angel in this incredible way! Another interesting point is that Carlos had come to Baja Del Sol from Puerto Vallarta four months prior to Tina and Roger's meeting with him. Even more amazing was that Carlos was going to be leaving Baja Del Sol at the beginning of December of that same year. Had Tina come to Baja Del Sol right after the case was concluded, she probably wouldn't have met Carlos. If she had decided to come to Baja Del Sol at the beginning of January the following year, she still would have missed him. The window for meeting Carlos was about five months.

"Looking back today, it was a long time ago, but on the other hand, it is like yesterday," Tina said. "The pictures in my mind and the words and sounds around me will never leave; they will always be a part of me. These special people who crossed my path will forever be my friends." Tina snuggled even closer and quietly said, "Thank you, Roger, I love you." She kissed him again.

*"DREAM AS IF YOU WILL LIVE FOREVER, LIVE AS IF YOU WILL
DIE TODAY." JAMES DEAN*

EPILOGUE

Looking back, Tina had been on an unbelievable ride—starting with the crash, then recovering from serious injuries, fighting the courts, and finally finding the men who saved her life.

Writing this story has been a revelation of years filled with parallels that she wanted to share with you, the readers:

good vs. evil
corruption vs. justice
devils vs. angels
life vs. death
tragedy vs. triumph

In the end, Tina met the most exceptional human beings, ordinary people who had extraordinary strength and values. Doing what was right and what a person felt compelled to do from the depths of his heart transcended every barrier—cultural, racial, religious, language, and, yes, even a border between two countries.

The Michael R. Santonio Courthouse in Richfield County, New York, where this case was handled for a period of more than eleven years, sits near Martin Luther King Expressway. In 1961, Dr. King said, "Injustice anywhere is a threat to justice everywhere."

According to a crime-investigative website, members of the Richfield County Surrogate Court have been accused of committing deeds that include judicial steering, corruption, denial of due process, and obstruction of justice.

December 2008: The Surrogate Elect of Richfield County was arrested on election fraud charges.

Looking through the Las Cruces Directory for Attorneys, 2008, Cisco Samsel had been fully reinstated as an attorney by the State Bar. Speaking to the State Bar, they said a man could change, and at the time he received the reinstatement, the requirements were less strict. The Las Cruces State Bar reinstated his license to practice law in 2004.

The basic truths that one could not escape were that all judges are not fair, some courts are corrupt, and attorneys are good and evil. The justice system is not always just, and the past can mold your future, but you must let it go to survive.

GOD BLESS AMERICA!